Coda

By the Author

Coming Up Clutch

Coda

Visit us at www.boldstrokesbooks.com

CODA

by

Anna Gram

2026

CODA

ISBN 13: 978-1-63679-926-1

THIS TRADE PAPERBACK ORIGINAL IS PUBLISHED BY
BOLD STROKES BOOKS, INC.
P.O. BOX 249
VALLEY FALLS, NY 12185

FIRST EDITION: JANUARY 2026

CREDITS
EDITOR: RUTH STERNGLANTZ
PRODUCTION DESIGN: STACIA SEAMAN
COVER DESIGN BY TAMMY SEIDICK

Acknowledgments

This story began when I asked the question: *If you could speak to your younger self, what would you say?* Honestly, I don't know what I'd say, but the question caused some reflection on who I was then—a young woman navigating feelings for other women that felt both right and scary—to who I am now, a forty-something woman who feels comfortable with her sexuality—though she still gets nervous speaking to attractive women. All of this culminated in asking myself another question: What if I ran into the first girl I ever had a crush on today? Thus, *Coda* was born.

While I did the emotional heavy lifting, this book would not exist without extra help. Thank you to Bold Strokes Books for accepting this story. Thanks to my editor, Ruth Sternglantz, for talking out the finer points with me and making sure I didn't add any "unnecessary drama."

Thank you to my beta reader, Mary, for setting eyes on this and giving your honest opinion. You're the best audience an author could ask for. To everyone I mentioned this idea to and talked it out with. Unfortunately, there were so many I don't remember everyone but know that our conversations were encouraging and beneficial in getting this story here.

Finally, I need to thank my mom. You listened. You supported. Most importantly, you loved unconditionally.

For those who love fiercely.

Prologue

Twenty-seven years ago
University of Central Arkansas

Parker Thompson sat in the corner booth with her eyes closed and her head lightly bopping to the rhythm she tapped out on a sugar packet. The latest drum cadence they'd performed in marching band was intricate, precise, a far cry from the simple rim taps that had accompanied her onto the field in high school. This cadence matched the intensity of the formations she and her bandmates were expected to execute at the university level. The staccato hits on the snares blended seamlessly with the rhythm of the quads and the booms of the bass drums. Too bad she didn't have the skill to be a percussionist—her hand-eye coordination wasn't quick enough to rattle off all the necessary beats. She was lucky she could do one tap per drumstick on the snare, but the three, four, and five tap combination proved to be too much for her brain. So she chose the trumpet, and all she had to worry about then was how fast her tongue could separate the notes. She still hammered out a beat once or twice—like now—when she was nervous, but she stuck to just her hands and fingers. No extra tools required.

The cadence reached its natural end, and Parker smiled. A peace settled over her. It always did when she played music, and she needed that peace, that calm, now more than ever. Parker took a deep breath, opened her eyes and ran into the glare of a big, burly bald gentleman in a trucker cap, a deep scowl contorting the skin across his brow. While Parker enjoyed music, being a soloist was never her end goal, but she'd obviously been tapping loud enough to garner some attention. Embarrassment took over her peace, and she sheepishly dropped the packet to the table and said a meek apology. She checked her watch and let out a long breath. Five minutes to go, so no extra drumming was necessary.

Parker had been bold, leaving the letter. At least, that's how she viewed it. Her feelings for Hannah McArthur had built to a fever pitch for months. In fact, as Parker looked around the semicrowded Yucca's Grill, she smiled. This was where those feelings started to take root. Seemed only fitting she tell Hannah to meet her here. Or maybe Parker should've said the band room, since that was where her heart leapt into her throat when she first laid eyes on Hannah—standing atop the podium, commanding everyone's attention, including a very timid Parker.

No, she thought. Anyone could walk into the band room at any time and interrupt the conversation. Best to meet her here.

Yucca's wasn't anything spectacular. The food was okay, but the selling point was it was local and cheap—two requirements for first year college students. It was here Parker had found enough courage to sit in the chair right next to Hannah. She hadn't talked much, but when Hannah turned and gave her a warm, welcoming smile, Parker sat up straighter and said a more confident hello.

Hannah had laughed, but not in a malicious way. Her laughter was kind, and she immediately engaged Parker in conversation. The words didn't matter, but the fact that Hannah—a senior drum major—took the time to speak to Parker made her feel special. The kind of special that stirred something in Parker's core. She didn't have a name for it, but she knew she liked it.

From that moment on, Parker made it a point to see Hannah as much as possible. Mostly, she found Hannah in the Snow Fine Arts Building in between classes. Every so often, Parker would see her in the library or the commissary. She'd nearly melted the night of the Greek house field day when she got so dizzy after a relay game and nearly fell to the ground, only to fall into Hannah's arms instead. She'd sunk into the sensation of being held with such care that Parker never wanted to leave.

But then winter rolled around, and Parker didn't have any classes with Hannah, and their paths didn't cross on a daily basis anymore. The absence of those moments left a void in Parker's heart, and she did something she never thought she'd do. She pledged the same sorority as Hannah. Even that didn't come without its own headaches.

Parker had asked for Hannah as her big sister, but the pledgemaster decided to pair Parker with someone else, Stephanie Lamar. She was disappointed at first, but Stephanie was a great big sister, showing Parker all that Tau Beta Sigma had to offer. But strangely, what solidified their friendship was Stephanie calling her out for her crush on Hannah. Stephanie didn't berate or humiliate her, just gently confronted her with the observation that Parker seemed a little too focused on Hannah. Stephanie had supported Parker's coming out and her confession that she had it bad for Hannah, but she also warned her off.

"She and Mike are engaged," Stephanie explained. "You're setting yourself up for heartache."

Parker heeded Stephanie's warning and her pursuit ebbed. Then, two months after Parker's initiation, the rumor of Mike and Hannah's breakup caught her attention. This was her chance, her moment to confess her feelings. Let the chips fall where they may.

A letter. A simple folded piece of paper that lay on Hannah's desk in her office held the secrets to Parker's heart and one request. Meet Parker at this diner, in this booth, on this night. Face to face.

It was either the boldest thing she'd ever done, or ridiculous. Either way, Parker couldn't take the emotional agony anymore. She'd listened to her brain: Be sensible, settle for friendship. Now, her heart leapt at the chance to reveal itself, and it was pushing her brain aside, despite the many protests it threw out. *What if she doesn't show? What if she does and laughs at you?* These were two of the biggest questions rattling in Parker's brain and nearly had her leaving Yucca's early. She couldn't do it, though. If nothing else, Parker needed to hear what Hannah thought and risk the fallout.

The bald guy stood and left, and Parker immediately picked up the sugar packet, resuming the drum cadence. She breathed as she looked out the window into the darkness, her mind conjuring images that made her smile. Hannah running into the diner, desperately scanning the tables. Her eyes landing on Parker and a big smile forming on her lips. *I knew it was you* she'd say, and then she'd climb into the booth across from Parker, take Parker's hands in hers, and kiss each one. *I was so scared I was alone in my feelings, but to know you feel the same...I'm so happy. Now we can be together.*

A pair of headlights glided across the tinted window, breaking Parker out of her daydream. She sat up straight and checked her watch. Right on time. A figure exited the car, but Parker couldn't make out any distinguishing features. Their physique and build, however, suggested a woman. Butterflies took flight in her stomach. The cadence on the sugar packet increased in tempo. The bell hanging above the door rang, and she tossed the packet aside and plastered on the biggest smile.

Parker did recognize the person standing at the counter scanning the patrons, but it wasn't Hannah. Surprise was Parker's first emotion, followed by confusion. Stephanie's gaze stopped when she saw her. The sympathy in her eyes told Parker everything she needed to know as Stephanie walked over and took the seat across from her.

"Hannah's not coming, is she."

Stephanie shook her head and sighed.

"Oh, Parker. I wish you would've talked to me before you did this. Do you know the risk you took leaving a note like that?"

A low simmer of anger sparked in Parker's chest at being scolded like a child.

"Because you would've talked me out of it," she said. "And with the rumor of her and Mike breaking up, I knew this was my chance."

"They didn't break up."

Parker startled, confused. "They didn't?"

"No. They had a big argument in front of everyone at the house party last Saturday, but there was no breakup."

"How do you know?"

"Because I was there. Mike got drunk and started saying things he didn't mean. Hannah was upset that he was plastered and let him have it. Someone made a joke about how there was trouble in paradise, and I guess that's how the rumor got started, but there was never any indication they were breaking up. Especially since Mike called her and apologized the next day."

"How do you know that?"

"I'm the one who told him to do it," Stephanie admitted.

Parker's jaw dropped. "So you're the reason I'm not sitting here with Hannah?"

"No, I'm the reason Mike isn't here confronting you about leaving a love letter for his fiancée."

Panic rose in Parker's chest.

"Why would Mike confront me?"

"Because he was with her when she found the note."

"He was?"

"Yes. At first he laughed it off, but then he said they should keep the meeting so *he* could let this person know it wasn't okay."

Parker felt dizzy. From what she'd gathered, Mike was a pretty decent guy. Hannah dated him, so he had to be. But he was also a frat guy. She'd seen him when he got hold of a piece of gossip. He was worse than a nosy neighbor, telling everyone what he'd learned about someone, the person's feelings be damned. If he knew she'd left the note, everyone in their circle would know in two days. The humiliation, along with the rejection, was too much for Parker to bear.

"Luckily, I walked in as they were arguing about what to do," Stephanie continued, breaking through Parker's thoughts. "Hannah said to just leave it alone. That once she didn't show up, the person would realize she doesn't return the feelings, and it'll all be over. Parker?" She paused. Parker looked up. "It is over, right? Now that you know she's not interested?"

Parker nodded and turned to look out the window. She felt the tears well up but kept them at bay. She didn't need Stephanie to see her cry.

"Yeah. It's over. It was a long shot to begin with."

"For what's it worth, I think you were very brave to put yourself out there."

Parker laughed sarcastically. She wasn't brave. She wrote an anonymous love letter to a woman who never thought of her as anything but a friend. A woman who, along with her boyfriend, would probably laugh in her face along with everyone else. No, Parker wasn't brave. Or bold. She was a coward. A foolish coward.

"I appreciate you looking out for me."

Stephanie gave a sad smile. "You're my little sis. I'll always look out for you."

They sat quietly for a few minutes, Parker getting her emotions under control. "Do you have any suggestions for your little sis on how to proceed?"

"Now you want my advice?" Stephanie asked skeptically.

"I do, please."

Maybe it was the somber tone of the response that made Stephanie reply with more sympathy.

"Keep your distance. Hannah probably suspects it's from you, and she's not telling Mike. But one look at you, and he's going to know something is wrong."

"And it wouldn't be hard for him to put two and two together."

Stephanie nodded.

The thought of not being near Hannah was agony, but Parker knew it had to be done. She'd taken her shot and failed. As she looked out into the darkness, she let the tears fall. First loves always hurt. In time, she would move on. Live her life. And never cross paths with Hannah McArthur ever again.

CHAPTER ONE

Present day
Los Angeles, California

Parker sat back in the ergonomic chair, took off her headset, and sighed the loudest depressing sigh.

"Finished the edit?" David Klotz, her business partner and friend, asked.

Parker nodded. "All I have to do is export the session to the drive, and it's ready to take to the final mix tomorrow."

She hit a few keys on the keyboard to start the save process, then checked her phone for any news alerts. She rolled her eyes as a big headline emboldened in red letters read: *SAG, WGA not in Agreement with MPSA. Strikes Continue.* She tossed her phone down on the desk and opened the newly saved session to check for errors.

"This sucks," Parker mumbled. "You'd think they'd be able to get this figured out in four months. Before that, even."

"I know," David said, his unruly brown mop unmoving, stiff with excess product, as he nodded his head in agreement. "People want what they want, and unfortunately no one's willing to compromise."

Parker flopped back, frustrated. When it'd been announced the writers were set to strike, she and editors like her believed it'd be short and production workflow would continue as scheduled to release new shows in September. There was no way they'd have another drag-out fight with everyone still recovering from the pandemic. Then the actors announced their strike the following month, and it became apparent this was going to last a while.

Not great news, when Parker and David were trying to get their new music editing boutique off the ground.

"When did the producer say they'd start up production again for *American Gore Tales*?" Parker asked.

David shrugged, his black oxford bunched around his shoulders. She never understood why he always dressed up, even working from home.

"The hope was to start again before the holiday hiatus, but now it's not looking like until after the new year."

"Great," she mumbled.

They'd gotten a contract for the horror anthology as their first account and were set to work through the end of the year. The producer/show runner loved them so much, he'd promised to give them first ask on all his future projects. Now the anthology—like everything else in this town—had stopped cold. The steady stream of work Parker and David expected was gone. With the last episode in the anthology completed until further notice, the entertainment industry was a barren wasteland until the strikes ended.

"So, what are you going to do with your enforced vacation time?"

Parker heard the lilt of humor in David's question, but she also detected an edge of worry. Chalk it up to exceptional ear training as a musician. She wasn't surprised to hear the unease. All she had was a one-bedroom apartment in North Hollywood and two cats to take care of. Even with student loans looming, Parker's lifelong frugality would help keep her afloat until the strikes, hopefully, resolved. David, however, had a son in private school, a new wife, and all the adult things most people their age strove for. So while he joked about vacation, Parker was certain he'd be up early on the internet tomorrow, scouring sites for job positions on low-budget independent films.

"I honestly don't know," Parker admitted. And she truly didn't. She'd probably try to do what David and others like her would be doing and find something to tide her over, but it wasn't very appealing to fight others like her for work. Nor was it appealing to sit and do nothing but wait. Neither felt right.

David narrowed his eyes at her. "What have you always wanted to do this time of year but couldn't because you were always working?"

Parker looked at the ceiling. Los Angeles in October was always a conundrum. The calendar said it was fall, but it didn't look or feel like fall, no matter how much this city loved going all out for Halloween. If there was one thing she would do, it would be to have a full fall experience. And she knew one place she could have that.

"I think I'd want to go back home."

"To Arkansas?"

She nodded. "Fall in Arkansas is the real reason it's called The Natural State. The weather is cool but not freezing. The leaves are bright red, orange, and yellow. You can go just about anywhere in the state and experience the colorful array of leaves, but the northwest is the best because of the Ozarks. You really experience the beauty of nature."

"You can get the same thing in Maine. Or Vermont. Practically anywhere in the Northeast," David said.

"Possibly. But they don't have the Razorbacks."

David laughed. "You and your football."

"'Tis the season," Parker said. She transferred the completed session over to the drive, then held it out to David. "You want me to drop this off at the stage on my way home or let you handle it?"

David grabbed it from her hand. "I'll take it in the morning. This late, the mixers wouldn't upload it until then anyway."

"Is there anything else you need me to do before I head out?"

He shook his head, the worry he'd tried to hide earlier more apparent on his face. "No, I'm good, but I want you to seriously think about that trip. See the foliage, enjoy the sports thing. Maybe even look up an old girlfriend."

Her first instinct was to scoff, but the comment triggered a memory. Not of an ex-girlfriend—she didn't have any of those from college— but someone Parker knew. Someone she'd liked. And someone she hadn't thought about in a long time.

"I know it's not ideal," David continued, causing Parker to lose her thought, "but use this opportunity to do what you want because, once this strike ends, you won't have much time to go anywhere for a long time."

Parker stood and grabbed her jacket off the back of her chair. "I love the idea of being that busy, and I'll remain hopeful that your premonition comes true."

"And the vacation?"

Her shoulders sagged as she relented. "I'll think about it."

She opened the door and patted David on the shoulder reassuringly as she passed. "It's going to be okay."

He nodded and smiled sadly. "I'll let you know when I hear something."

A short nod and Parker left the small editing suite and walked through David's house back out to her car, hoping David did hear something. For him as much as for her.

❖

Parker barely had her keys on the hook by the front door before two balls of fur—one tortie and one black—halted at her feet, crying mercilessly. She groaned and bent to give them each a pet on the head, but the bellowing continued.

"The food will drop in a minute, I promise." On cue, the food dispenser in the kitchen relinquished its bounty, and the two felines scurried away in the direction of the noise.

"I can feel the love," she said sarcastically. While her cats were distracted—Xena, the tortie, taking up all the space in front of the food bowl, while Midnight waited her turn—Parker stripped off her computer bag and unpacked her laptop along with its hardware before flopping down on her couch. The sectional was way too big for a single bedroom apartment, but she'd fallen in love with it and knew it'd be perfect when she made the leap to homeownership.

She fished her phone out of her pocket and pulled up the Zillow app with her saved listings for the North Hollywood/Burbank area and whistled softly when she noticed the bungalow that was once out of her budget had just reduced the asking price.

The strike was affecting everything right now.

It was perfect for her and her babies. Three bedrooms, two baths with an open concept kitchen/living room, hardwood floors. But the thing that caught Parker's attention was the detached shed in the backyard that had been outfitted to be a home editing studio, complete with central air, audio wiring, and dampening sound materials encased in the walls. The fact that this hidden gem was now within her budget had Parker believing in fate, signs, and every other form of miracle that could be conjured.

"Looks like I'm going to have to wait a little bit longer," she said. Buying a house without an income was ridiculous and irresponsible.

She set her phone down on her left and felt the dip of the cushion on her right. Xena sat there, licking her chops and squinting her eyes.

"Did you leave any for your sister?"

Xena turned her head.

"I'll take that as a no."

Parker stood and rounded the couch to see Midnight sitting in front of the feeder and staring forlornly at the empty dish. She sighed, then walked over and kicked the side until a few pellets of kibble fell out, and Midnight immediately dug in.

"Glad to be of service."

She moved into the galley kitchen, grabbed the Factor meal from her fridge, and put it in the microwave. As she set the timer, her phone beat out the familiar rhythm of its ringtone. Parker returned to the couch and smiled genuinely for the first time all day when she saw the name on the screen.

"Hey, Steph. How's it going?"

"Probably a lot better for me right now than you, my Hollywood friend."

Parker rolled her eyes at the incessant need for Stephanie to call her *Hollywood*. When they'd reconnected two years ago via social media, Parker had naturally told her about being in Los Angeles and working as a music editor. Despite also telling Stephanie she in no way was considered Hollywood, her friend insisted on keeping the nickname. It was annoying most of the time, but after the news about the strikes, it was a comfortable—only mildly annoying today—distraction.

"You'd be correct in your assessment," Parker replied. "My last day for the unforeseen future was today. I just got home."

"So you're on a forced vacation?"

She pulled out her dinner from the microwave. "If by *vacation* you mean freaking out about making sure I don't burn through my savings, keep the lights on, and cats fed? Then, yes, I'm on the perfect vacation."

Parker switched the phone to speaker as she sat at the table and peeled the film off her dinner. As she picked up her fork, Xena and Midnight jumped up and stood like sentinels over the phone while Stephanie spoke.

"I have an alternative proposal for you."

"What did you have in mind?"

"The University of Central Arkansas is having its homecoming next week. They're going all out this year with pep rallies, carnivals, parties, capped off with the big football game Saturday night. And..." Stephanie paused.

Parker detected some mischief in her tone. "And?" she prompted.

"And—it's also the fiftieth anniversary of the Gamma Tau chapter of Tau Beta Sigma."

Parker stopped the fork to her mouth. "Am I supposed to get excited?"

"You're a former member. I know *I* thought it was exciting."

"I'm an *inactive* member. There's a difference," Parker said, mouth full. "Hell, I didn't even graduate as a member of any of the music groups in the music department, which was a requirement."

Parker didn't like to dwell on that time. Stephanie had been the only true bright spot, and the main reason she'd stayed a member three years after Hannah graduated and left. Stephanie had taken Parker under her wing like any good big sister should. She'd shown Parker kindness, taught her confidence when everyone else saw her as an immature kid desperate for attention—something that took years for Parker to admit.

"I know your experience with TBS wasn't great," Stephanie said. "But you've grown up. You have a career. Don't you want to show them that you're so much better than their impressions of you?"

Parker laughed. "I never wanted to get revenge by being successful. My success is for me and me alone, not an *I told you so* to people who probably don't even remember me."

"Fair point. Then don't do it for them. Come and see me," Stephanie pleaded. "We have a lot of catching up to do. You've turned into a wonderful person, Parker. Not that you weren't a wonderful person before, but you know what I mean."

Parker scoffed. "Actually, I don't, but I'll pretend I do so you can stop digging yourself deeper."

"See? It's things like that I miss about you. You were never one to get revenge or sulk. You're compassionate, supportive, and fearless."

"Fearless?"

"Yes, fearless. I believe you know what I'm referring to. A specific love letter comes to mind."

Parker set down her fork and pushed the plastic tray aside. She *did* know what Stephanie was referring to. "The ramblings of a lovesick kid are more ridiculous than fearless. Especially since I couldn't show my face to Hannah after that."

"How about now?"

"What about now?"

"Could you face Hannah Wells now?"

The last name didn't surprise Parker. She knew Hannah and Mike

"Hannah! Thank God you're here."

Hannah stumbled back on her heeled boots a little as the full force of Keith Booker stopped inches away from her.

"Yes, I'm here. What's wrong?"

She took in his heaving chest and worried he might need an ambulance.

"It's Stephanie," he gasped. "She's having a minor wardrobe malfunction, and it kicked off this whole ball of nerves about her speech tonight, and I can't get her to calm down. Can you come talk to her, please?"

Hannah nodded. "Morgan, go ahead and go in. We'll be there shortly."

"You're going to leave me to fend for myself against your friends?"

"Only for a few minutes. Now, go."

She shoved Morgan toward the door, then followed Keith down the hallway on her right to Stephanie's office, hoping this would be the biggest crisis she'd have to deal with for the rest of the night.

This is ridiculous.

Parker drained the small plastic cup of complimentary wine she'd grabbed when she'd first arrived and shook her head. The only reason she was here, in this room—at this event—was Stephanie, and she'd yet to show. She'd been courteous enough to text Parker and say she was running late but didn't give an ETA on when she *would* be there. Parker looked at her phone and groaned. Fifteen minutes since that text and still no Stephanie.

She sat at a perimeter table and looked at the huge empty space in the middle of the floor for everyone to congregate. Luckily, it was also the table farthest away from the DJ, which was across the space. While the music wasn't of the bump-and-grind variety, Parker was jetlagged, and her ears needed a vacation. The soft melodic chords were a nice reprieve. Unfortunately, they were also putting her to sleep. This would be a good time to find a familiar face.

She sighed and watched groups expand and shrink in size as men and women walked up for a few minutes, talked excitedly—sometimes laughed—then walked away to repeat the process with another group nearby. Parker scanned the faces, all unrecognizable, so she couldn't just walk up and pick up a conversation. Well, she could, but then she'd get strange stares, people asking who she was. And if they did recognize her, she'd inevitably get the question *Didn't you go inactive and leave the band?* No, best to sit and wait…alone. She was used to it, but she could also be alone at home. She checked her phone again and saw another five minutes had passed. She'd give Stephanie another ten, then leave.

"Excuse me? Is it alright if I sit here?"

Parker looked up and saw a young woman with pleading blue eyes. She gestured to one of the empty chairs, and those eyes looked relieved as the teen took it and pulled out her phone. She looked young, even by college standards, with long, dark auburn hair and a cherubic face. The ripped jeans and bomber jacket didn't give anything away either.

"You're not an alum, are you?" Parker asked.

The girl chuckled. "No. I'm a sophomore in high school. I just turned sixteen last month."

Parker nodded, understanding now. The girl turned her attention to her phone with a deep crease in her brow. Parker leaned over slightly.

"What are you watching?"

"My friend sent me this video of a music piece in this film he directed. He says that there's this weird point where a C chord is played, but it's quick, so he's not certain if he's hearing it or his brain is creating it. He asked me to look and tell him if I see the chord."

"See?" Parker asked. She'd never heard of someone *seeing* music.

The girl nodded. "I can see all sounds."

She said it so matter-of-factly, and Parker wanted to see this ability in action. "Do you mind if I watch with you?"

"Are you a synesthete?"

Parker opened and closed her mouth. "I'm not sure what that is, but I'm going to say no. However, I think I know what your friend is looking for, and if I'm right, I can help diagnose the problem."

"Oh, okay. Then, sure."

She scooted her chair to the side, and Parker slid closer.

"I'm Morgan, by the way."

"Parker."

They shook hands, and Parker accepted the offered earbud. As they turned to watch the video, Parker noticed the moment immediately. Morgan did, too, as she reared back and blinked rapidly.

"I'm guessing you saw something?"

"I did," Morgan confirmed. "It was quick, but it was there. I saw a spot of red. Did you hear the C chord?"

"Mm-hmm. My guess is whoever edited the picture also edited the music. When they made the cut, part of the C chord got cut off instead of being removed entirely. He just needs to go in and clip it out and crossfade the music sections."

Morgan looked at her in awe. "Wow, he'll be so happy to hear that. How did you know what to do?"

"I'm a music editor."

"What's a music editor?"

Parker smiled. She expected the question and was happy to discuss it. "The best way to describe what I do is that I conform music to specific scenes in movies to highlight the action on the screen. What your friend did here is what I do professionally."

Morgan scrunched up her face. "Huh. I didn't know that was a thing."

"Most people don't, and if the music editor is really good, they never will. But the next time you watch a movie, watch the credits at the end. Every film has a music editor or two."

"That's cool. Did you learn this here?"

Parker shook her head. "I studied music and theater here. Then I went to graduate school in Savannah, Georgia. That's where I studied music editing before moving out to Los Angeles."

"Do you know if they teach this at UCLA?"

"They teach it in their film and television department, but it's not uncommon to find composers and musicians doing it as well. My business partner went to school for composition, but he's been doing music editing for close to twenty years."

"That's good to know," Morgan said flatly.

"Why is that?"

"I want to go to UCLA for music. I feel like it's the best place for me to explore everything music related."

"Do you know what you want to do?"

"I like playing the clarinet, but I *love* composing."

"Did you compose this piece for your friend?"

Morgan shook her head.

"I was busy with regionals when he made this film, so I couldn't contribute. But he said he'd keep me in mind for future projects."

"Can I hear some of your pieces?"

"You really want to?"

"Of course."

Joy filled Morgan's features. She pulled up the music app on her phone and opened *Morgan's Playlist*.

"These are my favorite. They create the best color palettes."

It was the second time Morgan had referred to music as color. Parker did her best to hide her confusion. All she wanted was to hear what this lovely young woman created.

Goose bumps formed on Parker's arms as she closed her eyes and listened. She got washed away by the melodic, smooth transitions of major chords. Emotion welled up inside her as the arpeggio swept up into a perfect fifth, then dove into a major third. By the time the piece reached its end, she was in complete awe of Morgan's talent.

She removed the earbud and squeezed her eyes to stave off the remnants of the emotion.

"Wow. That was…"

"Good?" Morgan asked cautiously.

"More than good," Parker said. "This is a great piece for your portfolio. Make sure to include it when you start your application process."

Tears formed in Morgan's eyes, and Parker smiled, happy to give her validation for her talent.

"I see Morgan on the verge of tears and another person right beside her. I'm guessing you have been privileged to hear one of her musical creations."

Parker looked up at the gruff voice and saw a gentleman standing in front of them. Morgan smiled, so she obviously knew him. Parker looked closer, sensing a familiar face. He sported a buzz cut, and he was heavy. Round face, relatively small eyes. When he smiled, he had a slight chip in his front tooth. Parker's eyes widened. She stood up and got a closer look.

"Keith Booker?"

His eyes smiled as he said, "How's my li'l sis Parker doing?"

A rush of emotion propelled Parker forward into Keith's arms. He'd been her big brother when she'd pledged. Always the sweetest member of Kappa Kappa Psi. Always looking out for her, making sure she wasn't getting overwhelmed. Parker didn't realize how much she missed him until this moment. She pulled back and took him in.

"Wow, you've changed."

Keith, ever the good sport, laughed. Somewhere behind her, Parker heard Morgan snickering, too.

"Yeah, I have. Waistline got wider. Hair got…shorter. But that's by design." He rubbed his hand across his scalp. "You've changed, too."

Parker did a quick spin to show off her smart outfit. She'd decided to go with the red chinos and black shirt with the sleeves rolled up to show a little of her arm tattoo. While Keith opted for a tie, Parker had decided to have the vest as the main focus.

"Would you like to sit with us?"

He took the seat next to Parker and smiled brightly at Morgan.

"So, what have you two been talking about?"

"Well, you were right," Parker said. "Morgan played me some of her music, and I was floored."

A deep blush reddened Morgan's cheeks at the praise.

"Yeah, she's always been talented. I've been trying to get her to score some of my students' projects, but they have some weird aversion to high school kids working on their *masterpieces*."

Keith rolled his eyes on the last word.

"As long as Morgan is disciplined, it shouldn't be an issue. Deadlines and schedules are key." Parker stared at Morgan. "My mom always said talent will only get you so far. Hard work will get you the rest of the way."

"Hear, hear!" Keith said, raising his plastic cup in mock salute.

"Is that how you became a music editor?" Morgan asked.

Parker nodded. Keith's eyes lit up.

"You're a music editor? That's great. Work on anything I'd know?"

"Maybe," Parker said coyly.

"*Well*"—Keith drew the word out—"can you tell me more about it?"

"Me, too," Morgan said. "It sounds really fascinating."

Parker scooted her chair closer and was about to launch into her favorite music cues and the stories behind them when a shrill voice interrupted her.

"Oh my God. Is that little Morgan?"

Morgan rolled her eyes, said a quiet *sorry* to Parker and Keith, then faced their intruder.

"Hi, Aunt Emily."

Morgan slowly rounded the giant table. She squeezed her eyes shut and stood ramrod straight as Emily pulled her into a bone crushing hug.

"Oh my gosh," Emily gushed. "You've gotten so big. How have you gotten so big? I saw you last year."

She held Morgan at arm's length and scrutinized every inch of her.

"I'm still me," Morgan replied. "Just a little taller."

Emily cackled. Parker cringed, wishing she was wearing her earplugs.

"I see that sass has gotten stronger with age."

Emily made a show of looking around, bypassing Parker entirely, not surprising, and landed on Keith.

"Professor Keith. How's life treating you over in the film department?"

Keith stood and gave Emily a polite hug. "Can't complain. I have my students learning the importance of postproduction this semester." He turned and looked at Parker. "Is that something that would be within your field of vision?"

Parker stood and joined them. "I do have some expertise in that area, and I can attest to its importance. Absolutely."

She noticed Emily studying her intently.

"And who might you be?"

Parker waited a beat and took in the too tight black dress, big lips, and bottle-blond tresses.

"It's good to see you again, Emily. It's been a long time."

The blue eyes with too much eye shadow widened, and her lips morphed into a polite smile. "Parker Thompson. As I live and breathe. I didn't expect to see you here. I thought you went inactive."

Parker breathed deeply through her nose to stave off the retort sitting on the tip of her tongue.

"Stephanie invited me as her guest."

Emily nodded politely then turned her attention back to Morgan. "Sweetie, where's your mom?"

"She's with Dr. Lamar. Something about a wardrobe malfunction, but I think she's nervous about giving her speech, so my mom is calming her down."

At the mention of Stephanie's name, Parker interrupted the conversation. "Is Stephanie alright?"

"Oh yeah," Keith said reassuringly. "I think she's just nervous. This is her first year as faculty advisor for Gamma Tau."

Emily nodded, still eyeing Parker suspiciously. "Well, do tell your mom I'd love to speak with her when she arrives."

"I will," Morgan said.

One final polite smile to Parker, and Emily left. As soon as she was occupied with another group, Parker, Morgan, and Keith burst out laughing.

"She hasn't changed much since college," Keith said.

"She hasn't changed since *high school*," Parker said.

"You knew her in high school?" Morgan asked, trying to catch her breath.

"She was a year ahead of me, and we didn't get along well at all."

"Was she this…"

"Pretentious? Full of herself?" Parker finished. Morgan nodded. "Pretty much. Though not as…"

"Plastic?" Morgan supplied, and they fell into another round of giggles.

Suddenly the music cut off, and a voice boomed above the din of conversation.

"Ladies and gentlemen, will you please gather around!"

"Oh, that's my cue." Keith set down his wine and straightened his tie. "How do I look?"

"Very handsome," Parker said.

He ran toward the entrance and joined Stephanie as she came through the doorway, a genuine smile on her lips. Parker had to give her credit for being able to stand upright in stilettos.

"Hello, my fellow sisters, old and new, and those who were lost for a time"—she looked at Parker and smiled—"we welcome you here tonight."

As Stephanie's voice gained confidence, Parker noticed a woman moving in behind her. When she entered fully into the light of the room, Parker's heart plummeted into her stomach.

It couldn't be. Could it? Stephanie's words faded into the background, and Parker watched as Emily ran up and pulled the woman in a reluctant hug. If the face wasn't a dead giveaway, Emily's reaction to seeing the woman was. Still, Parker needed to be certain.

As inconspicuously as possible, she leaned over to Morgan and whispered, "Hey, do you happen to know who that woman is with Emily?"

Morgan smiled and replied, "That's my mom. Hannah Wells. Looks like Emily found her."

Oh shit. Parker turned away quickly, hoping she hadn't made eye contact, and focused on Stephanie.

Morgan was the daughter of Hannah Wells. Of course.

❖

Who is that?

The question sounded sultrier than Hannah expected. Good thing it was in her head.

Stephanie stood in the middle of the room giving a poignant, heartfelt speech about family, sisterhood, and lifelong friends, but none of it registered in Hannah's brain. Nor did Keith's words about support and teamwork as Hannah ogled the tall, androgynous woman five feet away, standing next to Morgan.

The woman was stoic, her attention on Stephanie, and Hannah allowed herself a moment to gaze unobstructed. She followed the line of fitted red chino pants that highlighted sinewy muscle. The dress shirt showed a little hint of collarbone thanks to the open flap style at the neck. The black fitted vest should've disappeared on the black shirt, but the flowery gold designs drew the eye's attention, yet not too much to make its wearer stand out.

The woman clasped her hands in front of her, and Hannah noticed a tattoo spiraling up her right arm. She couldn't make out the details, but there were music bars and notes. She tilted her head to follow it, but the sleeve blocked any further exploration. Suddenly, the woman fidgeted and shook out her shoulders. Her eyes darted around the room and landed on Hannah. Her lips thinned. Could she feel Hannah's gaze?

"She's gorgeous," Hannah whispered.

"What was that?" Emily asked.

Hannah totally forgot Emily was right next to her. She shook her head and said, "Nothing. I was just making an observation."

A very sexy observation.

Thankfully, Emily shrugged and turned her attention back to Keith. Hannah sighed in relief. She wasn't necessarily hiding her bisexuality, but it was still fairly new. So new that not a lot of people knew about it, except for Morgan and Stephanie. And that was all who needed to know while she navigated this newest development so late in her life.

To say it was unexpected was the understatement of the century. She and Mike had been separated for about four months when she'd met a wonderful woman. Hannah had thought her response was the typical new friendship feeling combined with not having to answer to someone who controlled every aspect of her life. Soon, though, she'd realized she wanted more than friendship. Nothing had come of it, but it'd unsettled Hannah enough she'd confided in Stephanie and was grateful to have her friend be so supportive.

"I'm glad you told me," she'd said. "I know you don't think you'll ever act on any feelings, but don't be surprised if a woman comes along to spark enough interest to try it out."

She'd rolled her eyes at the statement. It wasn't like Hannah was trying out a new bike. She was attracted to women. And that would require time to get used to. Seeing this woman now, Hannah had to wonder if she hadn't given Stephanie enough credit with her initial assessment.

The entire room broke out into applause. The speeches were over. Keith and Stephanie thanked everyone for coming and veered off in opposite directions. Hannah moved in the direction of tall, dark, and sexy but was stopped by a light hand on her wrist.

"Don't run off just yet," Emily said. "We haven't seen each other in years. Let's catch up."

Hannah nearly groaned in frustration. She didn't know how long this woman was going to be next to her daughter—the perfect in—and Emily was blocking her from that attempt. With as much cordiality Hannah could muster, she gently extracted her arm from Emily's grasp and plastered on her biggest smile.

"How about we meet up for coffee tomorrow. Just the two of us. Then we don't have to shout or be interrupted."

There was a light in Emily's eyes as she nodded her agreement. "That's a wonderful idea. Usual spot?"

"Usual spot."

Emily squealed and gave Hannah a quick hug before running off to other former classmates and sorority sisters.

Hannah turned and took a deep breath. She smoothed her dress pants and shook out her hair, and then she walked across the band room to finally meet the mystery woman. She nearly stutter-stepped when she saw Stephanie embrace her. Stephanie knew this woman?

As soon as Hannah arrived, she wrapped her arm around Morgan's shoulders.

"Hey, sweetheart, sorry about earlier. This one"—she pointed to Stephanie—"needed a little extra encouragement."

"It's okay," Morgan replied.

"How many of my friends gushed over how you've grown and gotten so pretty?"

She moved to pinch Morgan's cheek but was quicky swatted away.

"Only one. Aunt Emily. And she didn't pinch my cheeks. Keith came over and said hello, but I think he was more interested in talking to Parker than me."

"Parker?" Hannah asked. She looked at the tall woman, who smiled shyly and extended her hand. Recognition clicked hard in Hannah's brain. Her hand paused halfway.

"Parker? As in…"

Hannah didn't know how to finish that sentence. Her mystery woman was Parker Thompson. She had to be. Hannah didn't know any other Parker from her past, which made this meeting…Well, the best way to describe it was complicated.

She composed her features, completed the handshake, and took in the changes, convincing herself it was normal to ogle someone in that capacity. The face was leaner, hair exponentially shorter with salt-and-pepper gray that caught the light. And she was tall. Had Parker always been that tall? When she looked up and saw Parker's eyes, Hannah's heart stopped. She knew those eyes. Deep, brown, and full of hope. Hannah used to know what that hope was for. Now, she didn't have a clue.

"Good to see you again, Hannah. You look well."

"Thanks."

"Parker is a music editor in LA," Morgan said. "She helped me figure out Justin's issue with his video project."

Hannah looked between Morgan and Parker, still dumbfounded.

"I see. And how did she do that?"

Morgan gushed about how Parker told her to fix an issue Hannah knew nothing about. All she could do was nod and watch her daughter fawn over her—obviously—new best friend.

"It really wasn't difficult. I'm sure Justin would've figured it out eventually."

"But not as fast," Morgan replied. "Thanks for being a hero."

Parker shrugged.

"Yes, thank you," Hannah said, finally finding her voice.

Parker squinted at her. Her focus felt intense and caused Hannah's skin to tingle. Her breathing shallowed. She wished the floor would open and let her drop to the center of the earth.

"Will you excuse me for a minute?"

Hannah didn't wait for a reply and rushed to the bar in the far corner and ordered a glass of white wine. She gulped the liquid courage greedily and finished half by the time Stephanie appeared at her side.

"Did you know she'd be here?"

Stephanie winced and nodded. "I actually invited her. Are you upset?"

"Not in the least," Hannah lied. She polished off the wine and slammed the glass down, ordered another, then turned and watched Parker. A quick buzz was taking effect, and Hannah's breathing slowed enough she didn't feel in danger of hyperventilating. She grabbed the fresh glass and sipped it this time as she went over the last few minutes in her mind.

Parker Thompson was here. After all this time. All Hannah remembered of her was an eighteen-year-old kid who followed her around like a puppy dog. She took in Parker's current appearance again. She wasn't a kid anymore, if the heat simmering low in Hannah's core was any indication.

"I should've warned you," Stephanie said.

Hannah scoffed and turned back to the bar. "Yeah, a heads-up would've been nice."

"I'm sorry. Honestly, I wasn't sure you'd recognize her."

Hannah took a deep breath and set down the empty glass. "I'll admit, I didn't recognize her at first, but as soon as Morgan said her name…"

She needed get her emotions under control. It was bad enough Morgan seemed to really like Parker. Hannah didn't have to add on unexpected attraction if she was going to survive the week. Because if Parker was attending the cocktail party, she *definitely* would be at the other alumni events.

She turned to Stephanie and noticed a small crease in her brow. "What?"

Stephanie leaned in and whispered, "Are you attracted to her?"

Hannah's first instinct was to scoff, but she didn't. Apparently, her silence was all the confirmation Stephanie needed.

"Oh my God. You *are*."

"No, I'm not."

"You totally are." Stephanie's lips turned up into a grin. "This is a total surprise."

"You're telling me." Hannah signaled for another glass of wine. "I cannot fall for Parker Thompson."

"Why not?"

Hannah did scoff at that question. "Because I don't need another relationship with a codependency issue. I dealt with that for years, and I'm not doing it again."

Stephanie's eyes softened. "While I agree with your assessment of Mike, I don't think you have to worry about Parker."

"I think your opinion is biased."

"Yes, Parker's my friend, but so are you. And I'm telling you, she's not the same lovesick kid you remember."

"How can you be so sure?"

"Has she tried to get in touch with you over the years?" Hannah shook her head. "And she wouldn't do that because she knows it would be unwelcome. I've gotten to know her again as an adult, and I'm telling you, she's different. She's more caring, more aware, and pretty awesome if you ask me. And, yes, that last part *is* me being biased."

Hannah smiled. There was some validity to Stephanie's statement. After all, Hannah wasn't the same teenager she was back then. She looked over and saw the easy smile Parker gave Morgan before turning and looking toward Hannah. Then the smile dimmed.

"You may be right. But I'm not willing to find out."

"Okay," Stephanie agreed. "I won't push you, but I do hope you give her the benefit of the doubt. She's a good person, and she's not bad to look at either."

Steph gave a wink with her parting shot and walked back over to Parker and Morgan.

Hannah leaned against the bar. She couldn't deny Stephanie's assessment—at least the physical part. But she'd need to get to know Parker to discover the rest, and therein was Hannah's problem. Because getting to know Parker after the spark ignited was asking for trouble.

❖

Parker felt squirmy.

It was an apt description because she knew she was being watched. She did her best to listen to Morgan and Stephanie talk about school and music while looking around the room. When she locked eyes with Hannah, she knew she'd found the source.

"How long does it take to record an entire score for a film?"

Morgan's question filtered in slowly, and Parker tore her gaze away from Hannah.

"Um…it depends. Most orchestras are scheduled for only a few hours a day, and the union is adamant you stick to the schedule. So it can take from a couple of weeks to a month."

"And the musicians get paid for each recording session?"

Parker stole a glance to the bar, relieved to see Hannah's back to her. "That's out of my purview, but I think they get paid by the project like most people in the business. You'll have to check their union."

Stephanie must've sensed a little bit of Parker's distress. She immediately intervened and distracted Morgan. "Hey, I'm parched after that speech. Would you mind grabbing me a water?"

Morgan sagged at being dismissed, then reluctantly walked away.

Once she was out of earshot, Stephanie asked, "You okay?"

Parker nodded. "Yeah. Good speech. I don't know why you were nervous."

"Did you actually hear any of it, or did Hannah showing up distract you?"

Parker crossed her arms and repeated the opening of Stephanie's speech. "*Since its charter was formed in 1975, the Gamma Tau chapter of Tau Beta Sigma has stood behind its promise to uphold the bonds of sisterhood and support musicians in their endeavors, whether they be in music or beyond.*"

Stephanie clapped lightly while Parker flourished a bow. When she raised her head, her gaze ran smack into Hannah, who quickly turned away. Parker sighed and shook her head. She didn't know what was going on, but she was sure she wasn't going to like it when she found out.

"Are you mad at me?" Stephanie asked.

"Why would I be mad at you?"

"You're being very squirmy right now." Ah, good. It was the right feeling. "We can leave if Hannah is making you uncomfortable."

Parker laid a reassuring hand on Stephanie's shoulder. "I'm not mad at you, and she's not making me uncomfortable." She was surprised she'd said it with a straight face. "It's just…"

How did she finish that thought?

"Just what?"

"This will sound ridiculous, but during your speech, I felt Hannah's eyes on me. It felt like she was checking me out."

Stephanie laughed but stopped when Parker didn't crack a smile. "Are you sure it's not wishful thinking on your part?"

"I told you, I'm not harboring any romantic feelings for Hannah.

They died a long time ago. But"—Parker looked over at the bar and took in Hannah's appearance. She looked amazing in her slacks and purple blouse. She had curves in all the right places, and when she smiled, Parker noticed little lines around her mouth—"I have to admit, she looks really sexy."

Stephanie poked her in the arm and glared at her. "You just said you don't have romantic feelings for her."

"I don't, but I'm a red-blooded lesbian. I can admire a beautiful woman without it meaning anything. As a matter of fact"—she looked Stephanie up and down and bit her lip—"that dress is smoking hot. The purple brings out your eyes. And your legs show just enough to entice." She waved her hand in a fanning motion.

Stephanie laughed. "Okay, okay. I get it. There's nothing there to worry about with Hannah."

"Exactly. But if it makes you feel better, I'll play it safe and keep my distance for this week."

"You don't have to go to that extreme."

Parker looked over and saw Hannah laughing with Morgan. It was the most unguarded she'd seen Hannah since they'd laid eyes on each other. She didn't want to make Hannah lose that sense of freedom. If staying away meant Hannah was happy, Parker would stay away.

"Believe me. It won't be a hardship."

CHAPTER THREE

"Woohoo! Go, Bears!"

Hannah stepped away from Morgan and created a gap for the crowd of students running past them in the opposite direction. Morgan's normally stoic expression softened into a smile at all the exuberant activity up and down Main Street in downtown Conway. Hannah laughed as she saw students waving pom-poms. She'd received one herself at the pep rally earlier and waved it in Morgan's face. Morgan quickly pushed it away, but her laughter told Hannah she wasn't too upset by the antics. Considering how the night began, it was nice to end it on a positive note with everyone hyped up to see their team beat their opponent on Saturday.

"So? Final verdict on the evening?"

Morgan rolled her eyes and hooked her arm through Hannah's.

"Okay, I'll admit, tonight has been fun."

Hannah chuckled and kissed Morgan lightly on the head. She was glad Morgan had a good time. Even though she hoped her daughter would see what UCA could offer this weekend, Morgan's happiness was more important, especially since she and Mike were no longer together. Even now, Hannah was impressed with how well Morgan adjusted from a two-parent household to two separate households.

"It's not like I don't see both of you all the time at school," Morgan had reasoned. It was true, their situation was unique even by divorce standards. Still, Hannah worried, especially when Morgan came home from visiting her dad for a few days and, sometimes, didn't look as happy as when she left. Morgan never revealed the reason for her unhappiness. The only thing Morgan would say was "Just Dad being Dad," and she would leave it at that. Hannah hated that response because she knew Mike was still frustrated over their separation and probably took it out on Morgan. But she'd never gotten confirmation. Morgan was tight-lipped, and any confrontation with Mike would make the situation worse. So she'd do her best to be there for Morgan, cheer her up, and support her when she *did* decide to reveal the reason.

"You've been quiet for too long, Mom. What are you thinking?"

Hannah pushed thoughts of Mike and turmoil away. She chuckled at Morgan's astuteness and patted the hand at her elbow.

"I was quietly agreeing with you is all. It has been a great evening."

They walked slowly down the sidewalk, the entire street decked out in various shades of purple and gray streamers, balloons, and flags. The sign for Yucca's Grill came into view, and Hannah's stomach rumbled expectantly.

"So you had a good time?"

"Absolutely," Morgan replied. "I'm glad I remembered my earplugs. Otherwise, I don't think I'd have lasted five minutes in that gym and would be begging to go home."

Hannah was relieved as well. Though she would've taken Morgan home if needed, she really wanted this night out and was happy her daughter remembered to take care of herself once they arrived at the gymnasium for the pep rally.

"Parker looked like she was having a good time."

Heat bloomed on Hannah's face.

"Yes, she did."

The boisterous environment of the pep rally should've been a great distraction, but Parker had stood front and center next to Stephanie, keeping her at the forefront of Hannah's thoughts. Parker had laughed and cheered, even did a little jig to the hip-hop song playing through the loudspeakers.

"What was she like in school?" Morgan asked.

Hannah sighed and looked up to the sky. "Honestly, it's hard to remember."

It was the truth, unfortunately. Outside of band, the sorority, and Parker's unrequited feelings, Hannah really didn't know a lot about her. "I remember she was quiet. Observant. Always listening to what people had to say but rarely contributed to the conversation."

Hannah vaguely remembered a time when they were all camping, and Parker sat with them around a fire. She had laughed and ribbed the other women there, but she didn't reveal too much about herself. Come to think of it, Hannah didn't really know anything personal about Parker. Strange, since they were technically sorority sisters and part of their initiation was to show trust and reveal personal details. Even then, Hannah couldn't remember what Parker had revealed.

"Mom?"

Morgan's voice brought her back to the present.

"What, sweetheart?"

"I asked, do you think we'll see Parker again this week?"

"I would assume so," Hannah answered. "Stephanie did invite her and is her big sister."

Morgan laughed. "Good point. We see Stephanie so much already, we'll probably see Parker just as much."

Hannah bit back a groan at the idea of seeing Parker so much this week. It wasn't that she wanted to avoid the woman, but Hannah didn't want to add any fuel to her own burgeoning attraction.

"I'm sure Parker will be around and ready to answer whatever questions you have for her."

Hannah opened the door to Yucca's, and Morgan entered first. She let out a little huff and stopped just inside the doorway.

"Looks like you're right, Mom."

Hannah squinted and followed Morgan's sight line. There, in the corner booth, sat Parker.

❖

Parker read the news headline on her phone and blindly reached for a french fry in her basket. *Talks Resume Between Guilds and Producers: Progress Made.*

Relief flooded her body. Finally, some positive news. She pushed the basket away and focused intently on her phone, trying not dwell on the irony of the fact that in avoiding Hannah, she'd ended up in the one place that had the most impactful memory of her—even if that moment only played out in Parker's head.

While she had expected to run into Hannah, Parker was surprised it didn't cause her to fluster or panic. In fact, she was having fun. The pep rally had ignited her school spirit—as was intended—and she found herself cheering on the Bears with the rest of the student body. She *did* remember her earplugs when the band started blaring the horns and percussion. It had been a great distraction. Until it wasn't.

Every so often, Parker was certain a pair of blue eyes were watching her. Her body tingled, and the squirmy feeling from earlier returned. She'd been too much of a coward to confirm it, content to lose herself in the jubilation. The rising confusion, uncertainty, and flat-out wondering what the hell was going on had Parker begging off Stephanie's dinner invitation in favor of quiet solitude. She needed to get away, to decompress. That's how she'd wound up in the same diner, in the same booth. Thinking about Hannah once again.

"Hey, Parker. Fancy seeing you here."

Parker looked up and saw Morgan smiling down at her. She held a red basket overflowing with fries and a hamburger in one hand and a white paper cup in the other.

"You mind if we join you?"

Parker tilted her head and saw Hannah walking toward them.

"Ah, sure."

"Great."

Morgan slid into the booth next to Parker. Hannah's smile was hesitant as she slid into the seat across from them. An awkward silence settled around them as Morgan dug into her food. Hannah took small bites, her eyes darting to Parker.

"So, are you enjoying your time back at UCA?" Hannah asked.

Parker shifted a little on the squeaky leather seat.

"So far, so good. A lot has changed. I was afraid this place had closed down."

Hannah shook her head. "I think every Greek would protest if that was even rumored. They bring their pledge classes here."

"I remember that."

"Mom says you were a pledge when she was a member," Morgan said.

"That's right," Parker confirmed. "But she graduated the year I joined."

For the first time, Parker was certain she and Hannah were sharing the same thought. *Let's not talk about this, please.* She focused on Morgan, hoping to bring the conversation to the present.

"I'm sorry we got interrupted earlier, Morgan. Was there anything else you wanted to ask me about my work?"

Morgan took a sip of her Coke and swallowed her burger.

"Yeah. You said music editing is more of a film specialty. How do I get into it? Does it require extra schooling?"

Parker sat up straight and cleared her throat. "It can, but most stumble into it, which I'm sure your mother would not approve of, but in the industry, that's how most people learn their specialties."

Hannah looked up—finally, eye contact—and raised an eyebrow.

"I am not endorsing Morgan skipping college. While a college degree is not a big emphasis in the industry, it is helpful in speeding up the job search."

"How's that?" Hannah asked.

"Music editors use a suite of programs that some of my colleagues learned on the job, in different roles, and it took them years to break down barriers. Having professional training with these programs and other basic tools will totally smooth the path to landing a job."

"And they teach these classes at UCLA?" Morgan asked.

"They do. They should with all the famous alumni they have pouring money into the department."

"Wow. Sounds like all my bases are covered once I get into UCLA. I'll be on a prestigious music department track and learning a cool side hustle."

"Not to mention you'll have an awesome person in the area in case you need a place to crash."

Hannah looked at Parker expectantly. "You'd do that for her?"

"Absolutely. She'd just have to share my attention with two needy cats."

"I like cats," Morgan said.

"Just cats? No wife or girlfriend?"

Parker shifted her eyes to Hannah.

"I don't date a lot, I'm afraid."

Hannah widened her eyes. "You're joking, right? I mean look at you. You're suave, dapper, have tattoos. And you live in a city that is very welcoming to the LGBTQ community. You have to at least have… someone."

The rapid-fire comments caught Parker off guard. She wasn't sure what to say as Hannah looked at her, clearly expecting a response.

"Mom," Morgan whispered, "why are you being weird?"

Hannah opened and closed her mouth. Her gaze shifted between Morgan and Parker before it dropped to the table, and a light blush colored her cheeks.

"I'm sorry. That's none of my business."

While Parker agreed, she was also curious about Hannah's motives for being so personal.

"It's okay. I don't mind answering. The truth is my work schedule is unpredictable. I sometimes work sixteen hour days for six days straight, so it's hard to find time to meet women."

"Six days?" Morgan asked, surprised.

Parker nodded and noticed Hannah's shoulders relax. "I have deadlines to keep, so sometimes I have to work on the weekend. Plus, I'm not a big club or bar person. I prefer to be at home or go to sporting events or be out in nature. If I can find a woman who likes those things and understands that I may have to work long days, then I'm going to marry her."

"I'm sorry your hours are so bad," Hannah said, "but it seems very rewarding."

"It is. That's what makes the trade-off worth it."

Hannah's lips pressed together, and she gave a small nod. Apparently Parker's answer satisfied her curiosity.

The bell above the door drew their attention, along with the rowdy teenagers entering the restaurant.

"Hey, Morgan," one of them shouted.

Morgan looked up and smiled around her fries. "Hey, Kim, it's been so long." She waved enthusiastically at a young woman with blond hair, who waved back. "Can I go hang out with my friends for a bit?"

"Of course, sweetheart."

Morgan slid out of the booth and ran toward her friend. Hannah turned and watched as they walked over to another table in the back corner. When she turned back around, her smile had dimmed somewhat. Tension settled over the table as Parker found herself alone with Hannah for the first time that evening. In fact, it was the first time they'd been alone…ever. And it was an opportunity not to be wasted.

Hannah stared at the table once Morgan left. Her cheeks were warm, and knowing Parker was staring at her only heightened her sense of embarrassment. She hadn't set out to be so inquisitive about Parker's personal life. She'd hoped Parker would say there was someone special, someone she was spending her life with. Then Hannah could have let go of these conflicting feelings and moved on.

Hannah looked up once the heat dissipated and looked into Parker's eyes. She'd expected annoyance. All she saw was indifference. Parker gave nothing away, and she relaxed back against the leather seat and gazed at Hannah.

"I apologize if I embarrassed you."

"You didn't embarrass me," Parker replied.

"I embarrassed me, then. I have no right to bombard you with an inquisition."

Parker nodded and pursed her lips. "It has been a while since I was subjected to questions that were…intensely curious."

Parker smiled then. A soft, genuine, lovely smile. It broke the tension at the table, and Hannah relaxed against her seat as well.

"Thank you," Hannah said warmly. Sincerely.

Parker waved her hand to brush it off. "I guess in some ways, I'm not surprised. I believe you were the one who asked me the tough questions during my initiation."

"I did?"

Parker nodded. "When I was being considered as a pledge, you asked why I wanted to join Tau Beta Sigma. I said it was because I wanted built-in friendships. Or something along that line."

Hannah racked her brain. Was she the one who asked that question? It sounded like something she'd ask, knowing how much she loved the sorority.

"And then, when I made it to the night before initiation, you asked me that question again, and I changed my answer."

"Do you remember what it was? Because I don't," Hannah admitted.

Parker bit her lip.

Did she do that every time she had an intense thought? Hannah hoped not because it was doing things to her right now.

"I honestly don't remember," Parker said, "but I think it was something profound and had more depth than my original response because you gave me a small nod and a smile after I spoke, which told me I said the right thing."

"I wish I could remember what you said."

Parker shrugged. "Must not have been as profound as I thought after all this time. But my point is, when you want to know something, you ask the questions. I obviously had no problem answering them. Trust me, when I don't want to answer something, I'll let you know."

"Thank you. I appreciate it."

Loud laughter caught Hannah's attention, and she looked over her shoulder at the table where Morgan sat. She smiled, watching her daughter engage with her friends and look so at ease. So comfortable.

"I noticed Morgan has some of that same tenacity. She asked so many questions about music editing at the party, I had to check my brain to make sure I was giving the right answers."

Hannah chuckled and turned her attention back to Parker. "Morgan is…special. More than people realize."

"Is Morgan neurodivergent?"

Hannah steadied her breathing and gazed directly into Parker's eyes. "Why do you ask?" She wasn't opposed to answering the question. People asked all the time. Her protective instincts, however, kicked in—she was unsure of Parker's intent or how she'd react to the answer.

"When she showed me the video earlier, she said she was trying to *see* the music. I didn't fully understand what that meant. I also noticed the bright orange earplugs she wore at the pep rally. I recognized them because I have the same brand, but I don't think Morgan wears them for the same reason I wear them in those situations."

"Why do you wear them?" Hannah was stalling, trying to get a feel for Parker's attitude toward Morgan. So far, she didn't appear to be anything other than genuinely curious.

"My ears are my livelihood," Parker explained. "In the gym, I expected the decibel level to be over a limit my ears can't handle long-term. So I protected them." Parker's brow furrowed and she leaned across the table and whispered, "Is that why Morgan wears them? Is she sensitive to sound?"

Hannah took a deep breath. She must've looked annoyed or reluctant to answer because Parker immediately said, "You can tell me to mind my own business, I won't be offended."

"No, it's okay. You were kind enough to answer my questions, it's only fair I answer yours."

"Yeah, but Morgan is your daughter. And if you're wanting to protect her, I totally understand if you want me to leave it alone."

Hannah's heart swelled at Parker's understanding and willingness to let it go. Which was probably why she had no problem revealing the truth.

"Morgan has synesthesia, specifically chromesthesia. She sees music as colorful moving shapes."

Parker's eyes widened, and her mouth formed a perfect *O*. She clasped her hands on the table and hummed quietly. Hannah looked at her quizzically. Was that a good hum or a bad hum? The flex of Parker's forearms drew Hannah's attention for a brief second. When she looked back, a wide grin greeted her.

"That is so cool."

Hannah blinked and sat back. No one had ever reacted that way.

Weird was the most common response. Occasionally, someone would think Morgan was intriguing, which could be viewed as positive. *Cool*, however, had never been used.

"You think it's cool?"

"Absolutely. I only ever see notes or scenes play out in my head when I hear music. To be able to *see* music in a physical sense—it has to be pretty amazing sometimes."

Hannah was gobsmacked. "For the most part, it is amazing. There are times, though—like at the pep rally—it can be overwhelming, and she needs to take the necessary precautions."

"The earplugs."

Hannah nodded. "Too much exposure to music that is overly bombastic or repetitive, she gets queasy. Found that out the hard way."

Parker winced. "That bad?"

"Yeah. Not long after I had her tested, we went to a big Fourth of July celebration where they were playing all the big fanfares. We were sitting next to the speaker, Morgan pigged out on hot dogs all day, and—"

"You don't need to finish that sentence," Parker interrupted.

Hannah laughed. She felt comfortable talking to Parker about this, which was surprising because she'd never done so with other people, though not for lack of trying. Once Hannah said the word *neurodivergent*, people shut down or changed the subject, treating Morgan's ability as if it was taboo to say out loud. Parker reminded Hannah that what Morgan had was a gift and should be seen as such.

"How did you discover she had this ability?"

"Um…" Hannah took a moment to collect herself. "When she was five, she was learning about music and instruments in school. I asked her which one she liked the best, and she said the clarinet. When I asked why, she said *I like how the yellow looks when the notes come out.* I thought it was cute, but she would always describe notes as colors after that. I decided to get her tested, and that's when we found out she was a synesthete."

"She's lucky to be able to translate music in such a compelling way. And she's also lucky to have a mom who sees it as a gift and not a disorder."

Hannah ducked her head, knowing her blush was evident. Her emotions were raw, but that was par for the course when discussing Morgan. Only this time, they were raw because she was happy to find someone accepting Morgan's ability. Not because she had to defend it. She swallowed the lump in her throat and shook out the cobwebs. Hannah needed to turn this conversation in a different direction before she turned into a blubbering mess.

"You said you have cats?"

Parker shrugged at the sudden subject shift and flowed with the change. "Yes. They're the only children I have to worry about."

"But I bet you have tons of pictures."

"Absolutely."

Parker picked up her phone and turned the screen to Hannah. Hannah cooed over the giant tortie leaning against a pillow like a queen on her throne. Then she laughed at the picture of a little black cat rolling on her stomach with her paws covering her face.

"What are their names?"

"The tortie is named Xena, and she has the attitude to live up to it. And the black cat is called Midnight, but I shorten it to Midi a lot. Faster to get out when she's misbehaving."

"Oh, I doubt that cute thing could misbehave."

"Come to my house at three in the morning and see if you change your mind."

The thought of being in Parker's home, in her bedroom, at any time caused Hannah to gasp. "Well, I'll just have to take your word for it," she said.

Parker pulled the phone back, and Hannah got a good view of the ink on her arm.

"That's a very interesting tattoo."

Parker turned her arm over and smiled. "Oh yeah. Not too surprising that a music editor would get a music tattoo, but I'm happy with how it came out."

Hannah watched the bars and notes sway and twist with Parker's movements, but she still couldn't get a clear idea what the piece sounded like. She set her outstretched hand on the table.

"Is it okay if I take a closer look?"

"Sure."

Parker rolled up her sleeve a little more and gently laid her arm in Hannah's grasp. Hannah nearly gasped when the smooth skin made contact with hers. Luckily, she held it in as she slowly turned Parker's arm, scrutinizing every detail. She brought her other hand up and caressed the notes, noticing a progressive rhythm from A to C, down to B. Her hand continued to move slowly up Parker's arm to her elbow. It was only the gentle thud of the phone hitting the table that prompted Hannah to look up. There, in Parker's gaze, she found a torrent of emotions she couldn't fully understand. The mixture was so palpable, Hannah audibly gulped and returned her eyes to the tattoo and continued her exploration. She twisted Parker's arm. The notes followed the line of muscle along her forearm, giving the perfect road map as she caressed the spot along the elbow, below the sleeve. "This part must've hurt. With the bone protruding."

Her fingernails grazed underneath the sleeve, and she felt goose bumps form. Suddenly, Parker's hand rested lightly on hers, stopping Hannah's progress.

"What are you doing?" Parker asked.

The question was said so softly, Hannah looked up to make sure she'd heard it at all. This time, when she locked Parker's gaze, there was no mistaking the emotions Hannah saw. There was confusion, desire, and was that a hint of sadness?

"I was admiring your tattoo," she whispered.

Fire sparked in Parker's eyes. Her fingers curled slightly around Hannah's. Slowly, she pushed Hannah's hand back down her arm, past the wrist, the palm, until it rested gently on the table.

"What's going on, Hannah?"

"I'm just catching up with an old friend."

The excuse sounded like bullshit to Hannah's ears. Parker must've heard it as well. She leaned back, out of Hannah's reach. She gathered her phone and keys and slid out of the booth. "I need to go."

Hannah was taken aback. She reached for Parker but missed.

"Please, don't go. I'm sorry I upset you."

Parker fiddled with her keys and sighed. "It's fine. Tell Morgan good-bye for me."

Hannah watched her leave, totally confused.

"Where's Parker going?" Morgan asked as she walked over to the booth, confusion etched on her face. "Why is she leaving? What happened?"

Hannah turned and sighed. "Honestly, I don't know."

CHAPTER FOUR

Parker had hardly slept.

When six o'clock rolled around the next morning—after a cumulative four hours of actual sleep—she'd given up and made the trek to Conway for her breakfast date with Stephanie. The thirty-minute drive gave her time to contemplate the source of her abrupt departure from Yucca's the night before and what had triggered it.

Despite Stephanie's assurance Hannah hadn't been ogling her at the cocktail party, the interaction at the diner had Parker believing otherwise. It hadn't started that way. Morgan's inquiries about music editing—even Hannah's questions about her relationship status—felt normal. There was no electricity arcing between them. Hell, there wasn't even a tingle. Only when Hannah admired her tattoo, complete with sultry tone and caressing, did Parker realize Hannah was flirting with her. If she was still eighteen, Parker would've waved it off as wishful thinking, like Stephanie suggested. Yet she wasn't eighteen anymore. She was forty-six years old and had been flirted with enough times to recognize it, and Hannah was flirting.

Parker wasn't sure how Stephanie would take being wrong about Hannah *this* time.

She parked in the visitors' parking lot over by Carmichael Hall and walked the length of Student Lane until she could cut across to the Snow Fine Arts Building. It was a little cold, but nothing her flannel shacket couldn't handle. She approached the front door and saw Stephanie standing inside the lobby. She knocked and was greeted with a warm smile.

"Good morning," Stephanie said brightly and gave her a one-armed hug. "Sorry about the early hour. I have a class at eight."

"It's okay. I'm usually up for work by now anyway."

"Breakfast in the commissary okay?"

"Actually," Parker said, "would it be alright if we grabbed something to have in your office? There's something I want to tell you, but I don't want a lot of ears."

Stephanie crinkled her brow. "Is everything okay?"

"Oh yeah. I just…something happened, and I want to get your opinion on it, but it's nothing life shattering."

"Whatever you want. Let's take the long way, so you can see the changes to the building."

They turned and walked down the long hallway. The linoleum floor was still the same, thought it looked updated. Too bad Parker couldn't say the same for the cream-colored paint on the concrete brick walls. Those looked pretty faded. They hit the main lobby in front of the recital hall, and Parker noticed the faded burgundy carpet had been replaced with durable gray wood flooring.

"When did they decide to put furniture in here?" Parker asked, seeing the tall tables and love seats.

"When they started using the recital hall as a concert venue and got a liquor license. Didn't want to force people to stand around during intermissions."

Parker nodded, impressed with the smart yet elegant look.

"About the same time," Stephanie continued, "they enclosed the exterior patio to have more space to congregate and to discourage audiences from wandering down the halls and bothering students in practice suites."

Parker noted the change from wood to brick as they stepped into what felt like a little atrium with floor-to-ceiling windows. "A lot has changed," she whispered.

"Yes, it has," Stephanie replied. "Some good. Some bad…"

"Some confusing," Parker finished.

The crease in Stephanie's brow was back. "Let's go grab that breakfast because something is obviously bothering you, and I don't want to have to cut it short because I have to go teach my class."

They exited the double doors of Snow and walked over to the student center across the quad. The lines in the commissary weren't long, so they made quick work of getting their food and going to Stephanie's office.

"I like the blue," Parker said when they walked in. The dark navy walls made the light-stained bookshelves pop nicely.

"Thanks. I know I can't do anything about the brick look, but I picked a color dark enough for people not to notice the mortar lines." They took their seats and popped the lids on their food. "Stop talking about my office. I have forty-five minutes until my class begins. Spill."

Parker took a quick bite of her egg white scramble, then said, "I ran into Hannah and Morgan at Yucca's last night."

Stephanie slowly bit into her toast, then set it down. "How did it go?"

Parker didn't miss the cautious tone.

"It was nice. Morgan peppered me with questions about music editing. Hannah asked me about…other things."

"What, exactly?"

"Whether or not I was in a relationship in LA. It didn't feel intrusive, but it was weird."

"Uh-huh."

"I chalked it up to natural curiosity and wanting to catch up, but then something else happened, and now I don't think it was simple curiosity anymore."

She sighed and set her takeout container on Stephanie's desk. "At one point in the evening, Morgan went off to hang out with some friends. Leaving me and Hannah alone."

"Uh-oh." Stephanie gulped what food she had in her mouth. "What happened?"

"She flirted with me."

Stephanie shook her head. "Parker, please tell me—"

"No, Steph, I need you to listen," Parker interrupted. "I have *no* feelings for Hannah. We were talking about Morgan, then she asked to see pictures of my cats. That's when she saw my tattoo and asked to get a closer look. I was okay with that—people are always asking to see it—so I let her examine it closely."

"That's not really flirting."

"The way she caressed my arm was more than just a simple perusal."

"How do you mean?"

Parker rolled up her sleeve, showcasing the beautiful artwork the tattoo artist had done.

"If you were curious about my tattoo and asked to see it, how would you do it?"

Stephanie set her container next to Parker's and grabbed her wrist, turning it side to side. Every so often she'd run her thumb over the notes—roughly—as if trying to rub them off. When she let go, Parker clasped Stephanie's wrist.

"This is what Hannah did."

Parker slowly turned Stephanie's wrist over and back, eyes focused in concentration. She glided her fingertips over Steph's forearm, lightening her touch as she went higher to the elbow. When Parker looked up, Stephanie's eyes were glazed over. Parker quickly pulled back and waited for her opinion.

"Wow," Stephanie whispered. "I feel all tingly with goose bumps. Did you feel this?"

Parker nodded. "I wish I didn't. Do you have any other explanation why she'd be so…tender like that?"

Stephanie shook her head and rubbed her temple. "No, but I do think you're right, and she was flirting with you."

"Can you clue me in as to why?"

"Unfortunately, no."

Stephanie's tone told Parker she knew more than she was saying. "What's going on?"

"I can't tell you, but only because it's not my story to tell. You and Hannah need to talk, and I promise once you do, it'll all make sense."

"Great," Parker groused.

"You don't seem too happy about this."

"I'm not. Why would I be?"

"This is what you wanted."

Parker adamantly shook her head. "No, this is what I wanted in 1997."

Stephanie crossed her legs and gestured with her hands. "Just so I'm clear, Hannah flirting with you is a bad thing?"

"Yes, it is."

"Why?"

"Because it's Hannah."

"What does that mean?"

A long sigh escaped Parker's lips as she hung her head. "If this was any another woman, someone I didn't know, didn't love once upon a time, I'd enjoy it. Maybe even flirt back if I was attracted to them. But this is Hannah Wells. She was my first love. To have her flirt with me without any explanation as to why? After all these years? It feels cruel." Unshed tears blurred Parker's vision as she continued, "I have a great career. I busted my ass to build it. And I love it. But a big reason why I am a success is because I've had my heart broken too many times, and I refocused all my energy on music editing. Because music has never been cruel. Music embraces me for who I am, and I won't settle for anything less than finding someone who does the same."

She swiped at the tears that escaped and noticed Stephanie's eyes shimmering as well.

"I'm sorry, Parker. I didn't know."

"I stopped wearing my heart on my sleeve a long time ago, so you wouldn't know."

Stephanie gave a pinched smile as she grabbed some Kleenex out of her pocket and handed a couple to Parker. "So, what are you going to do now? Refortify your efforts to stay clear of Hannah?"

Parker snorted and dabbed her eyes. "Yeah, that's worked well so far."

They both laughed.

"Yeah, and Morgan is your biggest fan right now."

Parker folded the tissue, blew her nose, and sighed. "I'll do the only thing I can do. I will be me. If Hannah wants to forget it ever happened, then I'll forget it. If she wants to talk about it, I'll talk it over. But I'm done chasing. I'm done reading too much into a woman's actions toward me. I'm Parker Thompson, music editor. And that's all I need to be."

Stephanie nodded. "Well, I for one am proud of you, Parker Thompson, music editor." She put a reassuring hand on Parker's shoulder. "This version of you is wonderful. And anyone would be lucky to have you."

Parker nodded her agreement, but in her mind three words lit up in bright lights.

Not Hannah Wells.

❖

Hannah paid attention to the way the sixteenth notes flowed out of the saxophone.

"Remember, Brent, it's not a slur. It's smooth. A light tongue instead of a staccato."

Brent pushed the glasses up on his narrow face and sighed. He rolled his shoulders, which were probably sore from being hunched over for the last forty minutes—his tall, lanky frame wasn't built for dipping the saxophone the way it was intended. He wrapped his lips around the mouthpiece and tapped out the beat with his foot. A deep breath later, and he was off again.

Hannah listened, but it wasn't necessary. Brent was one of her best musicians. He knew the audition piece front to back, side to side, and diagonal. There was no way he wasn't going to make first band at regionals. When he reached the sixteenth note passage again, he accented each note with a little tongue flick instead of simply breathing through the reed and pressing the buttons on his saxophone. Hannah smiled, loving the way he listened. Loving his passion.

Parker has passion. It wasn't the first time she'd thought of Parker that day, but it was the first time she'd thought about the way she smiled when she'd interacted with Morgan, and her genuine curiosity about Morgan's ability. It was so beautiful and endearing. Maybe that's what had propelled Hannah to be a little reckless. She closed her eyes, seeing the hurt on Parker's face.

She'd lain in bed that evening and realized she'd been flirting with Parker. The way she'd caressed Parker's tattoo? Oh yeah, totally flirting. And since Parker didn't know about Hannah's bisexuality, she probably thought she was the butt of a big joke. If so, Hannah needed to apologize. Soon.

She tuned back in, as Brent finished the last note in the piece, and checked the time on her phone.

"Really good, Brent. We have three minutes left. Is there anything else you want to go over?"

He rubbed his shaved head. "Can we go over a couple of those minor scales again?"

"Sure. Which ones?"

"The hard ones?"

Hannah laughed. "Okay. We'll start with E-flat minor and see how far we get."

Brent pulled the sheet with all the minor scales listed and prepared to play. He was up to C-flat when Hannah's phone vibrated with a text. She looked at the banner on the screen and saw Mike's name and mentally rolled her eyes. He knew she was in the middle of a private lesson, but that didn't seem to matter to him. Instead of answering, she let it go and returned her attention to Brent.

"Good. Now do it in descending order."

Brent did as instructed but stopped when there was a knock on the rehearsal room door. Hannah turned and saw Mike's face in the narrow window. He motioned for her to come out. She shook her head and pointed at her watch, indicating she had a few minutes left. Mike knocked again, more forcefully. Hannah sighed and turned back to Brent.

"We can stop if you need to go," he said.

"No," Hannah replied. "You paid for my time, and you have three minutes left. I want you to play through the scale, up and back, three times. Then we can stop."

Brent nodded and licked his reed, then floated through the notes like he was on a cloud. Hannah smiled. He practically danced in his chair while he played his instrument. When he concluded, he held the last note and let it fade naturally.

"Well done, Brent. You're doing great."

He blushed under the praise and gathered up his sheet music.

"What do you want me to work on before our next lesson?"

Hannah opened her mouth, then paused and smiled. "You know what? You choose."

He pulled the neck of his saxophone off with a loud pop. "Me?"

She pointed at him. "You've got this, Brent. You put in the work, and you're going to blow them away at regionals. What I want you to do is look at this piece, look at the scales, and anything you're not one hundred percent comfortable with, rehearse it. But also remember to take time for yourself."

His glasses slid down his face as he furrowed his brow. "Time for myself?"

"I want you to have fun. Away from music. Go out with friends. Hang out with your family. Do other things that make you happy."

The shy smile came back as Brent said, "Thank you, Mrs. Wells."

Hannah inwardly cringed at the *Mrs.* but didn't call Brent on it. It would take time for all her students to get used to the change. The alarm on her phone notified her that their time was essentially done. She broke down her own saxophone and stowed it in its case, then cracked open the rehearsal room door.

"I'll see you in orchestra class. And remember what I said. Take time for yourself. Okay?"

Brent nodded. "I will. See you in orchestra."

She followed Brent out of the rehearsal room and headed toward her office on the other side of the band room. But a quick glance through the window in Mike's office door revealed a flustered Mike at his desk. His hand was plastered to his receding dark hairline, and his bulky frame sat low in the massive office chair behind the metal desk.

Sucking up her courage, Hannah dropped her saxophone in the storage cupboard and walked past the chairs and music stands and stood in Mike's doorway.

"What was so important that you needed to interrupt my student's lesson time and not wait until after?"

Mike's free hand landed on a paper slip and slid it to the end of the desk toward Hannah.

"I need you to look over this form and make sure I filled it out right. It needs to be mailed by Friday."

Hannah looked at her watch. Morgan would be arriving soon so they could drive over to the homecoming carnival. "I'll take care of it tomorrow."

She turned to leave and heard, "Why not do it now?"

Hannah looked to the sky. Typical Mike. Always waiting until she was leaving to get the last word.

She turned back and said, "Because I have plans tonight."

"So do it now and then go."

"I need to be ready to leave once Morgan gets here. If it's not due until Friday, it can wait until tomorrow."

She turned away again.

"It'll only take a few minutes now, and then it's done."

Hannah breathed hard through her nose. "You know, you can always just mail it. You don't need a second set of eyes."

Mike scoffed. "I never do these things right. You know that."

"Well, it's time you learned. You're in charge of marching band. I'm in charge of orchestra. You get to deal with any forms for your competitions just like I have to deal with the forms for mine. That's what we agreed on in the divorce."

He looked like he wanted to give a retort, but nothing came.

"I'll see you tomorrow, Mike." She turned and walked over to the conductor's podium and grabbed her jacket and purse.

"Would you please look it over? I don't want to disappoint my students with my fuckup," he yelled.

Hannah groaned and clenched her fist. He was such a bastard for using his students against her.

"Leave it on my desk, and I'll look at it in the morning."

She forcefully pushed open the door, hearing Mike shout, fruitlessly, after her before it closed. Needing a moment, she leaned against the wall and took deep, calming breaths.

"Mom? You okay?"

Hannah turned her head and saw Morgan walking toward her, concern etched on her face.

"Yeah. I'm fine. Just needed a minute."

Morgan looked through the window into the band room.

"What did Dad do this time?"

Hannah rubbed her temple. She hated that her daughter asked that as her first question. She pushed herself off the wall and wrapped her arm around Morgan's shoulders.

"Nothing that can't wait until tomorrow," she said, then she guided them down the hall and out the door.

CHAPTER FIVE

The carnival was working its magic on Hannah. It wasn't necessarily the bright lights, loud music, or deep-fried food she'd most likely be paying for later. No, it was the unguarded joy on her daughter's face. The only thing Hannah wished was that she'd had time to go home and change into something more comfortable. She'd been lucky enough to remember the sneakers in her car. They didn't match with the gray slacks and floral blouse she'd worn to school, but she wasn't worried about winning any fashion awards. She was here to have fun with her daughter. So far, mission accomplished.

"Hey, Mom! I'm going to the ring toss booth," Morgan shouted over the music and the screams.

"Okay. I'll catch up," Hannah replied.

So far, Morgan was handling all the noise pretty well, but Hannah knew from past experience that could change instantly and had to fight the urge to hover. Morgan was sixteen and knew her own limits. Hannah had trusted her daughter for years to do what she needed if she got overwhelmed. Maybe it was knowing their time together before Morgan went off to college was short that had Hannah wanting to stay close in case she was needed. But she couldn't. She wouldn't. Morgan not only needed a mother who loved her, she needed a mother who respected her and allowed her to have her own space.

Hannah chuckled at how some things didn't change as Morgan got older. Sure, they had their arguments—what mother and daughter didn't—but with Morgan on the verge of adulthood, it would be easy enough for them to drift apart. Especially if Morgan got into UCLA. They'd always been close. Would their relationship suffer with distance? Hannah shook her head. She didn't need to fret over what-ifs just yet. She rounded the corner of the balloon dart booth and saw a familiar figure at the cotton candy stand.

"You know that's pure sugar, right?"

Stephanie turned around and shoved a big pink cloud into her mouth. "This is my cheat for the week. Give me some slack."

Hannah laughed as Stephanie grabbed another wad and held it out to her.

"Oh no. I'm still trying to digest the fried Twinkie Morgan talked me into when we got here."

Stephanie shrugged, then stuffed the second cloud into her mouth. "Did you just come from work?"

Hannah nodded, noting that Stephanie wore dark blue jeans and a fitted purple T-shirt with UCA on the front. Obviously, she'd been smart to bring a change of clothes.

"How was Mike today?"

Hannah groaned as they walked. "I almost made it out of there, but then he interrupted the last few minutes of my private lesson with Brent." Stephanie held out a pinch of cotton candy. This time, Hannah took the offering and tore little pieces off.

"I hope you didn't stop."

"No, I finished the lesson, and then when I went to see what he wanted, he slid the application for the Greers Ferry Marching Competition over to me to look over."

"Does he not know how to fill it out himself? He's been a music director for over twenty years now."

"Exactly. I told him I'd look at it tomorrow, but he was like *do it now*. I said I had plans with Morgan, and…"

"He tried to guilt you into it?"

"Yes. But I stood my ground."

"Did you? Or did you just do a delayed surrender since you said you'd do it tomorrow?"

Hannah wasn't surprised Stephanie asked that question. She'd pushed back, and that had felt like a win. Until now.

"I didn't push my priorities to the side for his. So I consider that a win."

"Uh-huh."

Hannah sighed and stuffed another piece of cotton candy into her mouth. "I understand what you're *not* saying. If the kids miss the competition, then the guilt should be on him, not me, since he didn't do the work. But I don't want to do that to those kids who've worked their asses off."

"Okay, okay," Stephanie relented. "I will give you a B-plus for standing up for yourself and your plans and doing tomorrow what can be done...tomorrow."

Hannah bumped Stephanie with her shoulder, happy her friend saw her baby step for what it was. Progress. They rounded the corner to the baseball throwing booth, and Hannah chuckled when she saw Morgan at the ring toss, elbowing another teenager Hannah vaguely recognized from their high school, with a big smile on her face.

"I'm glad I ran into you. I have a feeling now that Morgan found her friends, she's going to run around and leave me in the dust."

"Happy to see you, too," Stephanie replied. "But I'm not here alone."

She followed Stephanie's outstretched arm. There, at the ring toss, two spots over from Morgan, was Parker. She gasped and turned to Stephanie, who had a tight-lipped expression on her face.

"Parker told me what happened at the diner. Did you really flirt with her?"

Hannah turned away from the booth, from Stephanie, from everything. She squeezed her eyes shut. She really didn't want to drag this out now. When she opened her eyes, Stephanie stood in front of her.

Hannah sighed. "I acted impulsively last night, and I may have hurt Parker's feelings."

"So that's a yes?"

A small nod.

"I thought so. For the record, I didn't tell Parker you were bisexual, even though I know that might've cleared up any confusion she had."

"You didn't?"

Stephanie squared her shoulders and looked Hannah in the eyes. "It's not my place to reveal your sexuality to anyone."

Oh, thank God. A loud exhale escaped Hannah's lips. She would have understood if Stephanie did tell Parker, but Hannah was so happy she didn't. Because Stephanie was right. This was news Hannah needed to deliver herself.

They turned back to the ring toss, and Hannah bit her lip. Parker wore tight denim jeans and a long-sleeve gray thermal. She was saying something with a grin on her face. Probably trash-talking Morgan. The ease with which she smiled tugged at something deep in Hannah's core.

"The last twenty-four hours have been a whirlwind for my emotions," Hannah confessed. "And it's all because of Parker."

"Is that good or bad? I can't tell."

"Most of it's good. I think. I didn't know who she was when I walked into the party last night. All I noticed was how handsome she looked. I don't normally put emphasis on physical attraction, but I certainly changed my tune when I saw her in the middle of the room."

Stephanie nodded. "Yeah, I can understand that."

"When she introduced herself, I panicked and decided to keep my distance."

"Hmm. Parker had the same idea. How is it that you both ended up at Yucca's flirting in a corner booth?"

Hannah shrugged. "Temporary insanity. Morgan asked about her job, and somehow I ended up interrogating her about her personal life and embarrassed myself in the process. Parker found it amusing and saved me by switching the topic to Morgan. That put me more at ease, and for a moment, I didn't see a young Parker. I saw this grown-up, mature, sexy Parker. That's when I started flirting with her. Then she left." The relief of no longer keeping that all a secret washed over Hannah.

"Do you want a relationship with her?"

As Hannah was about to answer the question, she briefly caught Parker's eye. Then the guilt rushed in.

"I don't know."

Stephanie moved into Hannah's sight line, breaking the connection with Parker. "You need to figure out what you want. Neither of you is built to take risks on a *maybe*."

Stephanie was right. Hannah needed to stop all the incidental flirting, ogling, and whatever else her brain was telling her to do. What she really needed to do now was apologize.

Cheers erupted at the ring toss, and Hannah looked up in time to see Morgan dancing in triumph and being rewarded a giant stuffed bear. She and Stephanie approached the booth and laughed as Morgan's friend—Hannah was certain her name was Ashley—groused, "This game is rigged."

"Of course it is," Parker said. "It takes luck to win these games."

"And I got it all," Morgan replied and hugged her prize.

"Congratulations, sweetie," Hannah said.

"Great job," Stephanie added.

Hannah stared at Parker as she shoved her hands in her pockets and hunched her shoulders.

"Are any of you hungry?" Stephanie asked. "I could use some salt after that cotton candy."

"I could eat," Morgan said.

"I'm kind of full from the…"Ashley didn't get a chance to finish before Stephanie interrupted her.

"Great. Let's go get in line while you two find a table." Stephanie gestured between Hannah and Parker, then headed toward the food trucks at the back of the parking lot with Ashley and Morgan in tow.

"Subtle, Steph," Hannah mumbled.

"As an elephant," Parker replied, her lips turned up in a smile. "I think the tables are by the food trucks."

Parker moved in that direction, but Hannah placed a light hand on her arm and stopped her momentum.

"Actually, I'm not that hungry. Can we walk around and…talk?"

Parker turned and settled in at Hannah's side as they walked in the opposite direction of the food trucks. They dodged a few groups who refused to give them the right of way, as well as a few games out in the open. It was only when Hannah noticed the drop in noise level that she realized they'd left the carnival entirely, and she remained silent until they arrived at the cafeteria pavilion.

"Would you like to sit?"

Parker silently took a seat on the bench. Hannah sat on the opposite side. The picnic table was between them, along with a chasm of silence. Parker looked at her expectantly, and Hannah knew it was time.

"I'm sorry for my behavior last night."

"So, you *were* flirting with me when you looked at my tattoo." Hannah nodded. "Why?"

"It's not easy to explain."

"Try."

Hannah recoiled at the forcefulness of Parker's tone in that one word. "This is hard for me, okay? I apologized. What more do you want?"

Parker leaned on the table. "Hannah, do you know why your flirting upset me so much? And why your unwillingness to explain is so frustrating?"

Hannah shook her head. Parker clasped her hands until her knuckles turned white. She breathed deeply through her nose and rolled her neck from side to side. Whatever she was about to say, it was a big deal.

"Hannah, when we were in school together, I fell in love with you."

Hannah gasped. The words so simple but clearly so tough for Parker to admit. She looked around. She wanted to run, but there was nowhere to run to. She was going to face Parker, hear what she had to say, whether Hannah liked it or not.

"Did you know?" Parker asked.

Hannah picked at the wood plank under her fingers. "I may have suspected it."

"Then you also suspected I was the one who wrote the love letter you found in your office."

Hannah felt the weight of the admission in her chest. Yes, she'd suspected Parker. She was the only person who'd lavished attention on Hannah during that time, outside of Mike. But she'd never found out for certain. Didn't *want* to know, if she was totally honest. Now, though, sitting and hearing Parker confess the truth, it was as if the puzzle pieces surrounding that mystery from her past fell into place.

"Look at this from my perspective." The hurt in Parker's voice broke through Hannah's reverie. "Someone you secretly loved starts flirting with you but has no interest in you romantically. I'm not only hurt by the fact you were having fun at my expense. The fact that—on some level—you knew I had feelings for you, it makes it all the crueler. And I don't want to be associated with someone like that. It's taken me a lot of work to learn to walk away from people who have no problem hurting me."

Hannah was lost. She needed to fix this and fix it now. Parker stood and moved to walk past her, but Hannah quickly stood up and blocked her escape.

"Parker, please. Don't go. I can explain why I did what I did. I swear I wasn't being cruel. I was…please, sit down."

Parker did as requested, though there was an air of uncertainty Hannah felt as she did. Hannah fidgeted with her fingers. Where should she begin?

Parker must've sensed her trepidation because she reached and put a comforting hand on top of Hannah's. It wasn't firm or soft. It was just there, and yet it was also soothing. Hannah turned her hand over and scraped her nails against Parker's palm. Then Parker gently clasped their fingers together, and it gave Hannah the courage to reveal the truth.

"When I was going through my divorce, I discovered I was bisexual."

Parker's eyes held a hint of surprise.

"How did you come to this revelation?"

The analytical, detached tone didn't sit well with Hannah, but she suspected this was Parker's way of distancing herself until she had the full story. Hannah squirmed on the bench. She was uncomfortable—still—revealing this to anyone. A gentle squeeze of her hand, and Hannah regained her courage.

"I was at the annual state band conference down in Pine Bluff, doing what I normally do—helping my students, checking out the exhibits, some light networking for new gear and equipment—and I met this other band director named Amy."

Hannah took a moment to remember the short blond hair that feathered over intense blue eyes.

"She was from Jacksonville, new to Arkansas, and we hit it off. At first, it was like a new friendship. I had come alone for the first time in years, so it was nice to have company. We hung out, went to dinner every night, and we sought each other out during the rehearsals." Hannah paused and took a deep breath. "On the final day, I couldn't find her. I felt this intense sadness, and I didn't know why. Mike had been moved out for months by this point, so I chalked it up to being on my own, and Amy was new and exciting."

She paused again and gauged Parker's response. The lack of engagement that was apparent when Hannah started her story softened into understanding. She waited to see if Parker had any questions. When none came, Hannah continued.

"Right before the final concert performance, I found out why I couldn't find her. I entered the concert hall, and I saw Amy with her wife. I felt like I had been punched in the chest, but I couldn't show that to Amy. I was polite, smiled and responded to questions, laughed at jokes. But inside I was dying. To this day, I couldn't tell you her wife's name. The ringing in my ears was so loud, no sound made it through. I held it together long enough to make it to the bathroom, then I locked myself in a stall and cried. Hard. I didn't even cry that hard when I told Mike our marriage was over."

Tears fell on the picnic table. Reluctantly, Hannah let go of

Parker's hand. She opened her purse to grab a tissue. She looked up, and Parker's eyes held so much compassion, so much empathy. Relief flooded her chest, as well as a sense of connection to Parker for the first time. Of course she would be understanding. She went through the same thing with Hannah.

"Did you ever talk to Amy again after that weekend?"

Hannah shook her head. "She tried to contact me a few times, but I never replied. I couldn't. I was so ashamed."

"For falling for a woman?"

"For falling for a *married* woman. I couldn't carry on a friendship knowing I possibly wanted more."

Parker nodded. "Have you dated any women since your divorce?"

Hannah scoffed. "No. Stephanie has dropped hints whenever I mention I find a woman attractive, but nothing ever comes of it."

"Stephanie knows?" Hannah nodded. "That explains a few things, then."

"Like what?"

"I told her about the diner, and she didn't look surprised. Concerned but not surprised. Her knowing explains it. And also why she said I should talk to you."

"She's a good friend like that," Hannah said.

"The best."

The tension eased, replaced by such a feeling of hope Hannah had never experienced before. Hope for what, she wasn't sure, but it had her excited for possibilities, especially if they were with Parker.

"I...appreciate you sharing this with me," Parker said slowly. "For trusting me with this. I have a better understanding of where your mind was last night. But..."

"But...?" Hannah echoed.

Parker's throat bobbed, and Hannah could hear the emotion in her words. "I don't think we should try to be anything more than friends to each other."

Heaviness settled in Hannah's chest. "I understand. I'm sorry I made you uncomfortable."

"You didn't make me uncomfortable. If anything—now that I know the full story—I'm flattered by your attention. My eighteen-year-old-self is cheering so loud right now."

Hannah chuckled at the image of a young Parker running around and waving her hands in the air at winning the girl.

"Relationships need a solid foundation to succeed," Parker said and clasped her hands on the table. The hope Hannah thought had floated away started to fill her heart once more. "You're just out of a marriage, and you've recently discovered this new piece of yourself, which I think you should take your time and explore. But in doing so…" She paused and closed her eyes, as if the words were going to be as painful for Parker to say as for Hannah to hear. "You are not in a position to give me the solid foundation I want to have in a relationship. And I'm not built for no-strings sex."

Hannah closed her eyes and nodded. Parker's words stung, but she spoke the truth. She'd just gotten out of a marriage where the other person's emotions were all-consuming and top priority. Could she guarantee a relationship with Parker would be any different? Did she *want* a relationship right now?

Simple answer: no.

"I would love to be your friend," Hannah said, ignoring the twinge of disappointment in her chest.

"I'd love to be your friend, too."

Parker's lips formed the easy smile that got Hannah in trouble to begin with. She suppressed the urge to say something flirty and went with practical.

"We'd better head back and rescue my kid. Who knows how much junk food Steph has plied her with in our absence."

They stood and walked back to the carnival. This time when Hannah looked over at Parker, her back was straight, her smile wide, and her hands swung easily at her sides.

CHAPTER SIX

"You told her the truth?"

Parker was never so happy to be in a crowded room. It meant Stephanie's question was lost in the din of the dishes and conversation happening around them, though one look behind her at the suspicious eyes of alumni spoke to the volume at which the question was asked.

"Would you keep your voice down." She gave an apologetic wave to the couple behind her in the breakfast buffet line and whispered, "Yes, I told Hannah the truth. Honestly, it was a relief. It was as if there was this invisible cloud hanging over me, like my feelings for her were some dark secret preventing us from moving forward. And that feeling was only amplified when she revealed…"

Parker stopped and looked around the room again.

"That she's attracted to women?" Stephanie whispered.

"Yes, that. And you could've given me a heads-up."

Stephanie shrugged and grabbed a couple of slices of bacon from the heated tray. "I did, in a way. I told you to talk to her. And after I noticed she was ogling you pretty hard while you were at the ring toss, I gave her the same advice."

Parker warmed at the thought of Hannah giving her the once-over. She ducked her head to hide her smile.

"I saw that," Stephanie said, grinning herself.

"Saw what?"

"That smile. It's okay to be happy someone found you attractive. I'm happy for you both."

They found an empty table near the ballroom window and settled in. Parker was three bites into her eggs when she realized what Stephanie said.

"Wait. You're okay with this?"

She wasn't totally sure what *this* was yet, but it was strange Steph would be onboard so quickly.

"Of course I am."

"I thought you didn't want me to fall into old traps with Hannah."

"That was before I knew the feeling was mutual. It wasn't thirty years ago, and that's why I tried to protect you. So did Keith."

"What?"

Parker gawked as Stephanie chewed her bacon and nodded. As if he was summoned by the mention of his name, Keith slid into the chair between them, his plate piled high with every fried breakfast dish offered.

"Good morning, ladies. What are we discussing this fine day?"

"Parker's crush on Hannah," Stephanie said.

Parker glared at her, trying to convey without words for Stephanie to shut the hell up.

Keith's exuberance faded a little, and he whined, "You're not still hung up on Hannah, are you?"

Parker huffed. "No, I'm not."

"But Hannah likes her," Stephanie explained, "and last night Parker told her she was the one who gave her the love letter."

Parker felt the burning in her cheeks. Could she crawl under the table and disappear now, please? The urge to run was only amplified when Keith let out a surprised whistle.

"Wow, that's news to me," he said. "I didn't even know she was gay."

"I think she's bisexual," Stephanie clarified.

"Oh, that explains it better."

"Would you two stop," Parker shouted. Heads turned. Even Mike, who was sitting a few tables away, stared at her. She shrank down as far as she could. "This is a private matter between Hannah and me. I only told Steph because..." A thought finally caught up with Parker. "Did you tell Keith about my crush?"

Steph quickly shook her head. "I did no such thing. I would never betray your confidence like that."

"I figured it out on my own," Keith admitted.

"How?"

"Face it, Parker. You weren't subtle. I saw how you looked at her, how you watched her. I was worried for you, so I asked Stephanie if you had a crush on her. All she did was confirm it."

Stephanie added, "And I bet good money even though you only told her last night, Hannah had a hunch as well."

"She said as much when I pressed," Parker said. "So, everyone knew?"

"Not everyone, thank God," Keith said, his gaze drifting behind Parker as he cut up a slice of ham.

Parker turned, only to find Mike. His cheeks were bright red as he laughed hard at something one of the guys joked about. He'd gotten heavier with age, and the redness of his face hinted at something more than a jovial attitude. He looked up and spotted her, and the laughter stopped. He narrowed his eyes. Then his smile disappeared, and a deep frown formed on his lips. He stabbed his eggs so hard, Parker could hear the clank of the fork hitting the plate across the room. Parker gulped and turned back around.

"Did he ever suspect?"

Keith focused on his food and gave a small nod. She rolled her lips and sighed. Maybe Stephanie's warning all those years ago had some merit. Gently, she placed her hands on top of Keith's.

"Thank you," she whispered. He smiled and popped a piece of ham in his mouth, then winked.

"Now that you and Hannah have cleared the air, where do you go from here?" Stephanie asked.

"We've decided to be friends, which I think is the best thing for everyone."

"Well, that's a bummer." Stephanie threw the toast onto her plate.

Parker laughed. "Actually, it's not. She's recently divorced and trying to figure out this new discovery and what it means for her. It's something that can't be rushed or pressured. Friendship is the best thing for her right now."

Stephanie nodded, and she looked over Parker's shoulder. "I hope you're prepared to put your *just friends* mantra to the test because it's about to be taken for a test drive."

Parker turned and saw Hannah in the brunch line, and she found herself doing something she normally didn't do.

"Good morning, Hannah. Would you care to join us?"

The surprise on Hannah's face matched the surprise Parker felt extending the invitation. She wasn't one to force an interaction, but Parker wanted to make good on her promise and be the friend she knew she could be to Hannah.

"Hey, Parker," Hannah said as she walked over to the table. "I was hoping to run into you today."

"You were?"

"Absolutely. Morgan has been singing your praises and gave me a list of questions to ask you about music editing."

"Can I see that list?" Keith asked and snatched the paper away as soon as Hannah pulled it from her purse.

"I believe that was meant for me," Parker said. She snapped her fingers, and Keith handed it over.

The questions weren't too complicated. They were what she'd expect from someone around Morgan's age. *What's the hardest edit you've ever done? How long does it take to complete a film or show?* Parker could answer these in no time.

"When does she want these back?"

Hannah cut a piece of sausage and shrugged. "Oh, she didn't say. How about I give you her email address and you can send them?"

Parker nodded and folded the piece of paper but stopped when Keith snapped his fingers and gestured to the list. She rolled her eyes and handed it over.

"You're incorrigible."

"Yes, and you love me for it."

Parker laughed. She really did.

Keith scrutinized the list and hummed at a few of the questions. When he handed it back, he folded his hands on the table and stared at her.

"How hard is it for you to explain music editing?"

"Um, not too hard since I do it. Why?"

"Have you ever thought about teaching?" Keith asked.

Parker looked around the table, filled with educators.

"While I respect education immensely, I've never pictured myself in a traditional classroom setting. However, I have given guest lectures on music editing at Savannah College of Art and Design. It's where I got my master's degree."

Keith's eyebrows rose. "That's impressive. Would you be interested in doing something similar for my students?"

Parker nodded. "Absolutely. Despite my aversion to classrooms, I feel getting into the process more when educating future artists helps them in the long run."

"Wonderful. Do you have examples to show?"

Parker chuckled and leaned over to Hannah. "Remind me to make Morgan my new agent. She's great at getting me work without even being in the room."

"Does she get a salary with this new position?" Hannah quipped.

Parker held up one of the silver-dollar pancakes on her plate. "Does she accept pancakes as payment?"

"Ha! She's worth more than pancakes."

Parker laughed and speared a sausage with her fork. "I think I can handle eggs and sausage as well."

"Deal."

They shook hands, and Parker reveled in the warmth. These were her people. They made her happy, and she would always cherish it.

"In all seriousness, though, I usually keep a few sessions on my laptop. So, yes, I do have examples. You just can't record the lecture because all of it is protected under NDA until it airs."

"I think we can handle that," Keith said.

"Is it hard?" Stephanie asked.

"Is what hard?" Parker replied with another question.

"Music editing? Overall."

"The hardest part is learning the equipment. But if you understand how a musical cue is utilized in a scene, as well as how tempo and beats are organized, then it's not difficult at all."

"Musical cue. That's what they call the music that plays under a specific scene?" Hannah asked, then slowly slipped the fork past her lips.

"Uh, yes. And depending on how much a director wants to utilize music in their project, there could be as many as one hundred or as few as five or six, depending on what kind of feel they're going for."

"Are you sure you're not cut out to be a teacher?" Keith asked. "You're doing really well teaching us right now."

"Like I said, I'm fine with unconventional teaching. But in a classroom setting, I get too nervous. I had to do a teaching internship while in grad school. Standing in front of students, being their sole focus, I nearly passed out five minutes into the lecture."

"Ouch," Stephanie said.

"Okay, okay," Keith conceded. "So, a guest lecture it is. How long are you in town? I could probably have something set up as early as next week."

"Not that long, I'm afraid. I'll probably be heading back to Los Angeles as early as Sunday."

"But you just got here," Hannah said. Was that a twinge of disappointment?

"The negotiations between the producers and the unions have made some headway. If they reach an agreement by the end of the week, I need to get back and resume work on my projects and find others."

"Why look for others when you already have work?" Stephanie asked.

Parker fought the urge to vent her frustration over the strikes and how they impacted everyone's workflow, so she calmly explained.

"These strikes have affected a lot of editors like me, in all departments. We were still recovering from the pandemic, and now these strikes have made all editing jobs valuable commodities. The problem is there are more editors than jobs, so people will be vying for anything that becomes available. It's going to be wild."

The breeziness of the earlier conversation gave way to tension at this bit of news.

"Well." Keith dabbed his mouth and broke the silence. "I wish you the best of luck with your work and keeping it going. Maybe we can set something up for the future? I'll even fly you in myself."

"Let's start with Zoom and go from there."

"It's a deal," Keith said. "On that note, I need to get going. I have to set up the computer lab for my next class."

"Oh, I'll walk out with you," Stephanie said.

Parker stood and gave them each a hug, waving good-bye as they left the room. When she sat back down, Hannah stared at her with narrowed eyes.

"What?"

"I know you don't have time to prep something big, but would you be willing to come and talk to a few of my band students for thirty minutes or so?"

"I'm not sure. I just told you I have issues with giving speeches," Parker stammered.

"And I understand that, but Morgan is so enamored of your work. And while I know you can answer her questions, I feel this can also benefit my other students. Kids who love music like you do but don't want to do conventional jobs with it."

Parker rubbed her neck, still unsure.

"I know it's last minute, but I really believe anything you tell these kids would be beneficial to them. Please?"

Parker felt the butterflies stir at the implications of getting up in front of students again. Students who would be solely focused on her. She looked up, and the plea in Hannah's eyes dissolved the last of her resistance. How could Parker not do this for Morgan? For Hannah's students? For Hannah? Her worry about passing out didn't compare to being in the company of the woman quickly becoming her friend.

"You know what? Maybe it's time I conquer my stage fright. Count me in."

❖

Hannah arranged the chairs to be evenly distanced, then placed the music stands in between for sharing—making sure each chair had a good sight line to the podium. Confident her students would be comfortable, she stepped back and smoothed a hand down the front of her blue blouse. She took a couple of deep breaths. She was nervous. Why was she nervous?

Right. Parker would be there. On Hannah's territory. And she'd been the one to invite her. No one was more surprised than Hannah that she'd extended the invitation. It was an impulse, one Hannah had convinced herself was for Morgan's benefit. At least, for the first twenty-four hours after the initial invite. But there was more to it. Maybe it was Parker's blunt honesty at the carnival the other night. Or maybe it was their interaction over the alumni brunch. While Parker had been aware of her, she didn't make Hannah her sole focus. Though small, the gesture allowed Hannah to relax, unlike with Mike, who would've kept his attention on her and made her perform a role she found exhausting. She needed someone like Parker in her life. Someone who cared for her but didn't need her to lift them up.

A light knock drew her attention, and the butterflies took flight when she saw Parker leaning against the doorframe, all casual in dark jeans and a black Henley shirt, smiling.

"Hey."

"Hey yourself," Hannah croaked out. "You're here early."

Parker walked farther in and dropped her backpack by the podium. "Sorry about that. I wasn't sure what traffic would be like, so I left Little Rock early. I hope that's okay."

"It's fine." Hannah focused on the packet of sheet music on her podium. "I'm just setting up for class. You can sit in the back while I finish this up."

"Do you need some help?"

Hannah paused. She looked up and found Parker standing next to her on the podium. Her brow creased, and her mouth opened and closed.

"It's a simple question, Hannah," Parker joked.

"It is, but no one's ever offered before." Parker stepped back, confusion evident. "Never mind. Yes, I would love some help."

She pulled out the stack of sheet music she'd sorted the day before and handed a small portion to Parker. "These are the horn parts. They're along the back row. Trumpets on the far left, then circle around to the tubas on the far right."

Parker did as instructed and set the different parts on the corresponding music stands. "Was Morgan excited when you told her I was coming today?"

Hannah—who'd started setting the woodwind parts on the front stands—smiled. "She squealed so loud I thought she'd burst my eardrum. I'm guessing that's a good sign."

Parker laughed and continued her task. When they crossed paths in the middle of the semicircle, Hannah noticed a soft expression on Parker's face.

"This really takes me back. How often did we do this at UCA?"

"Too much," Hannah said. "But it was part of our duties as members of TBS."

"True, but I didn't mind doing it because you were the librarian. I wanted to show you I was dependable, and it turned into a valuable skill. It was how I learned about score order, which comes in handy when I'm on the scoring stage."

"How much of your job entails working with musicians?"

Parker flipped the sheet music over as she set it on the stand and sighed. "Nowadays, not so much. Most studios and producers have gone to electronic music because it's faster and cheaper. Only the real diehards insist on using orchestras to create the score."

"Diehards? You mean old people."

Parker laughed. "Not all of them are old, but I understand why you'd think that. There are some up-and-coming composers I've worked with who prefer live orchestra to MIDI or patches."

"What do you prefer?"

Parker bit her lip, and Hannah looked away as heat climbed her neck. "I prefer the orchestra. I'll admit instrument patches have come a long way and can emulate the sound of a flute or horn flawlessly. But they don't capture the performance. Musicians don't just play notes on a page. They inflect all their emotions. They flow, dance, embellish. A cue for an army marching into battle takes on a different meaning when performed by musicians. You feel the soldiers' fear, their anger, their bravery. You can't get that with a computer."

Hannah nearly wept. She'd never heard so much appreciation and love for music outside of her own.

"Sorry. I got carried away."

"No, it's okay," Hannah choked out. "That was very…beautiful."

They stared at each other for a moment, content to share a love for an art form they both enjoyed in different ways.

"Hannah, you said you'd look over this application and…oh, hello."

Mike's timing couldn't have been worse. Parker stood and rubbed her hands on her jeans. Hannah immediately took the spot next to her.

"Mike, this is Parker Thompson. You remember her?"

Hannah's protective instincts kicked in at the way Mike looked at Parker. It was almost as if he was sizing her up.

"Good to see you again, Mike."

He shook Parker's hand. It looked like he squeezed harder than necessary.

"Uh-huh. Anyway, Hannah, you said you'd look this over."

Hannah sighed. "I did. It looks fine."

"Then why didn't you mail it?"

"Because that's not my job, it's yours."

"It's due tomorrow."

How could a grown-ass man whine like a child.

Hannah exhaled loudly. Heat crawled up her neck again, only this time it was in embarrassment as she saw Parker trying not to pay attention to the argument.

"If you mail it out today, they'll accept it because of the postmark."

He huffed and shook his head. "I don't understand why you just didn't mail it after you checked it."

"As I said the other day, it's not my responsibility. It's yours." Hannah's voice rose in volume. Parker turned and walked over to the music chart on the wall. This really was embarrassing on so many levels. "I'm about to start orchestra class, and I need to talk to Parker. You said you wanted to oversee marching band, and this is part of that responsibility."

She turned away, effectively ending the discussion, and jumped when Mike slammed his office door. She was organizing the score sheet on her music stand in an effort to calm down when a light touch on her shoulder startled her.

"Are you okay?" The genuine concern in Parker's eyes calmed Hannah's anxiety.

"Yes. It's nothing I haven't dealt with for the last twenty-seven years."

"I don't remember Mike being so…"

"Rude?"

"No. Helpless."

Hannah snorted, and she sat in her chair and sighed. Parker grabbed another one and sat next to her. There wasn't a lot of time before her students arrived, but Hannah needed a moment to gather herself and maybe give an explanation.

"He wasn't always like this," Hannah said.

"I would hope not. I'd like to think you wouldn't marry him otherwise."

"It started small. We'd come home from work, exhausted, and he'd go off and play video games to decompress. I was okay because I had my own decompression activity."

"What was that?"

"I'd clean the house." Parker's pinched eyebrows were comical. "Believe it or not, it was relaxing. I didn't mind it during the week because he'd always help on the weekends. Then he only did it on Sundays. Then he stopped helping altogether."

"It became easier for him to let you do it."

"Yep. Soon, he stopped doing other things, too. I was the one making dinner every night. Didn't matter if I had more responsibilities that day than him, it was always me. When we'd get ready for contests and regionals, I always filled out the forms and submitted them. If he was having a class, he'd get so upset when I'd interrupt him, even though it was important. So, I'd make sure that anything I had to ask could wait."

"Did he do the same for you?"

Hannah shook her head. "He always interrupted my classes. And it wasn't always important or work related. Sometimes it was stupid stuff like *what are we having for dinner*, or *we need to figure out Morgan's daycare*. Took me a while to figure it out, but I think he hated not being the center of attention."

"Holy shit."

Sympathy and anger warred in Parker's eyes. Hannah fought the urge to reach out and smooth the lines from her forehead.

"It all came to a head when I got my National Board Certification."

Parker's eyes widened. "Wow. I don't know much about the education system, but I know that's a really big deal. Congratulations."

"Thanks," Hannah said. "Mike wasn't so congratulatory or accepting. He couldn't handle me getting a prestigious qualification over him. Things spiraled quickly after that. When his manipulations started affecting Morgan, that was the last straw. I had to get out of our marriage."

Hannah felt exhausted and relieved. She hadn't meant to tell Parker all of that, but it felt like the right thing.

"I'm sorry you endured that for so long."

"Me, too. And while I know the divorce was good for me, personally—as you can see, it's hard to get away from him professionally."

"He still thinks he can manipulate you to get what he wants."

Hannah nodded. "I tried to be sensible, to make sure we didn't have more interaction during school than required. He seemed agreeable to splitting up teaching duties. He'd get marching band and jazz band. I would take concert band and orchestra. He didn't realize that also meant he'd have to deal with competition applications that needed to be submitted, since I always did that."

Parker leaned forward. She raised her arms slightly then set them back on her knees. Was she thinking about hugging Hannah? Lord knew she could use it.

"I'm sorry you're dealing with this."

Hannah shrugged. "I've been working on saying *no* more, and you can see how well that's going."

"I think you're doing spectacularly," Parker said quietly.

"Thank you."

They both jumped at the loud, obnoxious bell in the hall. They heard stampeding footsteps, and soon the door pushed open. Kids flooded in. Hannah stood on the podium as her students grabbed their instrument cases and unpacked.

"Two minutes," she shouted.

Morgan filed into the second row with her clarinet in hand and a wooden reed in her mouth. She waved enthusiastically at Parker, who returned it with the same enthusiasm. Hannah, surprisingly, didn't get whiplash from the switch from despairing ex-wife to teacher, but she was happy to shed that identity. Also, she was happy for Parker's presence.

"Where do you want me?" Parker asked.

"There's a chair for you in the back. You can sit there until we finish, and then I'll introduce you."

"I get to watch you conduct? Cool."

Hannah looked at her, questioningly. "Why is that cool?"

"Watching you conduct the marching band was one of the things I found attractive about you. All that command and power? It was an aphrodisiac."

Hannah gasped as Parker hopped off the podium and walked to the back of the room like she hadn't just dropped a big, flirtatious bomb on her way. She refocused and looked at Morgan, who was grinning like a little devil. She hated how observant her daughter was sometimes. Checking to make sure Parker was settled in—her excuse to see Parker relaxed and smiling—Hannah raised her baton.

"Let's start with warm-ups. And 1-2-3-4."

Parker looked on in awe as Hannah seamlessly transitioned from warm-ups to composition. She hadn't been lying when she'd told Hannah her position as drum major was sexy as hell to Parker. Honestly, Parker couldn't figure out why she'd revealed it in the first place. Maybe it was because the cat was out of the proverbial bag, and there was a sense of ease at revealing those little tidbits without worry of being ridiculed or embarrassed. Or maybe she wanted Hannah to feel special.

The way Mike spoke to Hannah, as if she was an assistant and not the band director, grated on Parker. And the obvious embarrassment in Hannah's face at being ridiculed so openly in front of another person, well, it took every ounce of restraint for Parker not to get right up in his face and tell him to fuck off. It wasn't her place, but she wanted to bring a smile to Hannah's face. Luckily, she'd been successful.

With a flourish, Hannah executed a hard down beat, then smoothed out the transition with her arms. The poise and grace with which she commanded the musicians to follow her without a single word gave

Parker goose bumps. There was beauty in the notes pulled forth from the instruments, a harmony that—when perfected over time—would move people to experience emotions they'd never experienced before. Parker felt a tightness in her core, foreign yet familiar at the same time. She remembered this feeling being present the last time she'd seen Hannah take the podium. It scared her then, and it scared her now.

"That was wonderful," Hannah exclaimed, drawing Parker's attention. "I'm glad to see you've all been working on your sight-reading skills."

A round of metal clanks combined with leg pats rose up from the musicians as they executed a perfect orchestra clap.

"Let's go back to the beginning and work on the transition into the coda, please."

Hannah raised her arms in a standard conductor's pose, while everyone brought their instruments up to the ready. As the first few notes flowed out of the horns, a smile bloomed on Hannah's face, and Parker saw it—the absolute joy of teaching. It was in the way she cajoled them into playing without force, the way she spoke to them with affirmatives. Hannah was clearly in her element, and Parker was humbled to witness the magnificence that was Hannah accomplishing her life's work.

"Good work, everyone." Hannah laid her baton back on the music stand. Parker wanted to applaud the performance and the effort of everyone in the room but restrained herself. "I'm going to end class a little early today because we have a special guest."

Parker sat up straight and smoothed down her shirt. She heard the door behind her open and turned to see Mike standing, imposingly, in the doorway. What was his problem?

"Please welcome Parker Thompson."

Oh shit.

Parker quickly stood and walked to the podium. As she took Hannah's spot, she felt a hot breath in her ear.

"I put some water bottles underneath the stand, and there's a chair behind you if you feel lightheaded."

"Thank you," she whispered and relished Hannah's fleeting grasp of her arm as she went to sit next to Morgan.

"Thank you for allowing me to be here today. I loved hearing you play."

Parker gulped and looked out at all the expectant faces. She sighed and moved the music stand off to the side, then pulled up the chair behind her. "I'm sorry. I was so nervous that I missed what Hannah told you. Did she say I was a music editor or a lion tamer?"

The students laughed, and Parker's anxiety eased a little.

"I said you were a music editor and a graduate of UCA."

"But if you are a lion tamer, I wouldn't mind knowing about that," a young man with short, dark hair said.

More laughter followed, and Parker's shoulders relaxed.

She'd given this type of talk before—usually to one or two people at a time, not twenty. This felt like teaching a class, but all the intent eyes looking at her made her realize what she said was interesting, fascinating, and exciting. She stumbled over some of her explanations at the start but found her rhythm, so to speak, and was able to give a complete and thorough idea of what she did and why she loved it. The smiles and the awe in the eyes of the kids in front of her told Parker she had succeeded in what she set out to do: show these students careers in music were available outside of performance and teaching. When she finished and asked for questions, lots of hands when up. She fielded everything from *Where did you learn how to do this?* to *Who was your favorite composer to work with?* It was exhilarating, and Parker wondered if this was how Hannah felt when she was conducting.

"I'm afraid we only have time for one more question," Hannah announced. The students whined. "It's true. Does anyone else have a question for Parker?"

"What's the point?"

Parker looked up and saw Mike, arms crossed, still looming in the doorway.

"What do you mean?"

"I mean…what's the point? Can't the composer do the work you do themselves?"

"They could, but that's not practical, given the budgets set by producers. A composer creates the score and moves on to his next project. People like me continue on and allow them to continue to create."

"So you're just a glorified assistant."

The smirk on Mike's face told Parker everything she needed to know. He was trying to demean her in front of Hannah's students. Well, she'd handled people like him before and had a retort on the ready.

"No, I'm not an assistant. My rate is much higher, and I don't get coffee for anyone but myself."

Hannah hid a smile as Mike's faded quickly. He fidgeted in the doorway, and Parker knew she'd hit a nerve.

"I am more of a composer advocate. Once a composer completes their work, my job is to make sure that the integrity of the score stays intact. Pictures go through dozens of edits. Score cues get cut up in the process. I am there to make sure the intent, the emotion, still comes through in the scene. If I do my job correctly, then the audience will never be the wiser."

Her eyes found Morgan, and she smiled.

"But sometimes, our work gets hectic, and we miss a note or beat. That's when it'd be nice to have someone with unique abilities to help me."

A light blush dusted Morgan's cheeks, and she tilted her eyes toward the floor.

Parker glared at Mike, whose scowl dug deep into his brow, then quickly gave a smirk of her own. When she looked at Hannah, Parker saw an array of emotions in the deep blue of her gaze she didn't expect. Acceptance. Awe. And, surprisingly, expectation.

"That was so cool," Morgan exclaimed. She'd stayed behind to give Parker congratulations and ended up gushing about her instead. Hannah stifled a laugh at her daughter's exuberance juxtaposed against Parker's calm demeanor.

"I didn't sound too panicked?" Parker asked.

"You didn't sound panicked at all," Hannah soothed. "Nervous, yes, but not panicked."

Parker placed her hand on her chest and sighed in relief.

"I must say, I was impressed with what you said." Mike's gruff voice killed the jubilation quickly. Morgan even rolled her eyes— good thing she had her back to him. "Sorry I busted your chops at the end. I just couldn't fathom wanting to play second fiddle to a famous composer."

He laughed, and it grated on Hannah's nerves. It wasn't laughter born out of something funny. It was born out of the need to ridicule and make himself feel more important.

"Not all of us were meant to be center stage. I enjoy what I do. Besides, none of my clients treat me as a second fiddle."

"They don't?" Morgan asked.

"No. I have composers who ask me to work with them time and again because I understand their process. I understand their art. That, to me, is more valuable than any kind of fame or notoriety."

Tension coiled in Hannah's core. God, could Parker be any more perfect?

"Well, be that as it may," Mike continued, "I think it was a waste of time. These kids are here because they *want* to be musicians and in the spotlight."

"Not all of them. I loved playing music with a group, but I hated solo pieces. I knew I didn't have the chops to make it as a performer. I guarantee some of your students feel the same way I do."

"And what feeling is that?" Hannah asked.

"They love music, want to continue doing something related to music, but feel they have limited options. If I knew about music editing when I was here, I totally would've done whatever I could to learn it then. I'm not here to tell them not to be musicians. I'm showing them another option. That's all."

Hannah's heart swelled at the passionate defense.

"Do you think I could be a music editor?" Morgan asked.

Mike's head whipped around so fast, Hannah thought it'd come unscrewed. "*You* want to be a music editor?"

Morgan hunched her shoulders and stared at her Doc Martens. "It was an idea. Parker helped me figure out a problem with Justin's score the other night…"

"Oh, now I get it," Mike bellowed. "You're still hung up on this whole notion of going to UCLA."

Confusion registered on Parker's face. Hannah waved a hand, telegraphing she'd explain later. Right now, she needed to intervene before Mike said something he'd regret.

"It was a student film," Hannah said. "Justin asked for Morgan's help, Parker was there when she watched the video, and that's how this whole music editing idea came about."

"You're allowing her to have this pipe dream? I told you no."

"No, you said you wouldn't support it," Hannah replied. "But I do. If Morgan wants to try to get into UCLA, then what's the harm?"

"The harm is what happens when she doesn't. She'll be going up against kids who have been prepping for this their entire lives, not to mention the nepotism. Children of composers probably will have an advantage because of their names. Also I guarantee *none* of them will have the same…condition as Morgan."

Parker flinched. "You mean Morgan's gift, right, Mike?"

"It's not a gift," he argued. "I don't care what these two have told you, but I don't see it as a gift. If others found out about it, she'd be the laughingstock of the whole school. I guarantee it."

Morgan gasped and ran out of the room. Hannah heard the sobs start. Torn between going after Morgan to console her or stay and get into another argument with Mike, Hannah looked to Parker.

"I'll go check on her," Parker said.

Hannah—thankful for Parker's intervention this once—waited until she was gone before turning and going toe-to-toe with Mike.

"You are such a bastard. You know that?"

"Oh, don't get all high and mighty on me. You don't want her going to UCLA any more than I do," he spat. "I was only saying what you're afraid to."

Hannah took a couple of deep breaths, then said, "I may not want her to go, but it's not because I think her synesthesia is a hinderance. If anything, she's more talented because of it."

Mike fumed and paced back and forth. "Be that as it may, the truth is you don't want her to go."

"Only because I would miss her terribly. But that doesn't give me the right to dictate her life. She's worked her ass off and earned the right to try and make it into her dream college."

"And who's going to pay for that, huh? Even if we'd stayed together, there's no way we could afford it."

Aggravation radiated off him. Hannah needed to be careful, so she stayed calm.

"She can apply for scholarships. Her grades are outstanding, so she qualifies for both general academic and music department financial aid. Why are you so against her doing this? I know you, Mike. There's something you're not telling me, so what is it?"

Hannah realized it was the first time she'd truly asked him that.

He huffed and looked to the ceiling. Then, quietly, he said, "I don't want people to find out about her…"

He didn't finish the sentence and stared at her. Only it wasn't sadness in his eyes. It was shame. Embarrassment. Finally, it clicked for Hannah.

"You don't want people to know Morgan has synesthesia." Mike turned and walked away, but Hannah followed. "You don't want people to know your daughter has a defect. Is that right?"

His silence was deafening, the only answer Hannah needed. She fumed and clutched her fists to keep herself from punching him out for even *thinking* that about their child.

"You listen to me, Mike Wells. Morgan is a beautiful young woman who can play circles around both of us. And her *gift*—because that's what it is—only makes her better. If you don't see that, well, I wish I'd known this about you long before now because I would've left your ass sooner."

She stormed out of the band room, not allowing him to reply. He didn't deserve it. Didn't deserve Morgan, and she was Hannah's top priority right now.

Hannah exited the main building and made a beeline for the football stadium, knowing she'd find Morgan on the bleachers because it was her safe space when conflict arose. Sure enough, as she approached the section where the band sat during football games, Hannah heard voices. She slowed her steps, listening from underneath the seats.

"Your dad loves you."

Parker's voice. So soothing. So supportive.

"Then why doesn't he support me on this? Aren't parents supposed to do that?"

Morgan's sniffles tugged at Hannah's heart. She wanted to run up there and pull Morgan into the tightest embrace and reassure her that everything would be okay. But after the revelation Mike dropped on her, she wasn't sure she'd be able to say the right words without breaking down herself.

"I think…" Parker started speaking again, slower now, measuring her words. "Your dad is scared about you being so far from home. I think he's also worried about you going out there without a plan."

"I *do* have a plan," Morgan replied forcefully.

"No, you have a dream," Parker corrected. "It's a good dream, but it's one that requires a lot of work and preparation."

"Oh, now you don't want me to go, either?"

"I didn't say that." Parker shifted on the bleachers. Hannah couldn't see her, but the sound of the movement suggested she was turning to face Morgan fully. "Tell me why you want to go to UCLA."

"I want to go to a good music program with options."

"There are other schools that have the same tracks. I know the University of Arkansas has produced some good musicians and composers. Try again."

Morgan sighed. "My friend Justin is in the film school. He sent me all this information about their music department after he worked with a student composer on his first project. He knew I enjoyed composing, and he sent me information about the composition degree. But they have so many great tracks, I wanted to know more. It was like my mind was opened to possibilities I didn't think were there before, based on where I am. I know I could really thrive there."

Hannah smiled. She remembered the day Morgan had announced her desire to attend the prestigious university.

"Out of the materials Justin sent you—and I'm guessing you've been looking online at some of their programs and promo videos—what have you done to prepare for admission?"

Morgan stayed quiet. The bleachers creaked, and Hannah looked up to see Parker slide closer and wrap an arm around her daughter.

"I'm not telling you it's impossible because it's not. However, you are going to have to put in a lot of work to make your dream a reality. You need to get information about the application process because you may have to apply to both UCLA proper and the music school as well."

"Really?"

"Uh-huh. You'll also need to find out what the requirements are for auditions and submissions because they vary based on the track you choose. Not to mention there's scholarships and financial aid applications…"

"Okay, I get it," Morgan said.

Hannah took a deep breath. She'd forgotten how much work went into applying for college.

"And while I don't like how your dad said it," Parker continued, "he is right about the competition. There will be other students just like you who are talented enough to get in, as well as others who are related to alumni of the same program who have the name *and* the talent to give them an edge."

They were silent after that. Hannah worried Parker might have inadvertently talked her daughter out of pursuing UCLA, and Mike would love that.

"So, what are you saying?" Morgan asked.

"I'm saying, anything worth having is worth putting in the work," Parker replied. "I didn't become a success overnight. I had to work for years before anyone took me seriously. I did Foley and sound design until David Klotz took a chance and asked me to be his assistant. Now we're partners with our own music editing company."

Silence settled over them again. Hannah stood and waited to see if anything else was said. Finally, she heard Morgan's voice.

"You know something, you're right. And I do have time. Time to do all those things and then some. Time to get everything ready so when I finally apply to UCLA, I'm prepared beyond reproach, and they have no *choice* but to accept me."

Parker laughed. "And I will do my best to help you get there."

"Really?"

"Absolutely."

Hannah placed her hand over her mouth, stifling the sob that escaped. She couldn't believe how Parker had not only soothed Morgan's heartache over her father's hurtful words, but she'd inspired her to take the initiative and show the world how great Morgan Wells would be.

CHAPTER SEVEN

Hannah turned from side to side to see the dress from every angle in her bathroom mirror. It was the beautiful blue-purple hue that had caught her attention in the department store a couple of weeks ago. She knew it'd be perfect for the alumni banquet. The silky fabric slid under her fingertips as she traced the curve of her hips. It was snug, but not uncomfortable. She shook out her shoulders to adjust the thick wraparound straps into place. The style was nice, but the point where the fabric crossed highlighted her breasts a little too much for her liking. She scrunched up her nose. Was it too much? She'd be fifty in a couple of months. Could she pull off wearing something this alluring?

"Don't you dare think about changing."

Stephanie's voice crackled through the speaker of Hannah's phone. She looked down at the screen and noticed a finger pointing straight at her where Stephanie's face should be.

"I wasn't thinking about changing."

"Liar. You look sexy as hell, and with your hair draped elegantly over your shoulder, you're showing just enough skin to entice."

Hannah stroked the strands shimmering in the light, careful not to undo what took her an hour to straighten. Stephanie was right. She did look good.

"Thank you. You look beautiful, too."

Stephanie smiled demurely and backed up from the screen to give Hannah the full view. She'd chosen to wear her dark hair up in a twist with curled tendrils falling around her face. It was a beautiful hairstyle for the light gray floor-length gown that shimmered in the light.

"You know," Stephanie said, "if we weren't such good friends and I was attracted to you, we'd make the striking couple."

Hannah laughed. "I guess we would."

"It's too bad you and Parker decided to just be friends. But if you're trying to change her mind, you're on the right track."

At the mention of Parker's name, Hannah's smile fell. She quickly busied herself by cleaning up the makeup on the counter.

She hadn't seen Parker since she'd eavesdropped on her conversation with Morgan. She'd been a no-show at the alumni band rehearsal, and when Hannah had run into Stephanie at the homecoming parade, it'd surprised her that Parker wasn't with her. All she got was a vague explanation of Parker meeting with some old friends from the theater department, and she'd be at the banquet that evening.

"I haven't seen her since she came to the high school, and I'm worried she left without saying good-bye."

Stephanie snorted. "She knows I'd kick her ass if she did that. Plus, Parker doesn't seem like the type to run because someone was mean to her."

"She did when she was younger."

"Another time, another place," Stephanie said. "You keep thinking Parker is that shy, scared kid, when she's not."

"It's hard when it's the only reference I have."

"No, it's not. You didn't like me when we were in school, and look at us now."

"True, but we were in such close proximity and got to know each other over the years. I haven't seen Parker in nearly thirty. It's difficult to reconcile who she was then with who she is now in a matter of days."

"But you like what you've seen so far, right?" Sincerity laced the question, and Hannah nodded. "Then give her the same benefit you gave me. You're not doing yourself or her any favors by trying to keep her in this image from your past."

Hannah sighed. Stephanie was right, and maybe she was being too hard on Parker. Still, the doubt lingered.

"Do you think it's also possible I'm projecting onto Parker my fears of having another Mike on my hands?"

Stephanie whistled low. "That's pretty deep. Honestly, it wouldn't surprise me. But I don't think you have to worry about Parker being Mike, especially since she told me she gave him a good what for the other day."

Now Hannah smiled. "Did she also tell you about talking to Morgan after Mike blew up at her?"

"She didn't, but I believe she was respecting Morgan's privacy in doing so."

Hannah stopped fussing with her makeup and turned to her phone. "I really wanted to thank her for doing that, but she left before I had the chance. Now, it hasn't even been forty-eight hours, and I'm worried I won't get the chance. I nearly begged you for her number at the parade."

"I would've gladly given it to you. Sounds like you care about her more than you want to admit," Stephanie said somberly.

"I think I do. She's beautiful inside and out. She's warm, comforting, exciting, and truly cares for Morgan."

"Sounds like you're already leaving past Parker where she belongs."

"The problem is she's leaving in a few days, and I can't be having these kinds of feelings for her. It'll only lead to heartache."

Hannah's chest ached at the thought of never seeing her again. Was this how Parker felt when Hannah didn't return her affection?

"I know you're scared," Stephanie said, cutting into Hannah's thoughts. "You've had a rough go at love. The thought of having a strong pull toward somebody into a relationship that is all-consuming makes you rightfully cautious. At some point, though, you're going to have to give love a chance again."

Hannah sighed. She didn't have the energy to give anything other than friendship to Parker. However, the idea of friendship didn't sit well with her either.

"What should I do?"

"You're asking me?"

Hannah heard the smile in Stephanie's voice as she closed her eyes and nodded.

"My advice is have patience with yourself. Move at your own pace. Don't let anyone, especially me, tell you when it's time to put yourself out there again."

"And Parker?"

"If Parker is the person I believe she is, then she'll be patient with you, too."

Hannah bent down and smiled into the phone. "Thank you."

"It's what friends are for," Stephanie said.

"Are we ready to go?"

Hannah turned and gawked at Morgan standing in the doorway in a pinstriped suit with a purple bow tie.

"Wow. Stephanie, you have to see this. My daughter is looking very dapper."

Hannah held the phone with the screen facing Morgan. She spun on the heels of her Doc Martens, showing off the slicked-back hairstyle she'd chosen for the evening.

"Very dashing," Stephanie confirmed.

"Thank you," Morgan replied. "I'm ready if you are, Mom."

Hannah looked at Morgan, then smiled at Stephanie.

"We'll see you at the banquet hall, Steph. Thanks again."

"Looking forward to it," Stephanie replied, and then Hannah ended the call.

She grabbed her clutch and shooed Morgan out the door while she called the rideshare. As she got into the back seat, Hannah went over Stephanie's words. She was half right. She needed to be patient, but she also needed to be bold because it would help her take the leap when the time was right. She was ready for whatever the night had in store for her. Parker or no.

Hannah stepped out of the Uber, mindful of the cobblestone parking lot. She was glad she'd opted for a sensible black heel. She looked up at the barn-wood structure where the banquet was to be held. She remembered playing in the jazz band in this very hall her junior year for a couple of swing nights and knew the space was big enough to house the current band, alumni, and everyone in between.

"Oh my gosh, you look better in real life than through the phone!"

Hannah turned and saw Stephanie rushing toward them, grinning from ear to ear.

"That dress is perfect for you, Hannah. It goes great with your skin tone and hair. And Morgan? Wow. I think you're going to give Parker a run for her money in the dapper department."

Heat bloomed elsewhere in Hannah's body. "So, she *is* coming?"

"Yes. Don't worry. She texted me that she's on her way."

Hannah placed a hand on her stomach to calm the butterflies and pushed Morgan and Stephanie toward the entrance. "Let's get inside and find a table before they're all taken."

As soon as they entered the building, the shift from rustic to elegant was palpable. Sheer fabric and fairy lights decorated the walls that separated the main ballroom from a stainless-steel kitchen. Tables were set up around the walls with space available in the center for dancing later. Small floral centerpieces and electric candles sat in the center. The only real rustic decor was the giant stone fireplace in the front of the room, where the awards stage was set up.

They grabbed a table near the entrance. Stephanie talked to another alumni from Gamma Tau. Morgan waved to some of her friends at the next table. Hannah did her best not to fidget or check the door every time it opened. She wouldn't worry. Not yet.

Stephanie's phone pinged with an incoming text. "Oh! She's here."

The door opened, and Hannah tried to calm her nerves, but it was futile when Parker entered, looking drop-dead gorgeous. The deep purple suede suit jacket *had* to be tailored to Parker's body. It was the only explanation for how it tapered to the dip at her waist so perfectly. Same with the pants. There was no way dark slacks came off the rack and fit that snugly, showing off her thighs and calves perfectly. Parker pulled on the lapels of her jacket, drawing attention to the purple and gray necktie against the black dress shirt.

"She cleans up nice," Stephanie said.

Hannah nodded, unable to speak.

Parker looked around the room, and Hannah noticed her hair was shaved a little closer on the sides, and the top was sculpted into a faux-hawk. It was the glasses that were the killer. And when Parker's eyes landed on hers, the smile lines around them caused Hannah to cross her legs unexpectedly.

Hannah was so distracted by the presentation that she didn't see Mike and his buddies enter until they bumped into Parker. She stumbled forward, then steadied when Mike grabbed her arm. Hannah scowled as he made some joke—most likely at Parker's expense—and nearly jumped up to rescue her. But Parker shrugged it off, adjusted her jacket, and strolled over to her table.

"Are you okay?" Stephanie asked.

Parker waved her off. "Please. I've taken worse hits in boxing class."

"You take boxing?" Hannah asked. That explained the muscle definition.

"It's a good workout after a day of sitting for hours." She took the seat next to Hannah and smiled beautifully. "Hello."

The word was so simple, but the happiness behind it—along with the joy in Parker's eyes—made Hannah's chest fill with indescribable emotion.

"Hey."

Hannah wanted to cringe at the weak rebuttal. Parker wasn't deterred, though, as her eyes raked up and down Hannah's body appreciatively.

"I have to admit, you look stunning, Hannah."

She felt her cheeks heat up because the comment wasn't flirty. It was honest.

"Thank you. You're looking pretty dapper yourself."

Hannah's fingers itched to reach out and feel the soft velvet slide through her fingertips, but she couldn't do that. She was already in so much trouble thanks to Parker's kindness and big heart. Touching her would be Hannah's undoing.

Parker eyed her jacket and pulled on the lapels once again. "I thought the occasion asked for a little extra effort. Though I probably should've checked to see what you were wearing."

"Why's that?"

"Because we match."

Hannah looked down at her dress. Sure enough, it was the same shade of purple as Parker's jacket.

"Well, it's not the worst thing in the world," Hannah said, heat rising up her neck.

"Are you sure? People might think we're a couple. I could take the jacket off."

She moved to do just that, but Hannah reached out and stopped her progress, her hand landing on the jacket. Yes, it was as soft as she expected.

"It's okay, Parker. I don't care what other people think."

Parker dipped her head—was that a blush on her cheeks?—and shrugged the jacket back on. Hannah turned and made sure Stephanie and Morgan were still distracted, then leaned into Parker's personal space.

"I'm sorry about Mike yesterday," she whispered. "He usually doesn't blow up like that in front of strangers. And he's *never* been so dismissive of Morgan."

Parker shrugged. "I've dealt with supervisors with worse tempers. I can handle a father looking out for his daughter."

Hannah frowned. "That's what you think it was? Mike being overprotective?"

Parker scooted her chair closer until their knees touched.

"When I told my dad I wanted to move to LA, he said he didn't like it and wouldn't support me. Years later, I found out he said that because he was worried about me being so far from home, and he'd miss me. He couldn't formulate the words to say that at the time and apologized for being dismissive of my dream."

"And you think that's what's going on with Mike?"

"It's the only explanation I can come up with that makes sense because I can't fathom a father *not* supporting his child just to keep her under his thumb."

Sadness clouded Parker's gaze. The urge to reach out and touch her was strong, but Hannah kept her hands clasped in her lap. She'd nearly fallen into trouble when she touched Parker's jacket. She couldn't imagine what would happen if she held Parker for real.

"I envy your ability to see the good in people, especially when they're probably not as good as you think."

Parker gave a weak smile and sat back, putting distance between them. Hannah leaned into the empty space, unwilling to let the moment end. Her pursuit was halted, however, by the blast of trumpets from across the room. Parker ducked like she was being attacked, then laughed as the saxophones and trombones joined the fun.

"I guess the music portion of the evening has started," Parker said, loud enough to be heard over the music. Hannah laughed and watched Parker tap out the rhythm on the table and move her shoulders to the beat.

Morgan and Stephanie jostled them on the way to the dance floor, and Hannah got a wild idea. She bit her lip. Should she ask? Despite her earlier inclination to avoid touching Parker, the thought of ending the evening without at least attempting to do so didn't sit well with her.

She tapped Parker on the shoulder to get her attention. The smile that greeted her propelled Hannah forward with her plan.

"Would you like to dance?"

Parker looked surprised then laughed. "You don't want to dance with me."

"I don't?"

"I'd step all over your feet with these clodhoppers I have on."

Hannah looked down at the black high-tops with rainbow laces, the thick soles resting alongside her heels. She winced.

"I think you're right. That would be painful. How about when something slower is played? Less chance of injury then."

"If they play 'Moonlight Serenade,' I'm all yours."

Parker gave an easy smile and turned her attention back to the dance floor. Hannah watched Morgan and Stephanie do their best to keep the beat, but every once in a while her eyes darted to Parker, and she shook her head. Stephanie was right. Parker wasn't the same lovesick kid from college. She was a woman who knew who she was, knew what she wanted, and would do everything in her power to help those she cared about most. Hannah hoped she was one of those people.

The night went on with minimal drama. Everyone was having a good time. Hannah said hello to a few of her students who were there with their parents. Keith even stopped by to give Parker kudos on her outfit and get her contact information to set up Zoom meetings for his classes. After the dinner portion ended, more dancing ensued. This time, Stephanie dragged Parker out during a particularly fast-tempo tune. She looked uncomfortable, but she was laughing, too.

Despite the joy and fun, Hannah kept an eye on Mike as he made his way through the room during the evening. She wanted to make sure he didn't try to start something because it was evident—between the war of words yesterday and the bump tonight—he had a problem with Parker, and Hannah didn't want it to escalate. Thankfully, he stayed away from them, though he did make several trips to the complimentary bar.

After dessert, the chair of the music department gave a speech about how wonderful it was to see so many alumni. Hannah caught Parker's gaze a couple of times, and they exchanged smiles. It really had been a great homecoming. The current presidents of Tau Beta Sigma and Kappa Kappa Psi gave their own speeches, followed by Keith and Stephanie handing out the alumni awards.

Then Mike stumbled to the stage—obviously drunk—and took the podium. Keith tried to escort him off, but he wouldn't budge.

"This year, we decided to resurrect an oldie but a goody. The crushed can awards."

A groan went up around the room. Hannah hid her face. She—like most of the people in attendance—hated these awards. They'd started funny with titles like *Most likely to forget their gloves on game day* to *Most likely to march off beat*. Over time, though, they became cruel, pinpointing people's quirks and idiosyncrasies as something to be made fun of. After one particular nasty one titled *Will you please be my friend* was given out—and the receiver ran out of the room in tears—it was decided they should be stopped altogether.

"Don't be like that, people," Mike groused. "I've been working all night to get these awards made"—he held up a trash can full of empty beer cans—"but if you feel that strongly about it, I'll only hand out one."

He dug one of the cans out from the bottom of the trash and held it up above his head.

"This award goes to the person who doesn't know how to take a hint and has been after the same girl for the last thirty years."

Hannah thought she might faint. *He wouldn't.* She looked over at Parker's profile as she stared at Mike, unmoving.

"In school, this person followed the same girl every free moment she had. I'm pretty sure she wrote an anonymous love letter as well, but I can't prove that."

Mike stumbled to his left, and Keith caught him. He whispered something in Mike's ear and was pushed away for his efforts. Panic settled into Hannah's chest.

"This crushed can award for *Will you please love me* goes to Parker Thompson."

Silence settled over the room. Not even a gasp. All eyes turned to Parker. Slowly, she stood and calmly walked up to the stage. Keith greeted her, his eyes sad. Parker nodded and shook his hand, an unspoken assurance that she knew it wasn't his fault. Then she went to Mike, and he presented her with the beer can.

She turned it over in her hands. "You forgot the cardboard placard."

Mike shrugged and stumbled. "Last minute rush."

"Well, at least Hannah didn't have to wait until now to find out what a dick you are and had the good sense to divorce you."

Stephanie squeaked and quickly covered her mouth, but the laughter could be heard anyway. Suddenly, everyone was laughing. Even Keith couldn't hide his mirth. Hannah would even go so far as to say he looked proud. Parker turned and left the stage. Mike lunged toward her, but in his inebriated state he stumbled and took a nosedive off the stage. Beer cans scattered across the floor, and everyone burst out laughing. Parker kept walking, past the table, past Hannah, and out the door.

Hannah looked from the door to the group helping Mike to his feet. She was certain they were all waiting for her to come over and assist, but that wasn't her job anymore.

"Go after her."

Stephanie's command startled her.

"What?"

"Go check on Parker. Keith and I will tend to Mike."

Hannah felt a surge of relief. She turned one last time and saw Mike being led to the kitchen. Keith shouted that the show was over and instructed the band to get everyone up on their feet again. As the first notes of "In the Mood" echoed through the hall, Hannah ran to the exit, intent on finding Parker.

The night air was cool against Hannah's heated skin. She didn't realize it was so hot inside. The door slammed behind her and reduced the sharp brass notes to a muffle, allowing Hannah to hear a crash of metal on metal to her right. She took off in that direction and noticed a tall figure leaning against a silver sedan with her head bowed. Hannah slowed her pace—Parker hadn't left, thank God—and mirrored her position against the car.

They stood silent, unmoving. Hannah chanced a look in Parker's direction. She looked exhausted and had every right to be. Having to constantly thwart people's view of her, after years of putting in the work to leave that image behind, had to wear on Parker. In one fell swoop, Mike had reduced Parker to a few moments that happened years ago, and exposed her secret without thought or consequence.

Damn him.

Hannah scooted closer until their shoulders brushed together. "Are you okay?"

Parker inhaled deeply and tilted her head back.

"Can I recant my earlier statement?"

"About what?"

"About Mike not being able to voice his true feelings? Because he had no problem doing it just now."

Hannah leaned her head on Parker's shoulder and pulled her arm into a light grasp.

"I'm sorry. I didn't have the heart to tell you. Mike is not emotionally stilted. He's just an asshole."

Parker rested her head on top of Hannah's.

"How did you do it? How did you live with him all these years?"

Now Hannah sighed. She'd never been able to truly explain how her relationship with Mike deteriorated. How, even though she'd noticed the changes, she stayed with him. Maybe now, with Parker, she could explain it.

"When you marry someone, you're not just gaining a spouse. You're gaining a best friend. A partner. Someone who will be there for you, fight for you—and with you. Meet you halfway. Even with Mike's shortcomings, he was there for me. Until he wasn't. When the relationship became all about his needs and wants, at the cost of my emotional and mental health, I knew it was time to get out."

"Oh, Hannah."

Parker's voice conveyed sympathy. Hannah looked up, intent on saying she was better now, but the compassion in Parker's gaze stopped her protests. A lump formed in her throat, and she turned away at the threat of tears. She felt Parker's body heat as she moved up to stand behind her. Hannah closed her eyes, expecting to feel suffocated by her proximity. All she felt, though, was protected.

"May I hug you?"

Hannah gasped. Such a simple question, yet she heard the hesitation behind it. She didn't answer, not with words. Slowly, she turned and wrapped her arms around Parker's shoulders and sighed as two arms wrapped around her waist. For the first time in a long time, Hannah was being held in an embrace that didn't feel constricting or suffocating. No, this embrace felt strong. There was comfort. Most importantly, she felt safe.

At some point, they started swaying slowly. Hannah opened her eyes when she noticed the music from inside the building—the music she hadn't paid much attention to—had changed from an upbeat swing song to the smooth, slow rhythm of "Moonlight Serenade." She smiled and pulled Parker closer.

"Looks like we get our dance after all."

Parker hummed knowingly, and then they fell silent, letting Glenn Miller's melody wash over them. Hannah felt so peaceful, so content, she laid her head on Parker's shoulder.

"Can I tell you a secret?" Parker whispered, sending a shiver down Hannah's spine.

"Of course."

"I dreamed about this. Dancing with you. Holding you. This was all I wanted as a kid."

Hannah expected alarm bells to go off in her head, but instead, she felt a deep sense of being cherished and a longing to be bold. She pulled back, bringing them face to face for the first time. She smiled, and she couldn't stop herself from speaking a devilish thought out loud.

"This was *all* you wanted? Or did you want…more?"

The gasp from Parker would've been funny had her pupils not dilated at the same time. Her shoulders tensed and she stumbled to reply.

"Uh, your virtue stayed intact. I promise."

Hannah laughed at the absurdity of the comment. "Thank you." She slid her hand down, relishing the feel of the short strands of Parker's fade cut sliding under her fingers before she cupped her cheek. Her eyes darted to Parker's lips, a question poised on her own.

"What about kissing?"

Confusion warred with lust in those brown eyes, and Hannah took the initiative. She licked her lips, and desire coiled in her stomach as she slowly stood on her toes. Parker's breath shallowed and her eyes closed.

"Well, Parker?"

A slight nod, and Hannah's mouth was on hers.

It wasn't elegant, sensual, or deep. A simple pressing of lips together that sent shock waves through Hannah's system. Neither of them moved to deepen the kiss, as if there was an unspoken agreement that this kiss wasn't meant to be passionate. It was meant to fulfill a dream, a gift to their younger selves. Unfortunately, the unhurriedness allowed Hannah's mind to catch up with her actions, and the alarm bells that were absent earlier flared to life.

Questions raced through Hannah's mind. What was she doing? What did this mean? How did they end up here? Parker caressed her cheek and pressed the tip of her tongue against Hannah's lips, requesting entry. Suddenly, images Hannah had long forgotten flashed in her mind.

A young Parker showing up in the commissary, the library—everywhere Hannah was—at least once a day. Parker sitting by her at the pledge ceremony, looking at her so adoringly. The scenes faded, and in their place came images from her marriage. Mike hijacking her birthday by talking about himself instead of toasting her. Mike getting upset with her for planning events without him.

The pressure on her lips eased, then completely disappeared. Hannah bit her bottom lip and tasted salt and moisture. She rested her head on Parker's chest and quietly sobbed. "I'm sorry," she whispered.

The cool hand on the back of her neck calmed her.

"It's okay," Parker replied.

Hannah squeezed her eyes to stave off fresh tears. No, it wasn't okay, and the patience and comfort in those two words left Hannah with the heavy guilt of giving something only to pull away.

"I'm sorry," she said again, but Parker gently shushed her. She softly stroked Hannah's hair, soothing the turmoil.

"You don't need to apologize or explain anything."

Hannah felt more than heard the words as the lips she'd just tasted moved against the shell of her ear.

"You are a woman in the midst of self-discovery and rediscovery. And I am honored to see and experience that with you. Even if it's just this one moment in a longer journey."

Hannah looked up into understanding eyes. "I'm scared of where this journey will end. That it will take me away from you."

Hannah never made declarations, but this was pretty close. She didn't want to lose Parker, even though she knew, at this moment, she couldn't give Parker what she wanted.

"All the more reason why you must take the journey on your own, without me or anyone else to influence you."

Hannah swallowed the lump in her throat. Her heart was screaming at her to claim Parker as hers and figure the rest out together. Her brain, however, knew Parker was right. Hannah needed to know who and what she wanted. If that meant letting go of Parker for the time being, then so be it.

"You are too good. You know that?"

Parker chuckled and pulled her into a hug. "So I've been told."

Hannah closed her eyes and soaked up the feeling of completeness, of being in Parker's arms, knowing she'd have to let it go for however long it took her to figure her shit out.

"Mom! Are you out here?"

Hannah pulled away and turned in the direction of Morgan's voice. She turned back to that quiet understanding aimed directly at her. She opened her mouth, but Parker stopped her with a raised hand.

"Go check on Morgan. I'll be fine."

A tinge of disappointment sat in her chest at being dismissed, but she had no choice. Her daughter needed her, and she needed to walk away. With heavy steps, Hannah crossed the parking lot. She heard a car engine behind her, followed by the sound of tires on gravel. She turned back and saw a gray sedan pull out of the parking lot and onto the highway.

❖

Parker sat on the cold metal bleacher and stared out at the football field. She needed a moment to collect her thoughts, mainly—and not surprisingly—about Hannah.

She still couldn't believe it. Hannah had kissed her. One minute they were dancing, next minute Hannah's mouth was on hers. That was the point Parker needed to make clear in her mind. Hannah kissed *her*. And then she pushed Parker away.

Parker had done the right thing, said the right things to Hannah to make her realize what she'd done wasn't bad. But, oh, it still hurt. To have the dream become reality and then slip away...

She squeezed her eyes shut. She'd gotten over this pain before. She could do it again.

The sound of heels on metal caught her attention. She turned and saw Stephanie walking up the bleacher steps and slow her pace as she reached Parker's row, eyes filled with sympathy. Her lips pinched in a very *I'm sorry* type line as she sat next to Parker. They didn't say anything for a while. Parker assumed Hannah told Stephanie what happened when she'd reentered the banquet hall, and the text she'd received demanding her whereabouts was the result of that. Parker wasn't hiding, and she immediately told Stephanie her location. Now here they were, sitting quietly and looking out over the gray and purple football field.

"This field is really ugly," Parker said.

"Right? Who decided purple and gray turf was a good idea?"

"I don't know, but they should turn in their landscaping license."

Stephanie nodded, and they fell silent again.

"I ran into Hannah."

Parker nodded. "I figured as much. Did she tell you what happened?"

"That she kissed you, then stopped it from going farther? Yeah, she told me."

Despite the ache in her heart, Parker felt a modicum of pride that Hannah took ownership of her actions.

"The whole time I've been back, I kept waiting for the other shoe to drop. I just didn't expect it to be this painful."

Stephanie shuffled closer. "I'm sorry. For what it's worth, I was rooting for you."

Parker let out a mirthless laugh. "You're a good friend, Steph. I don't think I ever realized how much until now. Thank you for always being there for me."

"You're welcome."

Parker sighed. This was it. This was the last time she'd think about possibilities and Hannah Wells in the same breath. The thoughts always led to heartache, and she couldn't deal with it anymore. However, there was one thing she could do, even though the idea had the potential to leave a door open Parker wanted to close.

She reached into her jacket pocket and pulled out an envelope. "I need you to do me a favor."

Stephanie took the letter and rolled her eyes. "Please tell me you're not writing love letters again. Or at least tell me you've gotten better at it."

Parker shook her head. "No, my letter writing days are over. This is for Morgan. It's a list of music editors I know in Los Angeles. I reached out to them yesterday, and these are the ones that said they'd be willing to answer any questions she has about music editing."

"Is your name and info on here?"

"Yes."

"Good. Don't let what happened—or didn't happen—stop you from helping Morgan."

"Thought never crossed my mind."

Stephanie stuffed the envelope in her jacket and furrowed her brow. "Obviously, I have no problem giving it to her, but why can't you give it to her tomorrow at the game?"

Parker hung her head. Now came the hard part. "I'm flying back tomorrow morning."

"What?"

Stephanie's reaction was expected.

"It's all over the news. The unions and the producers reached an agreement. David texted me and said work resumes Monday morning."

"Well, I'm obviously happy for you, but do you have to leave right away?"

"I can't face her," Parker admitted. "She needs to figure out what she wants, and I need to do the same. Away from each other."

Any further protest died on Stephanie's lips, and she gave a small nod. "Do you need a ride to the airport?"

"No, I have a rental."

Stephanie stood and held out her hand. "Well, the way I see it, you have a broken heart, and you're leaving. This calls for alcohol, and lots of it."

Parker laughed and wiped a tear away, then took the offered hand. "Lead the way."

As they walked down the bleachers, Parker took one last look at the football field. Then and there, she vowed never to attend another homecoming again.

CHAPTER EIGHT

Six months later

Parker draped the sound cables across her neck and did her best to recall her audio engineering classes from college.

What goes in must go out. Input to output.

Her memory bank unlocked, and she plugged two cables into their respective outputs on her Pro Tools interface and fed their corresponding ends into the amplifier. She ran two more cables from the amp to the dual speakers on the left and right of her computer monitors.

"All right. Let's see if I did this right."

She walked around her stand-up desk—a splurge after she'd closed on the house—opened a session, and sent up a silent prayer as she hit the space bar. Soft, melodic strings faded in through the speakers, and Parker pumped her fist in celebration.

"Let there be sound."

She jumped and turned to see David standing in the doorway, looking unapologetic. She hit the space bar, and the music stopped.

"I still need to do a pink noise balance, but I'll wait until I get the room outfitted with furniture and padding."

Parker looked around the small space and smiled. This was why she'd wanted the property. The house was nice, but it was the converted shed that drew her attention. It had all the makings of a great at-home studio in the backyard. So if she ever had guests, she could work without disturbing them. She still couldn't believe how lucky she was to get it.

When she'd returned from Arkansas, she and David tag-teamed finishing up their projects in time for the holiday hiatus. Surprisingly, there had been more work waiting in the wings when they'd resumed in

January. David's reputation as an award-winning music editor brought in plenty of projects to get their little boutique off the ground. It was all falling into place, creatively and professionally, and Parker welcomed the distraction. At night, though, when the work was done, she was still haunted by what happened with Hannah.

"You're lucky I didn't see this listing first," David said, halting Parker's mind from traveling to the past. "Lisa only allowed me to use the loft for my office."

"Because you're going to need that fourth bedroom for another reason," Parker said. "Congratulations, by the way."

David ducked his head and blushed. "Thanks." He looked toward the main house. "How's the rest of the unpacking?"

Parker winced and motioned for him to follow her. When she opened the back door, she laughed at his shocked expression upon seeing the stacks of boxes.

"I got the couch and television set up"—she pointed to the sectional facing the wall where the flat-screen hung above a bookshelf filled with Blu-rays—"the cats have all their supplies unpacked, and I think I unpacked a box of dishes so I could eat."

"Did one of those boxes include drinking cups?"

Parker rounded the peninsula to the kitchen and grabbed two clean glasses from the cupboard. As she poured water from the pitcher, David continued talking.

"By the way, I heard from Morgan today. She and her mom are going to be in Los Angeles in a couple of weeks for a visit to UCLA, and she wanted to meet up."

"Yeah, she told me." Parker tried to play nonchalant, but it was fruitless. The thought of Hannah being in Los Angeles and seeing her caused Parker's stomach to roll...in a good way. Maybe.

"Are you okay?" David asked.

"I'm fine. Why?"

"I don't know, you went a little pale for a second. Are you worried about seeing Morgan again?"

"Of course not."

"Then what?"

Parker handed him a glass, then drank her water slowly and looked out the window to the backyard. She turned back when she heard David set his glass down on the counter. He sat on the stool and looked at her with such sincerity, it nearly broke Parker open.

"I know we really haven't had a lot of time to talk since your trip, with all the projects and moving. But now that we have a moment—and you can tell me to mind my own business—did something happen while you were back home?"

"Why do you think that?"

"I don't know. Maybe it's because, outside of Morgan, you haven't really talked much about your trip."

He was right, but it wasn't because she didn't trust him. She hadn't really talked about what happened with Hannah to anyone, outside of Stephanie that last night at the football stadium. Maybe it was time to let someone else in.

"Remember when you said I should look up an old girlfriend on my trip?"

He nodded. "You said you didn't have any."

Parker sighed and set her glass in the sink.

"Morgan's mom, Hannah, was the girl I had a crush on in college. I ran into her at the reunion, we got close, and…let's just say we ended up sharing an intimate moment."

David's surprised expression would've been comical if the stitches around Parker's heart didn't tug a little at the memory.

"By *intimate*, you mean…"

"We kissed. Nothing more. Get your mind out of the gutter."

David nodded.

"We haven't spoken since then, but I left a note promising to mentor Morgan."

"You left without saying good-bye?"

Parker still felt guilty about that.

"I'll admit, that wasn't my finest moment, but you texted me about work resuming, and I used that as an excuse to come back early."

David stared at her, sympathy evident in his gaze. "Have you asked Morgan about her?"

"No. Morgan doesn't need to be in the middle of whatever is going on between me and her mom. Besides, I promised Hannah I'd keep my distance from her."

"What for?"

"She'd just gotten out of a bad marriage and was discovering who she was. She didn't need me hovering and making the waters murky while she figured out who and what she wanted."

She waited for more questions, but all that greeted her was a contemplative stare.

"That's very admirable of you, considering her feelings over yours. Not too many people would make the sacrifice."

I know of at least one, Parker thought.

"So if I invite them both to join us for the scoring session at Sony that Wednesday, will that be an issue for you?"

Parker stared at David. The thought of spending any time with Hannah made her nerves kick up. But she was a professional. She could focus on her work and not Hannah being in the same room as her for a few hours.

You are a glutton for punishment.

"No problem at all," she replied.

"Good. I think that would be the best opportunity for them to sit in."

"You mean least boring," Parker quipped.

"That, too. Plus, they're staying close to LAX to save a little money, and Sony is closest to their hotel and UCLA."

Parker nodded. "Did she say when her tour was scheduled?"

"Same day, in the afternoon, so they'll come by in the morning and leave at lunch."

"You know we're also there on Friday. Why not have them come then?"

"They're coming in Tuesday and leaving Friday. Very whirlwind-esque."

Parker pondered this for a moment. Why such a quick turnaround? David mentioned them staying near LAX where a lot of hotels were discounted. Were they having financial issues? If so, how did this affect Morgan's desire to go to UCLA? She shook her head. It wasn't her problem. Only problem Parker had was seeing Hannah again.

"Having them there only for the morning session shouldn't be an issue," Parker said. "Morgan will absorb a lot in those few hours."

"I thought so, too. And if Hannah gets bored, you can show her around the lot." David winked.

"I don't think you have to worry about Hannah. She's a music teacher. She'll love it and go back and tell her students if Morgan doesn't beat her to it."

"Good, I'm glad we got all that figured out. Do you want to give Morgan the good news, or should I?"

"I'll let you handle this one."

He smiled and tapped his fingers on the counter. "Well, I'll get out of your hair. I'm excited to meet this kid in person."

"She's really special," Parker said.

He stopped and turned back before opening the door. "Are you sure you're okay with Hannah?"

Parker threw the pot holder at him. "I'll be fine. Now get back to your place before Lisa sends out a search party."

"She knows where I am. Unpack these boxes, will you? You're a homeowner now."

The door shut, and Parker slumped against the counter. When she looked up, two pairs of eyes—one hazel, one green—silently judged her.

"You have no business giving me that look. You weren't there. You don't know what happened."

They blinked, but the silent judgment lingered.

"Do you two want to help me unpack?"

The cats jumped off the counter and took their judgment with them.

"Yeah. I didn't think so."

Hannah was at a loss as she held up the short-sleeve blouse. It was nice, professional—she'd worn it to work a few times—but was it appropriate for Los Angeles in April?

"What do you think of this one?"

Stephanie scrutinized the shirt from across the bed. "Seems okay. Nothing flashy but also airy, so you shouldn't burn up if you're out in the sun too long."

Hannah nodded, folded the shirt, and put it in her suitcase.

"I have to say, it looks like you're packing for a month instead of three days. You know this puts a dent in your *trip on the cheap* theme if you're going to pay fifty dollars each way to check a bag."

Hannah looked at the clothes strewn across her bed. They ranged from jeans to slacks to shorts. She needed dressy clothes for the visit to UCLA, jeans and capris for exploring, and—according to David Klotz—business casual for the scoring stage. She stacked the clothes into piles on the bed, then pushed the shorter strands of her hair behind her ear. The new style still felt foreign despite it being done over the holidays. Now her fingers stopped below her ear where the freshly trimmed bob ended.

She caressed the spot below her left ear as Parker's face came unbidden. She'd touched Hannah in that exact spot when she'd cupped her face during their kiss. The memory played out in her head so many times since then, and Hannah always found a new detail in that moment. This time, she focused on how Parker looked at her as she said the words that let Hannah go. Despite her confident and supportive words, there was a glint of hurt in Parker's eyes. In a couple of days, she was going to see those eyes again. Would they still hold the hurt? Or would they have moved on?

"You okay?"

The tenderness in Stephanie's voice broke Hannah out of her reverie, and she tossed her phone across the bed.

"The weather in Los Angeles is very unpredictable this time of year, and the weather app isn't any help. I type in the city, and I get four responses."

Stephanie pulled up the aforementioned app and whistled at the screen. She stood and went to Hannah's closet and pulled out the small rolling suitcase and flopped it on the bed. Then she picked up two pairs of jeans and capris, and the blouse Hannah had just put into her big suitcase, and placed it in the small one—along with a couple of casual T-shirts and another green blouse on the bed. Next, underwear and socks went into the zip pocket, and then Stephanie closed and zipped up the entire thing.

"There. You have everything you need plus room for toiletries."

Hannah smiled and walked into her bathroom to gather said toiletries on the counter.

"I knew I called you over here for a reason."

"Well, this is just a bonus," Stephanie said, her voice getting louder as she approached the doorway. "I'm also your chauffeur to the airport and your psychologist should you get nervous about seeing Parker again."

Hannah nearly dropped her toothbrush to the floor.

"I hadn't thought about her that much until you mentioned it," she lied. "Now that you have…yes, I am nervous."

"Because you left her standing in a parking lot after you kissed her senseless."

"I did *not* kiss her senseless."

"But you wanted to."

She huffed and stumbled over a reply before finally saying, "That's beside the point."

"You're right," Stephanie said, her arms folded across her chest, her eyes serious. "The point is you left her standing there feeling rejected."

Hannah sighed and looked at herself in the mirror, which had been harder to do as the date for the L.A. trip grew closer and closer.

"For your information, it was Parker who let me go."

"Because she knew you weren't ready to be with her. A very noble act, if you ask me."

"Yes, it was."

"Do you plan to bring it up while you're there? Clear the air and all that?"

"I don't know if I'll have time."

Hannah wasn't lying. Their schedule was tight, due to expenses. Fly in Tuesday, go to the scoring stage and campus tour on Wednesday, take a day on Thursday, then fly out Friday. Not a lot of time for Hannah to meet with Parker to say a simple *I'm sorry*. But it wasn't simple. It was an apology laced with regret for not only running away but for also not telling Parker why she'd done it. Hannah knew if she asked, Parker would make the time to talk about the kiss. Did she want that, though?

"It's really shitty to leave Parker hanging, thinking she did something wrong."

Hannah slammed the toothpaste to the counter. "Why are you so hell-bent on this? It's not like there was a chance Parker and I would end up together."

"Not now anyway," Stephanie mumbled.

"Steph!"

"Okay, fine. The reason I'm harping on this is because this feels like something Mike would do."

Hannah sucked in a breath.

"You're a cautious person," Stephanie continued, "but you're not hurtful."

Hannah slouched against the counter, all anger leaving her body. Stephanie came and mirrored her position, leaning her head on Hannah's shoulder.

"I'm not pushing you to be with Parker. But you do need to clear up what happened. That way you can move on to…whatever."

"Whatever?" Hannah asked.

Stephanie shrugged and sported a cheeky grin. "Yeah. Friendship, relationship, fuck buddy. You know, whatever."

Hannah snorted. "I really wonder where you get your gumption from."

Stephanie laughed and hugged her close. "Oh, I get it from *my* mother. Definitely. But don't ever say that to her face."

"I know better, trust me."

They stayed that way, silent, and allowed the tension to ebb away.

"Are you sure there's no chance of…"

"No, there's not," Hannah interrupted. "But I'll do my best to fix this, okay? No promises, but if the opportunity presents itself, I will make things right with Parker, and maybe we can be friends."

"Thank you," Stephanie said, and squeezed her shoulder.

"Hey, Mom!"

Morgan's shout broke up the embrace and pushed Hannah back to her task.

"In here, sweetheart!" she called back.

The stomping of Morgan's boots on the floor slowed as she entered the doorway.

"Oh hey, Steph," she said, then turned her attention to Hannah. "I just got an email from David. He's put our names on the visitors' list at Sony. We're instructed to park in the garage off Overland Drive, then meet him and Parker at the security gate, and they'll guide us to the stage."

Hannah crossed her arms tight over her chest, ignoring the trip of her pulse at the mention of Parker's name. "That's great, sweetheart."

Morgan beamed and bounced on the balls of her feet. "I'm excited. Are you excited?"

"I'm excited for *you*. Are you all packed?"

"Please. I was packed two weeks ago."

They chuckled as Hannah placed her makeup case and travel brush on the edge of the counter.

"Then I guess all that's left is to eat dinner and go to bed, since we have to leave early for Little Rock."

Morgan scrunched up her nose, and Hannah didn't blame her.

"Ugh. You better get me something cool for driving you both so early before my wake-up time," Stephanie said.

As they entered the kitchen, Morgan and Stephanie settled in the chairs at the island, while Hannah prepared a frozen pizza.

"Mom?" Morgan asked.

"Yes, dear."

"Are you upset with Parker?"

Somehow Hannah didn't burn her hands when she placed the pizza in the oven. She looked at Stephanie, who just shrugged.

"Why do you ask? Did she say something?"

Please tell me she said something.

Morgan shook her head, and Hannah's hope died.

"I know she left without saying good-bye, and I thought you might be angry with her about that."

Hannah leaned across the island and grabbed Morgan's hands.

"I'm not angry with her. I was at first, but then she left you that list and an explanation, so I couldn't be mad at her."

The only person Hannah was angry at was herself. Parker's note had been amazing, but it was even more proof that Hannah had handled the situation badly.

"I'm glad to hear that," Morgan said, "because I have some news. Parker convinced me to put UCA on my list of possible schools."

"She did?"

"Yep. She said it'd be wise to do auditions for my other school choices because it'll allow me to get comfortable with the process. So when I audition for UCLA, I won't be nervous."

"I'm happy to hear this, and she's right. It's smart to audition for other schools. But how come when she says it, it makes sense, and when I say it, I get an eye roll?"

Stephanie patted her hand. "Because you're her mom. Duh."

"Exactly," Morgan said. "Also, it's just smart to not put all my eggs in one basket."

"Just the bigger ones," Stephanie said.

Hannah chuckled and kissed Morgan on her cheek, causing her to scrunch up her face. "When did you get so logical?"

"When I met Parker."

God, Hannah really needed to fix this thing between them. If for no other reason, for Morgan's sake.

The buzzer on the oven went off, and Hannah busied herself with the pizza. "Come on. Let's eat and get to bed. We have to be on the road to Little Rock by three in the morning."

CHAPTER NINE

Parker checked her watch as she and David stood near the security entrance at the Sony parking garage. She was nervous, no doubt about it. "What time did you tell them to be here?"

"Nine thirty. Don't worry, your girlfriend will be here shortly."

Parker rolled her eyes. "Please, do *not* make jokes like that around Hannah. This whole situation with her is delicate. I don't need her to think I go blabbing our private business to every person in Hollywood."

"I'll be on my best behavior, I promise. I was just trying to loosen you up because you look like you're about to jump out of your skin."

Parker appreciated his effort and told him so with a solid pat on his shoulder. She turned back to the entry gate and swayed back and forth, with her hands in her pockets to ward off the chill—and her nerves.

The weather had taken a turn again at the beginning of the week. Instead of sunny and warm in the upper seventies, a storm system moved through over the weekend—causing the temperature to drop twenty-plus degrees. Parker shivered and wished she'd picked up her jacket on the walk over from the stage. The thin, long-sleeved Henley and gray chinos did nothing to protect her from the wind.

"There they are," David announced.

Parker looked up in time to see Morgan walk through the security checkpoint. Hannah followed, putting on her visitor's name tag. Something was different. Good different. Parker's lips twitched. Her nerves were still there, but her heart swelled with something she hadn't anticipated. Happiness. Despite everything, Parker was happy to see Hannah again.

As Hannah stepped from the shadows into the sun, Parker noticed her hair was shorter. Much shorter. Not a pixie cut—closer to a bob. It bounced lightly as she walked. The wind carried a few strands into her face, and Hannah took a moment to push them behind her ear. When she looked up and saw Parker, she immediately stopped. She looked back at the guard, probably wondering if she could wait in her car. Her chest rose and fell, then she turned with a wide grin on her face as Morgan jumped into Parker's arms and squealed.

"It's so good to see you again," Morgan exclaimed, then promptly hit Parker on the arm.

"Ow. What was that for?"

"For leaving without saying good-bye."

"I kept in touch, didn't I?" She rubbed her arm and looked over at Hannah. She wouldn't meet Parker's eyes.

"Still should've said good-bye," Morgan said.

"Fine. You're right. I'm sorry. Just don't hit me again, or I won't introduce you to the person you're here to see."

David chuckled as he stepped forward. "Yes, please, don't greet me the same way you did this one."

Morgan's cheeks colored. "Sorry. It's so good to meet you in person, Mr. Klotz. Thank you so much for this."

"David, please. And is this your mom?"

Hannah stepped forward and shook David's hand. "Hannah Wells. It's lovely to meet you. I appreciate all you've done for Morgan, including this opportunity."

"Well, when someone sends you multiple emails a week, asking about your job, it's really hard to say no, especially since music editing isn't widely known."

"We are very appreciative," Hannah said. "Are you sure we won't be in the way?"

David shook his head. "I've already cleared it with the engineers. They're used to guests coming and going. As long as you don't interrupt the workflow, you're fine."

Hannah's shoulders relaxed.

"Shall we get going?" Parker asked. "The orchestra is arriving, and we start at ten."

Everyone walked in the direction of the soundstages. Parker allowed Morgan to take the lead with David and gestured for Hannah to go ahead of her. They passed rows of tall, blocky buildings with giant doors and numbers on the corners. Morgan hardly seemed to notice as she'd already started with the questions. Hannah watched on, a smile on her face.

"She's doing well," Parker said.

"Very well," Hannah replied.

"And how are you?"

Hannah looked over at Parker, eyes curious. "I'm good. It's been a rough few months, but nothing I haven't been able to handle."

Parker wondered at Hannah's statement. Rough how? Was Mike still being a jerk and making it rough for her at work? Was it her abrupt departure and lack of contact that made it rough emotionally for her? Something with Morgan? She wanted to ask, to know if she could help—or if she was the cause. Now was not the time, though. So Parker only said, "I'm sorry to hear that."

Hannah gave a small hum and kept walking.

Parker sighed. This was ridiculous. What happened, happened. Months had passed. She needed to get over it. She'd promised herself she wouldn't make it awkward, and she was doing just that. As they passed the stages filming *Wheel of Fortune* and *Jeopardy*, she blurted, "I like the new haircut. It looks lighter."

Parker mentally face-palmed, but Hannah chuckled and pushed a strand of hair behind her ear. Parker laughed herself, and the tension eased.

"It is. Lighter and new. I decided for a change around the holidays."

They turned the corner and passed the Coffee Bean. They watched Morgan and David talking in front of them. Parker smiled, and when she turned, she saw Hannah smiling, too.

"Thank you for doing this," Hannah said.

"This was all Morgan."

"Not *this* specifically," she clarified. "I mean, you could've just disappeared after. Instead, you continued to help Morgan. I appreciate that more than you could ever know."

"It was my pleasure to help her."

"I'm glad. I just wish…"

"Wish what?"

Hannah sighed as they turned down a side street.

"I wish I hadn't screwed up our friendship in the process."

Parker stayed quiet. She didn't know how to reply. Yes, Hannah had pulled away, but Parker had also tried to get more from her when she wasn't ready. She needed Hannah to know she was as much responsible for their friendship falling away. When she opened her mouth, though, she was cut off.

"We're here," David said.

Sure enough, they were in front of the John Williams Music Building. Damn. She wanted to clear the air with Hannah, but she had work to do first. She rolled her shoulders and vowed to initiate a conversation soon and clear the air.

"Let's go in, shall we?"

She motioned for Hannah to go through a tall metal door, and they ended up in a room that served as a pantry.

"If you get hungry or thirsty during the performance, there are sodas and water in the fridge and snacks in the cupboard," David said.

He waved them through another doorway into a carpeted room with a giant mixing console, and padding on the walls.

"This is the mixing booth. We'll be set up in here," he said. "And out there is the Barbra Streisand scoring stage."

Hannah and Morgan gaped at the size of the room and all the musicians taking up the space. Parker laughed.

"Pretty impressive, huh?"

"I'll say," Morgan replied. Parker noticed Morgan's fingers moving, as if playing an invisible instrument. Morgan was itching to get onto the stage. She walked over to Hannah, who hadn't taken her eyes off the room.

"Well?"

"Amazing," Hannah whispered.

Parker's chest swelled with pride as she followed Hannah's sight line to the musicians on the other side of the glass. "Yes, it is. I remember my first time on a scoring stage. I got goose bumps when the orchestra played the first chord. Still do, actually."

"I can see why. This is the kind of atmosphere you'd find with the Arkansas Symphony Orchestra."

"It's cooler than the ASO," Parker said. Hannah quirked an eyebrow at her. "When you hear the first note of a cue, you'll see what I mean."

Hannah chuckled and shook her head. Parker, surprisingly, felt very at ease in her presence. It was unexpected, yet relieving to know that what happened in October didn't affect Hannah's ability to have fun while she was here, nor Parker's enjoyment of her time with Morgan.

She looked over at Morgan as she conversed with David and looked at the score. Feeling she was well-distracted, Parker turned her body into Hannah and whispered, "The majority of the cues are pretty tame, but we are recording an action sequence today. The music is up-tempo and staccato in rhythm. Will Morgan be okay?"

"Of course she will. Why wouldn't she be?"

"I remember at the pep rally Morgan wore earplugs. You said certain music could get overwhelming to her senses. Do you think the cue I'm referring to could become an issue for her?"

Hannah's gaze softened.

"No, that shouldn't be an issue. If it gets to be too much, Morgan will step out of the room for a moment to collect herself or wait until the piece is finished."

Parker sighed in relief. "That's good to know. If she needs to leave, that's fine. We also have ibuprofen and Tylenol on hand if she needs it."

"Thank you. Not many people would take the time to do that for her."

The sincerity in Hannah's statement made Parker break the eye contact. God, how goofy could she get? She needed to act like an adult used to compliments. She focused on her shoe digging into the carpet and knew that wasn't happening today.

A loud fire bell went off, and everyone inside the scoring stage scrambled to their seats.

"It looks like we're about to start." Parker gestured to the couch behind her. "You can sit there while we work with the engineers."

"Thanks," Hannah said. "Anything we need to be aware of?"

"If you need to step out, be quiet and don't slam any doors. Otherwise, sit back and enjoy the performance."

Hannah smiled sweetly and Parker took her seat between David and Morgan, adjusting the score and having her pencil at the ready. As the orchestra tuned, she caught the excitement in Morgan's posture—back straight and toes tapping the floor. She looked back at Hannah and smiled, happy when it was returned.

❖

Hannah's butt was totally numb from sitting on the leather couch for three hours, but it was worth it. From the time the musicians tuned their instruments to the first notes of composition, she was enraptured with the one-hundred-piece orchestra and their ability to adjust and harmonize on the fly. It shouldn't have been too surprising. They were professionals, after all. They got paid to be this good. Still, Hannah believed she was witnessing something spectacular, something the everyday moviegoer didn't get to witness, and she felt honored to be one of the few.

Watching Morgan and Parker interact was a bonus. The care Parker displayed for Morgan upon their arrival told Hannah that there was a special bond between them, despite their short time together in Conway, a connection that went beyond physical proximity. When the orchestra reached the cue Parker had worried about, Morgan simply closed her eyes, limiting her senses. Hannah was certain Morgan would've left the room had it been any other situation, but a special event like this required a different tactic. When the recording was done, Morgan opened her eyes, took a couple of deep breaths, and resumed her attentive study. Every once in a while, Parker asked if Hannah wanted to see what they were doing, but she just waved her off, happy to be a witness to the joy her daughter had found.

The fire bell rang loudly throughout the room again, and the musicians stowed their instruments.

"What's going on?" Hannah asked.

"It's lunch break. Under union rules, everyone gets an hour," Parker explained. She motioned for them to exit through the pantry and wait outside while David finished his meeting with the audio mixer.

"What did you think?" Parker asked.

"So awesome," Morgan said. The smile told Hannah she was on a permanent high. So was Parker, if her matching grin was an indication. David bounded out a few moments later, just as energetic as the other two.

"Who's up for lunch?" he asked. "There are some good restaurants around here to check out."

Hannah looked at her watch and winced. "I'm afraid we're going to have to decline." Morgan opened her mouth, but Hannah cut her off. "We have the UCLA visit at three. You know, the *real* reason why we're here."

"Oh right," Morgan replied.

"I understand," David said. "Westwood isn't far from here, but LA traffic can make it tight."

Parker nodded her agreement. "We'll walk you back to your car."

They followed the same pathway through the soundstages toward the garage.

"Thank you so much for this," Morgan gushed. "I learned a lot."

"Glad we could help," Parker said.

"Is this your only project right now?"

David sighed. He sounded exhausted. "This is one of five."

"Five?" Hannah didn't even try to hide her surprise.

"Yep," Parker confirmed. "We're currently finishing up two streaming series, this feature, another show is about to start once we get videos, and David is, finally, composing music for a cable show that I'll be music editing."

Hannah's mind swam just from the list alone. "Is it normal to have so many?"

"No, it's not, but we have extenuating circumstances driving the need to get as much done as possible in a short amount of time."

"What circumstances?" Morgan asked.

Parker looked at David. "Our union is now threatening to strike, which would halt the entire industry."

Hannah didn't know much about the entertainment industry, but she knew a complete halt on everything wasn't good for anyone.

"While our union is doing everything they can to prevent a strike," David added, "the producers aren't taking any chances."

"We've also created a situation where we're going to be either finishing, beginning, or in the middle of all five projects in early June."

Hannah shook her head. Her brain couldn't follow the process. How would Parker and David execute it?

"I still think we should hire an assistant," Parker said.

"Assistants cost money that we don't have as a start-up. An intern would be better. We'd still pay them, but we don't have to worry about it breaking us."

"I'd totally do it if I lived out here," Morgan said off-handedly.

A gleam shone in David's eyes. Parker must've have seen it, too, because her face wore a look of panic, and she shook her head.

"That's not a bad idea. How would you like to be our intern, Morgan?"

The spontaneity of the question didn't ease Hannah's nerves. In fact, it had her grappling with an answer that would make her unpopular with Morgan instantly. "I'm sure Morgan appreciates the offer, but I'm afraid it's not feasible."

Morgan turned, ready to argue, but Hannah held up her hand. "Sweetheart, you know what our current situation is like. A Los Angeles summer isn't in our budget right now."

Morgan's shoulders slumped, and disappointment—yet understanding—colored her features. "My mom's right. While I appreciate the offer, I have to look at the bigger picture and…yeah. I have to say no."

"Well, that's too bad," David said, though he didn't look as disappointed as Morgan, or Parker for that matter. Hannah wasn't too surprised. David was a kind man, but he was a professional. Based on the workload he and Parker were taking on, they'd find someone else to intern in a heartbeat.

Hannah walked over and shook his hand. "Thank you again for the wonderful opportunity. It has been the highlight of the trip for me."

"You're very welcome," David said. "You have a very special young woman there. I look forward to seeing what she does in the future."

She gave a smile and stood back while Morgan said her good-byes. Hannah eyed Parker. The thought of touching her, even in a platonic gesture, sent her heart racing. In the end, she said a quick thank you, and Parker waved a silent good-bye as she and Morgan entered the garage.

"Why can't I do the cool stuff?" Morgan grumbled.

Hannah felt bad for not allowing Morgan to take the internship, but they'd scrimped and saved to just have three days out here for the UCLA tour. There was no way they could manage a second, longer trip.

"I'm sorry, sweetie. If you want, I'll start buying lottery tickets as soon as we get back, and maybe we'll get lucky."

Morgan laughed and hugged her around the waist. "It's okay, Mom. I'll just keep in touch with him and Parker more. It will be enough."

Hannah swelled with pride at Morgan's sensibility and compromise. She really had raised a good kid. As they approached their rental, Morgan slid into the passenger seat, but Hannah stopped when she heard footsteps running up the ramp. She turned and saw Parker jogging toward them.

"Oh, good. You didn't leave yet."

She doubled over, gasping for air. Hannah checked her watch. It was one fifteen. They really needed to get going, so whatever Parker had to say, she needed to say it now.

"I know you're in a hurry, but I want to talk to you about the internship."

"Parker—"

"I know what you said," she interrupted, "but I would like to try to find a way for Morgan to do it. She could really benefit from this."

The plea was so genuine in her voice and her gaze, Hannah crumbled. The least she could do was hear Parker's argument.

"Okay. Let's hear it." Her words came out pinched, but she didn't have a lot of time to get them lunch before the tour. Parker must've sensed her frustration.

"How about we meet later tonight at your hotel. We can discuss Morgan and the *other* topic you tried to start before I had to work."

Hannah nodded slowly. The opportunity presented itself. Time to take it. "We're staying at the Hilton by LAX."

"Perfect. We wrap things up here around seven. Say eight o'clock in the bar downstairs?"

"Fine," Hannah said. "We can meet, but I can't guarantee I'll change my mind."

Parker held her hands up. "I know. Thank you, though. You won't regret it." She turned and ran back down the ramp, throwing an "Enjoy the tour!" over her shoulder. Hannah sighed and turned to her rental car. Yes, they would talk about the internship, but they would also talk about their kiss. Hannah needed to do that before it drove her mad.

Parker pulled her Subaru into the Hilton and found a parking spot near the entrance. She bounded through the doors, then turned left and headed toward the bar.

She was nervous. No doubt about it. But this time it was because she needed to plead a case for Morgan. She also needed to let Hannah know this was not her idea—David's offering Morgan an internship had been a surprise to her as well. Now Parker needed to do damage control and convince Hannah there was no ulterior motive.

She scanned the crowds lit by candlelight at intimate tables for two. Thankfully, she saw a familiar figure sitting at the bar. Hannah still had on the jeans and blouse from earlier, but her hair was held back by a black headband, and she'd traded her sneakers for sandals. Parker looked on as Hannah brought a martini to her lips. Even though Hannah looked casual, the way she sipped her drink exuded an air of sophistication. Suddenly, Parker was thrust back to the first time she witnessed Hannah as drum major, when she first witnessed Hannah's superiority and elegance. A familiar stirring settled in her core. She shook it off. She was here for Morgan. Calmly, Parker strolled up to the bar and took the empty stool next to Hannah.

"Hey. Sorry I'm late. The recording ran a little long, and traffic was pretty heavy. It always is around LAX."

Hannah looked at her phone. "You said eight, and it's eight. You're right on time."

"To me, that's late, and I know you've had a long day."

Parker waved at the bartender and waited patiently while he finished with another customer.

"Yes, I have, which is why I don't mind this." Hannah raised her martini glass with a sly grin.

The bartender arrived quickly, and Parker ordered an old-fashioned, then swiveled on her stool and fully faced Hannah.

"How did the visit go?"

Hannah chuckled wryly. "If Morgan wasn't totally set on UCLA before, she is now."

"Really?"

"Oh yeah. The tour of the music department solidified it. She's still unsure which track she wants to take, but the guide said they offer admissions workshops to help prospective students understand admission requirements and the application process. They also give more in-depth details about each program track."

"Wow. I wish that had been available when I was applying."

"Me, too. Morgan gave her contact information so they could notify her when the next workshop is, so I have a feeling she'll make a decision once she's able to complete that."

"I'm glad to hear it," Parker said.

"How about you? What have you been up to these last few months?" Hannah asked.

Parker sighed. She could do small talk, then turn the conversation back to Morgan and put off the hard conversation a little longer.

"A lot, actually. I mentioned we've been working steadily since I returned. I've bought a new house."

"Congratulations."

"Thank you. Xena and Midi are happy to have more places to run and drive me bananas. Also, Keith roped me into doing class lectures for him."

"In all your spare time, huh?"

Parker laughed. "It's all done remotely, but I like it. I feel like the students understand the importance of music editing. He's trying to organize me coming back to do one in person, but my schedule is too tight for that right now."

"Be that as it may, it must feel good to be in demand. I'm glad to see you doing so well."

There was sincerity in Hannah's words and her eyes, but Parker couldn't help hearing a twinge of…What was that? Regret? "Thanks. I appreciate that."

The bartender set her drink in front of her, and Parker lifted it toward Hannah.

"Shall we make a toast?"

"A toast to what?"

"To Morgan. May she have all her dreams come true."

Hannah smiled, but it was tight. She raised her glass and clinked it against Parker's, then took another sip. Parker didn't know if it was the design of the martini glass—or she was hyperfocused on Hannah's lips—but the way Hannah's mouth wrapped around the rim nearly did her in.

"So, you want to talk about Morgan and this internship?"

Parker swallowed, the bourbon burning a path down her throat, and clasped her hands. "I do. First, I want to be clear—I didn't know David's plan before he announced the invitation out of the blue. I would have come and talked to you first."

Hannah's eye contact was intense. She slowly set her glass down and folded her arms. "I believe you. And thank you."

One hurdle down, Parker thought.

"Second, I know you're hesitant. However, as Morgan's mentor…"

"Which I thank you for continuing despite our, um…"

Parker was confused. "Our what?"

Hannah stared at her glass. "With what I did to you last year. I would've totally understood if you wanted to cut all ties, including to Morgan."

"One has absolutely nothing to do with the other."

Hannah guffawed. "Oh, please. You didn't reach out to her until after the New Year."

"Only because she finally reached out to me. That's how it works." Hannah's brow furrowed. Parker took a long swig of her drink, and then she explained. "Time out here is very precious. It's a lot of hurry up and wait, not to mention there are personal attachments that also need attention. I learned people are willing to teach, but I had to show the initiative. I had to show the hunger to do this. Morgan did that, too. As soon as I saw her email, I answered right away. So did David and anyone else she reached out to on that list I gave her."

Hannah's posture loosened. She didn't appear so defensive anymore. "I'm sorry. I obviously don't know how things work out here."

"It's okay. It took me some time to figure it out, too." Parker tilted her head and studied Hannah. While she wasn't defensive, she didn't look relaxed either. "Before I plead the case to have Morgan intern, I think we need to clear a few things up."

"I agree."

Parker sighed and spun her glass on the bar top. "Has it ever crossed your mind?"

"What?"

"The kiss?"

"More times than I can count."

Parker blinked rapidly and shook her head. Not the response she expected. "I'm guessing after all this time, you realized it was a mistake—"

"I don't think it was a mistake," Hannah said, cutting in.

"You don't?" Parker didn't attempt to hide her surprise.

"No. I *wanted* to kiss you, so I did."

The response was so nonchalant. Parker downed her drink in one gulp and slammed the glass on the bar.

Hannah laughed. "Weren't expecting that response, were you?"

"No, I wasn't."

Hannah set her glass next to Parker's. "Can I be completely honest with you?"

Parker was confused. Was she tipsy after one drink? "I would hope for nothing less."

Hannah reached out her hand. She hesitated, then pulled it back, clasping them in her lap. "I kissed you because I was attracted to you. I still am, and I can say that because this is my second martini and they are really strong."

Parker snorted, but she composed herself, knowing this was important for Hannah to say.

"I pushed you away that night *not* because I thought I'd made a mistake, but because I didn't want to make another one."

"What do you mean?"

"The scars from my marriage to Mike were fresh. Still are. I didn't want to start something with you knowing I wasn't emotionally ready to embrace it." Hannah slid her hands across her lap, palms up.

It was an invitation, and Parker accepted. She slipped her hands into Hannah's grasp. A shiver raced up her arms at the contact.

Hannah continued, "I know it must've been hard for you to say the things you did that night. To be the bigger person and let me go." Parker swallowed the lump in her throat and nodded. "But I need to thank you for that. Thank you for giving me the space and time to find myself."

"And what did you find?" Parker asked.

Hannah sighed and slid her hands back to her lap. Parker missed the contact immediately.

"I'm still working through a lot of the emotions I have, but I am certain I want to be friends with you."

Parker expected the feeling of disappointment to wash over her, but it didn't come. Actually, she felt relief. She hadn't screwed this up. Hannah didn't want to ban Parker from her life. She wanted to be friends. Parker could do that.

"I can be your friend," she said sincerely. Hannah's smile was warm, and her eyes conveyed a silent thank you. Parker signaled for the bartender and asked him for another round. When he returned with their refills, Parker said, "You know, the best way to work on being friends is to have Morgan do the internship."

Hannah shook her head. "I meant what I said earlier. It's not financially feasible for us to be out here for two weeks."

This piqued Parker's curiosity. She knew teachers didn't make a lot of money, but Hannah obviously paid for their LA trip. "Can't Mike chip in? I know he has hang-ups about Morgan going to UCLA, but is he so heartless as to not help her in some way?"

Hannah sighed and focused on her drink.

"He kicked in a little toward this trip as an apology to me for his behavior at the alumni banquet, but I can't ask him to underwrite an internship, and what would ultimately be a summer vacation for me. That would push the limits of his tolerance. And I can't float us for two weeks in a hotel. Not to mention a rental car, airfare, and all those other things I'm probably not remembering but will freak me out when I do."

Parker absorbed everything Hannah said, and a wild idea formed in her head. "What if all you had to worry about was the airfare?"

Hannah snorted. "I don't see how."

"I have a new house with two guest bedrooms. You and Morgan could stay with me."

Hannah's eyes widened, then she shook her head. "No."

"Why not?"

"Because…it's…"

"It's what? Me?"

Hannah looked away. "I'm ashamed to say this, but yes. What if it's all tense and awkward? What if we end up resenting and hating each other?"

Parker set down her glass and clasped her hands.

"You were honest with me, so I'm going to be honest with you. I'm attracted to you, too."

Hannah eyed her with skepticism. "Those old feelings still lingering?"

The comment cut a little bit, and Parker hated that. After all this time, Hannah still saw her as that kid she couldn't shake.

"On the contrary, those feelings are long gone. I'm attracted to the person you are now."

Hannah's mouth formed an *O*. Looked like she wasn't expecting that response.

"You're beautiful, passionate, and would move heaven and earth for your daughter. I'm enraptured by you."

Parker hid a smile as Hannah picked up her fresh martini and said a quiet "Thank you."

She leaned on the bar and waited until Hannah set her drink down, giving Parker her full attention.

"You know, Hannah, just because we're attracted to each other doesn't mean we'll end up together."

"It doesn't?" Hannah said, and…was that a lilt of disappointment?

"Be honest. Does the idea of being together excite you or frighten you?"

"Can it be both?"

"Yes, but which one is more predominant right now?"

Hannah looked to the ceiling, and Parker already knew the answer before she said it.

"Fear. I'm sorry."

Parker put her hands on top of Hannah's. When Hannah looked up, she said, "I wanted you to be honest, and you did that. Thank you."

Hannah gave a meek smile and interlaced their fingers.

Parker fought the urge to slide off the stool and close the space between them. Now was not the time to push things to a point Hannah wasn't comfortable with. Hell, she might never be comfortable with. Parker would continue to be understanding and patient, and—

hopefully—they would reach that point where fear wasn't a factor for either of them anymore.

She pulled back—missing the fit of Hannah's hand in hers—and raised her glass. "I propose letting Morgan do the internship. You stay at my place—I mostly work from home anyway. Morgan gets a once-in-a-lifetime opportunity. You and I get know each other as friends."

"Only friends?"

Parker matched her smile.

"I'm willing to leave the door open for other possibilities if you are. Do we have a deal?"

Hannah chewed on her lip, then raised her glass and clinked it against Parker's. "Deal."

Parker wanted to drag Hannah upstairs and give Morgan the good news, but she settled for dinner. "Let's order some food and go over the finer details."

Parker ordered them a couple of appetizers, and for the next hour, they went over what Hannah needed to do to spend two weeks in Los Angeles. Parker advised Hannah to fly into Burbank. "It's cheaper and not far from my house," she said.

By the time Parker left the hotel, she felt good about everything coming her way. June couldn't get here fast enough.

CHAPTER TEN

Two months later

"Are you sure this is a good idea?"

Stephanie's question blared through the car speaker as Parker pulled out onto Magnolia Boulevard in the direction of the Hollywood Burbank Airport. She rolled her eyes, even though Steph couldn't see it. Steph had asked the same question two months ago...and every week since.

She'd called Stephanie after Hannah and Morgan left LA and brought her up to speed, unsure what Hannah would tell her and how much. Flabbergasted was the best description of Steph's reaction when Parker explained David's offer. And Parker had to check the phone connection when she'd said Hannah had agreed.

"Will you survive living together for two weeks?"

At the time, Parker said, "Of course," easily, not fully realizing what the phrase *living together* entailed. She'd finished up her studio, unpacked her entire house—leaving only two boxes for Xena and Midnight to commandeer—put new beds in the guest rooms, and cleaned the bathroom from top to bottom. Then, last week, she drove by the airport on her way to a mixing session, and that's when it hit her.

Hannah and Morgan would be *living* with her. Eating meals, hanging out in the backyard, going to work, coming home, doing laundry. *Living* together.

"It's kind of hard to back out now," she said. "I'm on my way to the airport to pick them up as we speak."

The line went silent, but the connection said Stephanie was still there.

"Just be careful. Okay? I know you two put to rest the whole business from homecoming, and it's great you have a common goal with Morgan."

"But?" Parker prompted.

"I can't help but worry things will go *too* well, and you'll start romanticizing more than what's actually happening. I'm afraid one or both of you will get hurt."

Parker leaned her elbow on the window frame. How could she convince Steph she wasn't a kid anymore? Maybe she could use the same explanation she'd used on Hannah—without the romantic undertones.

"Steph, don't worry. This will be good for our relationship."

"Relationship?"

"That's what a friendship is, right? We want to build that while supporting Morgan in her opportunity."

"Are you *sure* that's all you want?"

Parker sighed. "You want the truth?"

"Yes."

"I haven't completely closed the door on the possibilities with Hannah. There's a mutual attraction between us. We're not going to ignore it because it'll make everything tense and weird. But I'm also not going to press Hannah into something she's not ready for."

"That's all I ask," Stephanie said. "I'm sorry to grill you, but I want to make sure you're both on the same page."

"We are."

"Good, because I'd hate to fly out there and knock sense into both of you for being stupid and careless with each other's hearts."

Parker laughed. This was the Stephanie she knew and loved. "I need to hang up. I'm turning into the airport now."

"Okay, I'll let you go. Have a wonderful time."

Parker disconnected the call and shook her head. The line of cars into the terminal crawled, and she maneuvered her vehicle into the pickup lane with some difficulty. When she spotted two familiar figures standing at the end of Terminal B, she ignored the kick in her pulse and focused on pulling to the curb. An SUV vacated a spot, and she claimed it for herself. She jumped out and opened the hatch. Hannah and Morgan spotted her and wheeled their suitcases over to her car. They looked exhausted, and Parker sprang into action.

"You made it. Leave the bags to me and get in the car."

They gave no argument and slipped into the passenger seats as Parker loaded the bags. By the time she had both suitcases secured and the hatch closed, a Mercedes was laying on the horn for her to move. She jogged to the driver's side, hopped in, and pulled out in record time. Only when Parker exited the airport did she feel comfortable enough to talk. "Welcome back to LA. I hope the flight wasn't too bad and that you're hungry. I thought I'd get you back and settled, then we can go down the street for din…"

Parker stopped talking when she saw her passengers were passed out. Hannah's head leaned against the window, eyes closed. A peek in the rearview mirror showed Morgan in a similar position. She laughed quietly and shook her head.

"Don't worry, ladies. We'll be home soon."

Hannah hated traveling. It was always stressful. She'd set three alarms but didn't sleep for fear of missing all of them. They'd gotten to their connection city with just enough time to run to the next gate, so she'd skipped breakfast and lunch. Worst part was her stress rubbed off on Morgan. Or was Morgan stressed about other things? She couldn't worry about that now because, thanks to all the travel, she'd promptly passed out as soon as they arrived at Parker's house.

She slowly came out of her slumber when she heard the door creak. The bed dipped, and Hannah opened her eyes. They quickly widened when she saw it wasn't Morgan or Parker but a large cat sitting demurely, blinking at her. She didn't dare move. Was this cat friendly? As if reading her thoughts, the feline cautiously walked up to Hannah and sniffed at her face. She smiled as the whiskers tickled her cheeks. Not the worst way to wake up. Hannah reached up and scratched its head and was rewarded with the loudest purring she'd ever heard.

"Are you my alarm clock?" she asked.

The cat continued to purr and rubbed its head against her hand vigorously. Then she flopped over onto her side and exposed her belly. Hannah acquiesced and petted the soft fur in long strokes. Her sleep dissolved into relaxation, and it wasn't long before she heard footsteps approaching her room. Her attention shifted from the cat to the door as Parker came into view in a black tank top and khaki shorts.

"Xena," she scolded, but it was weak. She walked in and sat on the edge of the bed. "I'm sorry if she woke you up."

Parker reached to pick Xena up, but Hannah stopped her.

"She's okay. Best alarm clock I've had in a long time."

Parker smiled and scratched Xena's head. "If you leave your door open, she'll sleep with you. Then she'll wake you up at six every morning to be fed."

Hannah chuckled and continued her strokes along Xena's flank. She stretched and purred louder.

"She really likes this."

Parker hummed, running her hand across the top half of Xena's torso. When their hands met in the middle of Xena's belly, they stopped and looked at each other but didn't pull away.

It was then Hannah noticed Parker's black tank top showed off a very beautiful expanse of skin, particularly the tattoo winding up Parker's right arm and ending in a spiral on her shoulder. She reached for Parker's wrist, the urge to run her hands along the music bars too much to resist in her sleep haze. As she made contact, Parker pulled her hand back and turned away. Xena, realizing her massage was over, quickly flopped over and jumped off the bed.

"Sorry," Hannah whispered. She sat up and turned away from Parker, who now stood near the doorway.

"It's okay. You caught me by surprise is all. Um, are you hungry?"

Hannah ran her hand through her hair and adjusted her shirt. "Yes, I am. You mentioned going out to dinner, I believe."

"I did, but I'm thinking that's a bad idea with how tired you are. I went down the street to Handy Market instead and got some barbecue. I hope that's okay."

Hannah swallowed. "Yeah. Sure. Barbecue sounds great."

"Good. It's just about ready. I only had to put it on the grill to reheat, so you can come out once you're a little more awake."

Hannah nodded, not trusting her voice not to betray her emotions, and listened to Parker's footsteps fade down the hall. When she was certain she was alone, Hannah stood and walked over to the window and peered out to the backyard. A silver grill with smoke billowing out caught her attention. Not because she was craving barbecue but because she saw Morgan standing next to it. A door opened and shut, and then Parker was standing next to her. They were discussing something humorous if Morgan's smile was any indication. Hannah sighed, scrubbed her hands over her face, and proceeded down the hall. Might as well get this adventure started.

The floorboards creaked as she entered the living room. It was open, but it also felt cozy with its light gray walls and shelves lining the perimeter. Blinds were open to her right, allowing what little sunlight was left to streak across the wood floor. As she looked into the kitchen, a black streak scurried past her and down the hallway, the sound of nails clicking against wood the only sound to make its presence known. She walked outside and looked at Parker, confused.

"I don't know what I just saw, but I'm hoping you don't have a rodent problem."

Parker laughed. "If it was black and small, that was Midnight. She gets the zoomies around this time."

Hannah sagged in relief. She'd never accuse Parker of poor housekeeping, but the thought of having to deal with mice was not on her agenda this trip.

"Come sit down, Mom," Morgan said. "Parker went and grabbed barbecue for us."

Hannah did as instructed and sat at the patio table. "Yes, she told me. What's on the menu?"

Parker raised the lid to showcase the racks full of meat. Hannah gawked.

"Is that for one meal?"

"No," Parker said, a light chuckle in her voice. "I wasn't sure what you wanted, so I grabbed a little bit of everything. Whatever we don't have tonight can be leftovers."

Morgan—eager as she was—held up her plate and took a couple of ribs and some tri-tip. Hannah requested the chicken, and Parker took a little sausage and chicken for herself.

As they sat around the table, plating sides and pouring drinks, a sense of comfort fell over Hannah. The scene felt normal, yet surreal. Never in her life did she think she'd be able to share a meal like a family with Parker. Yet here they were, and there were going to be more.

Surprisingly, the thought wasn't terrifying.

"So, what's the plan for the week?" Morgan asked.

"Lots of work," Parker said. "But there will be time for some fun, too. David's house is right up the street, and he's having a very belated housewarming party on Saturday. We're all invited."

"That's great," Hannah mumbled, her brain still muddled from the trip and her nap.

"And hopefully," Parker continued, a sly grin on her face, "we'll finish early enough on Friday for a surprise."

Morgan's face lit up. "What kind of surprise?"

"A fun one," Parker replied and gave a wink before digging into her chicken.

The conversation flowed around Hannah. She barely had enough energy to eat her food and listened in as much as she could. Maybe it was good she was so tired. Then she wouldn't focus on how natural dinner and conversation with Parker felt. It was like they were a couple. Like they were a family.

CHAPTER ELEVEN

Parker sat on the edge of her bed and stretched to the ceiling. The clock read 6:05 a.m. She groaned and looked out the window, the sky pinking as the sun came up. It'd been a long time since she got up this early for work. Six o'clock was reserved for feeding the cats while eight o'clock was her usual time to get up and ready, and start work by nine. With Morgan starting her internship, however, Parker wanted to get an early jump so she'd be able to assist Morgan in learning the ropes without falling behind. She turned side to side, loosening the muscles in her back. As she stood and slipped her feet into her slippers, Xena and Midnight stretched and yawned on the mattress.

"Yes, it's early. Which means you get breakfast soon."

Midnight squeaked at her—she never did grow into her meow—and jumped off the bed, following Parker to the shower. She stripped off her boy shorts and tank top and eased under the hot shower spray and hoped Hannah and Morgan had been able to get some sleep.

Dinner had been subdued, as she'd expected. Morgan peppered her with questions about her internship duties, and Hannah sat and ate quietly, content to let them control the conversation. Occasionally, though, she noticed a faraway look in Hannah's eyes. Was she thinking about the same thing Parker was? That the whole family dinner dynamic was a little too…comfortable? She hadn't looked upset or worried, so Parker didn't bring it up.

They'd both gone to bed shortly after, blaming jet lag and Morgan's eagerness to end yesterday to get an early start today. Parker nearly knocked on Hannah's door to see if they could talk about what happened earlier, but the light was off. So she decided to wait.

Parker rinsed the shampoo out of her hair and exited the shower. As she dried off, two sets of eyes glared at her from the counter.

"I'm coming," she said and quickly dressed in jean shorts and grabbed a tank top. She remembered the way Hannah stared at her tattoo. How her gaze caressed Parker's skin. She put the tank top back in the drawer and pulled on a normal T-shirt, then headed toward the kitchen.

She walked quietly to keep the floorboards from creaking and waking up her guests. As the hallway opened up into the living room, she noticed a solitary figure sitting in her dining nook next to the kitchen. Parker stopped, surprised to see Hannah up this early. She looked so peaceful, sitting and staring out the window, cradling a coffee mug in her hands. Her hair was pushed back by the same black headband, and she wore the cutest pair of pajama pants and matching shirt. Parker's heart swelled with an emotion she needed to tamp down, a dangerous one to harbor because, in this moment, all Parker thought was that she belonged there. Hannah belonged in her home.

Two loud, jingling collars raced passed her. Hannah looked up and gave a small smile. Parker rubbed her arm and walked into the kitchen.

"Good morning," Hannah said.

"Good morning." She walked past and felt Hannah's eyes on her as she opened the cupboard. "You're up early."

"I'm still on Arkansas time, so I'll probably be up this early for the next few days."

"At least you figured out the coffee machine. That'll make the mornings easier."

She popped the lid on the can of cat food, and the two felines circled her feet enthusiastically, crying loudly.

"Are they always that vocal?"

Parker laughed. "When it comes to food, they have no problem expressing their thoughts."

Xena and Midnight paced back and forth until Parker placed the bowls on the ground, and then they proceeded to slurp up every morsel.

"They're loud," Hannah said.

"Oh yeah. Be glad your bedroom is at the farthest point in the house."

Hannah's smile faded, and she clasped the coffee cup closer. Parker grabbed her mug and placed it underneath the Keurig machine, then sat across from Hannah.

"Everything okay?"

Hannah looked up, confusion evident in her gaze.

"I'm just surprised with how comfortable I feel here."

"Comfortable how?"

"Last night we sat outside for dinner and talked like a family. Now we're sitting and having morning coffee in your house—which is beautiful, by the way—like it's the most normal thing in the world for us to do."

Parker rolled her lips to stifle the laugh, but it didn't work. Soon she was holding her stomach as merriment bubbled out of her.

"What's so funny?"

"I'm so happy to hear you say that."

"You are?"

"Yes," Parker admitted, "because I was thinking the same thing. And I was worried it was going to freak you out."

"It did. You weren't freaked out?"

"Oh, I was terrified."

They fell silent, then Parker fell into another fit of laughter. This time, Hannah followed suit. Suddenly, they were both in hysterics. Parker turned when she heard a timid meow. Two sets of eyes glared at them like they had lost their minds, which only set off another round of laughter. It took a couple of minutes, but the laughter died down, leaving them both gasping for air and trying to come to their senses.

"Oh my God." Parker wiped the tears from her eyes and stared at Hannah. "We're off to a smashing start, aren't we?"

"Yes, we are," Hannah agreed.

Parker leaned closer but refrained from touching her. "Look, let's not overthink this. I'm glad you feel comfortable here. I *want* you to be comfortable. You can lie on the couch and read, sunbathe in the backyard"—*please don't do that*—"or walk down and window-shop in Magnolia Park. This is your home for the next two weeks."

Hannah's gaze softened, and she smiled sweetly. "Thank you. I will do that."

Parker stood and prepped her coffee on the counter. "I'm going to head to my studio out back. Before I go, do you have any questions?"

"Yeah, do you have any other coffee around here? This stuff is pretty strong."

Hannah held up her coffee mug and grimaced.

"I do not. What coffee brand do you like?"

"Oh, don't worry about it. It's not important. I can—"

"Hannah." Parker cut her off. "What coffee do you like?"

"Seattle's Best?"

Parker pulled out her phone and added it to her weekly shopping list. "I'll make sure to have it for you tomorrow morning."

Hannah waved her off. "You really don't have to—"

"Hannah, what did I say?" Parker firmed up her tone.

Hannah rolled her lips and ducked her head. "You want me to treat this place as my home for the next two weeks."

"Exactly. Now, if getting your favorite coffee will help do that, then I'll make sure you have it. Okay?"

"Okay. Thank you."

Parker nodded and walked out the back door.

"Hey, Parker?"

Parker ducked her head back in and was met with a more confident smile.

"Can you also add caramel flavored coffee creamer to that list?"

Now it was Parker's turn to smile.

"You got it. Can you have Morgan at the studio by ten?"

Hannah raised her glass in salute, and then Parker beelined it to her studio. As soon as she was safely inside, she leaned heavily against the door. *That went really well.* Maybe this whole situation would work out, after all. All Parker had to do was focus on their friendship and guard her heart from being broken...again.

CHAPTER TWELVE

Hannah sat and smiled, giggling to herself after Parker went to work. Wow, they were a pair. But in some ways, that was good. They understood each other in ways Hannah hadn't experienced in a while. A connection like that needed to be cherished and cultivated, not feared or avoided. The door was open for them. All they had to do was walk through it. And if this morning was any indication, they'd taken the first steps to do just that.

She took her empty mug to the sink and washed it out, then turned and noticed the rays of sun streaming through the back door window. She chuckled as Xena flopped down right on the sunny spot on the floor and rolled, exposing her belly. Hannah walked over and rubbed the soft fur warmed by the sunlight.

"I think you have the right idea."

A shuffle from down the hall alerted Hannah to another presence. A sleep-ragged Morgan entered the living room, and Hannah smiled as her daughter rubbed her eyes and stretched like a cat.

"What time is it?" she grumbled.

Hannah looked at the clock on the coffee machine. "Just past seven. Do you want breakfast?"

Morgan shook her head and continued to the kitchen. "I need caffeine."

"Help yourself."

Hannah looked out the window as the machine whirred to life behind her. Parker really did have a nice house, and a beautiful backyard. A firepit claimed the far end of the property, and the studio sat opposite, near the garage. Not a lot of grass, but Hannah understood California was more of a desert climate, and Parker's yard reflected that with succulents and planters filled with desert-tolerant flowers scattered around the yard. She wondered, off-handedly, if Parker entertained often with the high-end grill on the patio and the cornhole boards set up along the fence line. Maybe they could have David and his family over one night after they'd settled in.

Her musings were interrupted when Morgan took the seat Parker vacated earlier and breathed deeply the aroma of coffee. She hummed contentedly after the first sip and Hannah stifled a laugh as she sat opposite.

"Better?"

"Much. Is Parker up yet?"

"She's out in her studio and getting an early start."

Morgan set her mug down with a hard *thud* and stood abruptly. "Why didn't you tell me? I'm late on my first day."

She turned but Hannah grabbed her arm. "Relax. You're fine. She told me to make sure you're there by ten, so you have plenty of time."

Morgan wiped imaginary sweat from her brow and returned to her seat. "In that case, I will have some breakfast."

Hannah smiled wryly and went to the fridge to see their options. She touched her chest when she saw the shelves full of eggs, bacon, veggies. Pretty much everything you needed for a house full of people. It was only a full fridge, but it spoke to something inside her. Parker took time out of her day to care for them, make sure they had everything they needed along with herself.

Grabbing the eggs, bacon, and English muffins, Hannah decided to make a light breakfast—no sense in running up Parker's grocery bill on the first day. She settled comfortably into Parker's kitchen, as if making breakfast for Morgan in it was an everyday occurrence, and chuckled as the memory of their morning conversation entered her mind.

"What's so funny?" Morgan asked when Hannah brought her plate.

"Oh, nothing. You had to be there."

When ten o'clock rolled around, Morgan was showered, dressed, and ready to get to work. Hannah decided to accompany her, much to Morgan's annoyance.

"This isn't like the first day of school, Mom," she groused. "I don't need you to make sure I find my class."

"Ha! I wish your classes kept you this close."

She ruffled Morgan's hair, undeterred when she tried to dodge.

They opened the door and were met with a blast of cold air. Hannah wished she'd opted for something other than shorts and a sleeveless blouse. One look at Morgan rubbing her arms said she was regretting her summer attire as well.

"Oh, good. You're right on time." Parker beamed as she swiveled out of her office chair. "I hope the commute wasn't terrible."

Morgan picked up on the joke. "Traffic wasn't too bad, but I picked up a hitchhiker on the way. I hope that's okay?"

Parker's eyes raked up and down Hannah's body. "I think we can find something for her to do."

"How about I go and grab us some sweaters. It's freezing in here," Hannah said, ignoring her spiked libido at Parker's statement and gaze.

"I didn't know you were part Eskimo," Morgan said.

"Sorry," Parker replied, then walked over to a dresser and pulled out two hoodies. "It gets pretty hot in here with my computer system, so I keep the air conditioner going strong."

Hannah noticed Parker wearing a red fleece as she grabbed the offered hoodie. So, she wasn't immune to the chill either. Hannah zipped it up and caught hints of a woodsy fragrance.

"This smells nice."

Parker rolled her eyes. "Now I know where my deodorizers ended up. They have a strong cedar smell to them, and when I keep them in the chest it permeates everything. I'll get you another one."

Parker reached for the hoodie and Hannah quickly sidestepped her.

"You'll do no such thing. I like it and I'll keep it."

Parker held up her hands in surrender, then turned to Morgan.

"Ready to get started?"

Morgan nodded emphatically, and Parker guided her to the small desk with a laptop. It was set up right behind a big desk with monitors, speakers, and a piano keyboard taking up the enormous space.

"I'm going to start you out making cue sheets. I'll go over the process with you, and then I'll leave you on your own. If you forget something, I've made a cheat sheet for you."

Hannah noticed a slip of paper with writing on it she didn't understand. Probably shortcuts for the keyboard, but she couldn't tell from her angle.

"And," Parker continued, clicking the mouse and pulling up a screen with waveforms on it, "I took the liberty of color coding the tracks to the colors you told me you see during our conversation last night. I know you don't see the color based on instrument, but I hope it will be beneficial."

The urge to kiss Parker was so strong, Hannah took a step back. No one had ever taken the time to adjust for Morgan. Knowing Parker did made her even more attractive.

"It won't make a difference one way or another, but I do appreciate the effort," Morgan said. She sat and looked at the tracks, then hit some keys to look at the other screen with a list on it. The dimming of her smile told Hannah the excitement was wearing off and worry settled in as she looked at the foreign program. Parker must've seen it, too, because she pulled her chair over and sat down.

"You're not going to screw this up. If you make a mistake, or have a question, please ask. I know you have no problem doing that." The jab landed, and Morgan relaxed. "You're not expected to be perfect. I wasn't when I started, and I can guarantee neither was David."

"Really?"

"When you spend time with him, ask him what happened to the entire score from *Game of Thrones* after season one."

Morgan laughed and nodded. "Okay. Let's get started."

Parker launched into Music Editing 101, if such a course existed. She really would make a great teacher. Hell, she'd make a great anything. *Even a great partner?* Hannah sighed and turned to leave before her brain conjured up an idea that she had no business having.

"I'll leave you two to work. Will you be in for lunch?"

"Yes. One o'clock," Parker replied, her eyes focused on Morgan.

Hannah left the building, and the temperature shift was so drastic, she unzipped the hoodie and was about to remove it entirely. Then she stopped and breathed deeply again. She noticed the cedar, but under it was a tang of eucalyptus. Where did that come from? Was that Parker's scent? She slowly zipped it back up and wrapped herself in it. It was the closest she could get to Parker right now. Why not enjoy it? Why not take advantage of the gift she'd been given? Hannah had packed a book or two, and Parker did say she wanted Hannah to be comfortable. Getting swept away in a romance story while being surrounded by Parker's scent—there were worse ways to spend a vacation.

She walked back into the house and closed the door, causing two loaves of fur to startle and glare at her for daring to disturb their slumber.

"Sorry," she whispered—the ridiculousness of apologizing to two cats not lost on her—then beelined for her bedroom.

"Don't get too comfortable again. You're about to get some company."

❖

"How's your brain?"

Parker noticed Morgan was a little more bleary-eyed than when she'd walked in that morning.

"I think it's melted a little bit," Morgan replied.

They stripped out of their jackets and exited into the warm June sun. Morgan shielded her eyes as they walked to the main house.

"As you get more comfortable with the process, you won't be so hyperfocused."

"At least the score cues are easy to do. And the color coding did help, thanks."

"No problem."

"I just didn't expect the source cues to be so tedious. Three different composers with four different publishers, but one isn't actually a publisher, they are an administrator."

Parker laughed when Morgan slapped her forehead, then dragged her fingers down her face.

"I guarantee you'll never hear a top ten hit again without considering how many people had their hands in bringing it to fruition."

Morgan stopped and raised an eyebrow. "This is going to ruin radio for me, isn't it?"

"Pretty much."

Morgan rolled her eyes as she pushed the door open to the house. The smell of bacon greeted Parker's nose. She looked at Morgan and shrugged, surprised to smell anything cooking at all. They followed the scent around the peninsula and saw Hannah standing at the stove.

"Mom?"

Hannah looked up and smiled at them, then continued pushing the bacon strips in the pan.

"You two are just in time. I thought BLTs would be a good lunch option. Everything is prepped and ready"—she pointed with the spatula to the opposite counter that had tomato slices, lettuce and avocado— "so go ahead and make your sandwich while I finish this."

Morgan darted to the buffet and began her assembly. "What's the avocado for?"

"I thought it'd be fun to make them California-style."

Parker shook her head. "You've only been here a day, and you already know what California-style means. I'm impressed."

Hannah turned the stove off and removed the pan from the heat. "Don't be. I found out on our last trip here. Everywhere we went, they asked if we wanted California-style. I finally asked a waitress what that was, and she told me."

Parker nodded. The gesture was nice, and she'd make sure to say so. However, she didn't want Hannah to feel like she expected her to make them lunch—or dinner—every day they worked. Checking to make sure Morgan was distracted, she inched into Hannah's space.

"I appreciate you doing this," she whispered. "We could've easily reheated the leftovers in the fridge."

"I know," Hannah replied nonchalantly. "I *wanted* to do this. You've been working hard all morning while I've been snuggled up with your cats, reading a book. By the way, Xena is not a fan of the iPad."

Parker laughed. "Tell me something I don't know."

She regarded the food, the preparation, and the care with which Hannah was cleaning up the mess on the stove. The whole scene was very domestic, and Parker loved it. Not because she was picturing domestic bliss with Hannah—not a lot, anyway—but because she knew it meant Hannah had listened to what they talked about earlier and made herself at home.

"How many slices can I have, Mom?" Morgan asked.

"How many have you put on already?" Hannah retorted, then winked at Parker as if she knew the answer.

"Um, six?"

Morgan's wince made Parker snort.

"That's plenty," Hannah said. "And only two slices of tomatoes."

"Fine."

Hannah leaned into Parker and whispered, "The girl loves her tomatoes as much as she loves bacon."

"It's true," Morgan confirmed, then walked over to the table.

Parker noticed it was set with paper towel napkins, glasses of water, and bags of chips for three.

"Do you want me to make your sandwich?"

They were so close, Parker felt goose bumps on her arm as Hannah's voice sounded sultry in her ear. She panicked. When did a simple question feel so intimate?

"Parker? You okay?"

Parker quickly shook out of her stupor and reached for the bread. "I can do it myself. I *want* to do it myself."

Hannah's brow furrowed, then she shrugged and joined Morgan at the table.

"How was your morning, sweetheart?"

Parker heard snippets of their conversation as she assembled her BLTA. Morgan, despite her mental fatigue when they broke for lunch, spoke with exuberance as she regaled Hannah with all she'd been learning. She was certain Hannah didn't fully understand the specifics of how the percentages were divided among different publishers, but she hung on Morgan's every word as she recounted the information Parker had passed along.

"Why do publishers need other publishers to distribute their music?" Hannah asked.

"I don't know. Do you, Parker?"

Parker took a bite of her sandwich and thought for a moment.

"I'd have to consult a music supervisor, but I think smaller publishing houses make deals with bigger publishers to get their music in the right hands and keep their interests intact."

"Oh, okay," Morgan replied. "So, anyway…"

Parker ate contentedly and watched the mother-daughter interaction. Again, that feeling of domesticity, of normalcy, crept into her consciousness, and she welcomed it. She looked at Hannah, so enraptured with Morgan's enthusiasm. She could see the love they had for each other. Then, suddenly, she saw herself in the same picture. Her arm around Hannah. Hannah clasping her hand loosely, anchoring Parker to her and leaning into Parker's side.

I could really get used to this.

"Parker?"

She shook out of her daydream, and two sets of worried eyes stared at her.

"Sorry. I drifted off into space. What's up?"

Morgan looked at Hannah then back. "I asked what time we need to head back to work."

"Oh. Two o'clock. Then you'll get a couple more hours and be done for the day."

Morgan nodded and stood up. "Okay. I'm going to go rest my brain for a bit. Come get me when it's time to head back out."

"We will, sweetheart," Hannah said.

Morgan picked up her plate and put it in the sink, then gave a little wave as she walked down the hall, leaving Parker and Hannah alone.

"It happened, didn't it?"

Parker turned back to Hannah, confused.

"You had a daydream like I did yesterday." There was no accusation. Only a hint of a smile on her lips.

Parker leaned back. "I did."

"What did you see?" Hannah asked.

"Nothing too dissimilar from what you saw. A nice family moment. And I was part of it."

A smile formed on Hannah's lips, and she rested her chin on her hands. "And did you like being a part of this family moment?"

Parker's stomach coiled with a familiar nervous feeling. Flirting was probably ill-advised, but it was hard not to with Hannah practically inviting her in.

"I liked it."

"Just liked?"

Parker sighed and rubbed her hands on her legs. "I don't want to press, but I'm more than willing to go with whatever happens…to a point."

"And what point is that?"

Hannah batted her eyelashes playfully, and Parker chuckled.

"Whatever *point* you're comfortable going to. I'm more than willing to follow your lead."

Hannah hummed as she stood. She rounded the table and picked up Parker's plate, then leaned down into Parker's face, gazing in her eyes, one corner of her mouth turned up.

"Be careful, Parker. I tend to push boundaries when I want something."

Parker gulped. The hushed tone sent blood rushing south as Hannah turned and walked toward the kitchen. She needed to bail out of this conversation now before she did something neither of them were ready for…yet.

"I'm going back to the studio to get things set up for Morgan," she announced and walked to the back door.

"Okay. What time will you be done for the day?"

"Morgan will be done by four. I'll be working until six."

"Any requests for dinner?"

"I told you I don't expect you to cook for us."

Hannah leaned against the counter. "I know. I just feel like a mooch with you two working so hard."

"You're my guest. If you feel like cooking, go ahead. But it's not a requirement. Understand?"

Hannah nodded. "You sure do have a lot of rules for your guests."

"Only the problematic ones who don't know how to relax."

Hannah threw a dish towel at her, and Parker laughed when it landed harmlessly on the floor. When she returned to her studio, Parker leaned against the door and closed her eyes, waiting for her heart to slow. If this was how Hannah was when she felt comfortable, Parker was in for a long two weeks.

CHAPTER THIRTEEN

Developing her friendship with Parker ended up being easier than Hannah expected, once she got out of her own way.

She'd woken up early again the next morning but stayed in her room and waited until she heard Parker leave. She didn't want to interrupt Parker's morning routine every day. When she'd entered the kitchen two hours later, she saw a box of K-Cups in her favorite coffee brand on the counter and a bottle of caramel flavored creamer in the fridge. It warmed Hannah to know Parker went above and beyond to get that for her. And she *had* gone above and beyond. Not only did Parker uncover this bit of information through playful determination, but she made it a point to go to the store and grab it. That's when Hannah realized that she needed to stop worrying.

Since then, she'd gotten up every morning between six and seven o'clock. Sometimes Parker would be there, feeding her cats. Other days, Hannah would be the first one up, and she made sure to have everything out Parker needed to make her coffee. They'd talk, but it wasn't anything beyond the surface, mostly Morgan or the cats—they were Parker's kids, after all. Then Parker would head to her studio, and Hannah would start her day. She'd clean, read, prep for the school year by ordering sheet music or other supplies.

After a few days, her schedule felt like a well-oiled machine, which surprised her. Normally it took weeks for her develop a routine, but in Parker's house, with Parker and Morgan, it came easily. There was no anxiety over who was making meals and why. Conversations weren't stilted with things *not* said. Flirting happened naturally, with minimal second-guessing. There were moments Hannah wondered if she was pushing Parker toward something she wasn't ready for, but Parker seemed happy with their banter and gave as good as she got.

More importantly, they knew exactly where the other's boundaries were and respected them.

By the time Friday rolled around, Hannah didn't hide the fact that she was up early to spend time with Parker. It was really the only time they had to talk one-on-one without Morgan around—Parker was so tired after work.

Parker announced, "Thanks to Morgan, we're completely caught up on all the cue sheets, and it should be a short day. All I have to do is set up the main Pro Tools session for the mix and track a couple of cues for the streaming series, and we should be done by three."

"That's great," Hannah said. "We should do something. I don't think we've left this house since we arrived."

Parker winced as she poured creamer into her coffee. "I apologize. I haven't been a great host by keeping you cooped up here. I tend to get tunnel vision when I know a deadline is looming."

Hannah nodded. "I totally understand. You have a very demanding job. I'll admit I didn't understand how demanding until I witnessed it firsthand, but I do now."

Parker dipped her head and smiled sweetly. "Thank you. Still, you and Morgan deserve to go out and have fun while you're here. That whole *all work and no play* proverb is true. Luckily, I already have something planned."

"Oh, really? Do tell." Hannah sipped her coffee slowly and gazed at Parker over the rim of her mug. Parker raised an eyebrow and wagged a finger in front of Hannah's face.

"You're not going to get it out of me that easily, Ms. Wells," Parker said. "It's a surprise, and I intend to keep it that way."

Hannah stuck her lip out in a pout.

"Pulling out the big guns won't help you, either. You're just going to have to wait." Parker winked and walked to the back door.

Hannah turned and gave one last shot. "Well, how will you know if I'll like it or not?"

"Oh, you'll like it." Parker turned back and waggled her eyebrows. "I guarantee it."

Then she left.

The rest of the day, Hannah fought the urge to walk out to the studio and demand Parker tell her the surprise. After lunch—when Parker colluded with Morgan to not reveal it despite Hannah pulling the *I'm your mother* card—Stephanie's name appeared on her phone, and Hannah was thankful for the distraction.

"Hey, it's so good to hear from you."

"I wanted to call and see how things were going. Since I haven't heard anything, I thought you were either avoiding Parker or you'd finally said to hell with it and were having marathon sex."

Hannah rolled her eyes as Stephanie's laugher filtered through the phone.

"Not funny. Did you forget Morgan is here? I'd be too worried she'd walk in on us to have marathon sex."

"So you have thought about it."

Damn. Walked right into that one.

"No!" Hannah shouted, startling the cats out of their happy spots on the couch. "I mean, no," she said again at a reasonable volume. "We've settled into a nice routine here."

Hannah caught Stephanie up on everything that'd transpired since their arrival. She even mentioned the banter and flirting, which surprised her, but not as much as Stephanie's lack of retort.

"Sounds like domestic bliss to me."

"Stephanie…" Hannah said, her tone scolding.

Laughter filtered through the phone. "I'm just joking with you. I'm happy to hear you're not camped out in your room and that you've found a common middle ground."

"Me, too," Hannah replied.

"I guess the only question I have now is do you want to stay in the middle ground or do you want more?"

"What do you mean?"

Stephanie sighed. "Hannah, you kissed her. You're living in her house. You're basically coparenting Morgan right now, and you just admitted you're openly flirting with each other. That says something."

Hannah rubbed her head, frustrated to have this conversation again. "And what does it say?"

"You want to have a life with Parker," Stephanie argued. "At least admit it to me."

Hannah looked out the window to the backyard and made sure Parker and Morgan weren't about to walk in. She pulled on the edge of her hoodie. The same hoodie Parker had given her their first day. It still smelled like cedar…and Parker. She sat on the couch and scratched Xena's head, and her purring started immediately.

"You're not wrong."

"I'm not?"

The surprise in Stephanie's tone made Hannah chuckle.

"I know, I don't normally say that, but in this case, it's true. We've both seen this dream of being together. It's exciting, but also scary. I keep testing Parker's boundaries, and while it's fun—she tests mine, too—I can tell when I've pushed too far with her, and it's frustrating."

"Why frustrating?"

Hannah didn't answer right away, but when she did, her throat choked on the pent-up emotion. "Because she's perfect, and I could see having something amazing with her." Despite the ache those words caused, there was also a sense of relief.

"How does it make you feel, saying that out loud?"

Hannah heard the smile in Stephanie's voice.

"Mostly scared."

"Would you also say excited?"

"Why would I be excited?"

"Because you just admitted you're falling for Parker."

"I admitted it to *you*," Hannah replied cheekily.

"And to yourself," Stephanie said, a seriousness in her tone. "My question now is what do you plan to do about it?"

Hannah looked at the ceiling, trying to keep the tears at bay. "I honestly don't know."

Suddenly, she heard laughter outside, and it was getting closer. She straightened up and saw movement in the backyard.

"I have to go. They're coming back to the house."

"Okay, but let me say this. You should go for it. Don't overthink it. You've taken huge steps in a few short days. Keep pushing those boundaries. Or kiss her again but stay in the room this time." The voices were getting closer, and Hannah felt panic rise in her chest. "Be bold, Hannah. You both deserve to be fully and truly happy."

The line went dead as the door opened. Hannah stowed her phone and noticed something different about Parker and Morgan.

"What's going on?" she asked, taking in Parker's jersey with *Dodgers* across the front, and Morgan sporting a blue hat with an *LA* logo in rainbow colors.

"This is my surprise," Parker said, a broad grin on her face. "I'm taking you both to the Dodgers game tonight."

She held up a royal blue T-shirt with *LA Dodgers* emblazoned across the front. "I got this for you. I hope it's the right size."

Hannah took the shirt and turned it from side to side. She must've looked apprehensive because Parker's smile dimmed.

"Is something wrong?"

Hannah chose her words carefully, not wanting to insult Parker's gift and cause a rift before she mustered the courage Stephanie emphatically supplied her with.

"While I appreciate the gesture, I'm admittedly not much of a baseball fan."

She waited for the disappointment, but it didn't come.

"That's okay," Parker said. "Going to a Dodger game isn't always about watching the game. It's about the experience. I didn't even like baseball all that much when I went to my first game, but I still had fun because the stadium was awesome."

"Come on, Mom. It'll be fun," Morgan cajoled.

Hannah was still hesitant. Then Parker leaned in and whispered, "We'll go for an hour. If you're not having fun, we'll leave. I promise."

Parker's gaze was so hopeful, Hannah couldn't deny her. She looked down at the T-shirt in her hands and noticed their fingers were touching. That explained the tingling she felt up and down her spine.

"Okay," Hannah said. "Let's go. I'll go change into this."

As she walked down the hall to her room, she heard the distinct slap of a high five. She closed the door slightly and, reluctantly, removed the hoodie and slipped the T-shirt over her head. When she walked out, she got a nice round of applause and shook her head as everyone filed out to the car.

"Don't worry, Hannah. You're going to love it," Parker said, pulling out onto the highway.

"Yeah, Mom. It's a special event tonight."

"Oh? What event?"

Parker and Morgan exchanged knowing smiles and said in unison, "Pride night!"

CHAPTER FOURTEEN

"They really go all out for these events, don't they?"

Parker snickered at Hannah's comment. "This is LA. Nothing is done small."

"I can see that."

Parker watched Hannah take in the Pride flag streamers, electronic board announcing *Pride Night at Dodger Stadium*, and the DJ set up in the center field pavilion.

They'd arrived a half hour before first pitch, so they had plenty of time to walk around and explore the more recent remodels, which Parker hoped would convince Hannah that a baseball game wasn't the worst activity in the world. Early consensus put most of Parker's fears to rest as Hannah's eyes brightened at the visual stimulation. Excited fans passed them in various items of rainbow clothing. A peek inside the fan store showed Pride-themed Dodger gear on full display. Morgan spun around, taking it all in one sweep. It made Parker happy to know everyone was either LGBTQ or an ally.

They made their way toward the left field pavilion and the elevator bank where the crowd thinned. Parker looked over to make sure Hannah was still with them, and her mouth dropped. Hannah sported the Pride-themed baseball cap they'd been given at the entry gate. She tilted the hat so the brim covered her eye and showed off the underside, which sported the updated Pride flag colors, at the same time.

"It looks ridiculous, doesn't it?" Hannah began to pull it off, but Parker stopped her with a gentle grasp.

"It looks great, actually. You just surprised me."

Hannah released the hat and withdrew her wrist from Parker's hand, then she cocked her hip and gave them a sly grin. "I can't let you two have all the fun. Besides, as a new member of the LGBTQ family, I have to show my own pride."

Joy swelled in Parker's chest. The fact that Hannah admitted being queer, in the middle of a crowded ballpark, spoke volumes. Sure, no one they knew was within earshot, but saying it for *anyone* to hear? Parker knew how big a step it was just to be able to do that.

"You're looking sharp, Mom," Morgan said and dug out her phone. "I have to get a picture. My friends won't believe this."

Hannah struck a pose and blew a kiss at the camera.

"Let's get a selfie with all of us," Parker suggested. "That'll make them really jealous."

They squeezed in together, Hannah's cheek warm against Parker's. She wondered if Hannah noticed and shifted her eyes in time to hear the shutter click on the phone.

"I think my eyes were closed. Let's take it again," she said.

Parker reached for the phone, but Morgan pulled away and stared at the screen.

"No, your eyes are open."

Morgan's brow furrowed, then a slow smile spread across her face. Dammit, she noticed.

"Where are our seats?" Hannah asked.

Parker pointed high up in the stands on the opposite side of the pavilion.

"If they're all the way up there, why did we enter down here?"

Parker did a little two step and dipped her cap. "It's all part of the experience. Don't worry, we're near the elevators that'll take us to our section, but the exhibit for the latest World Series win is down here, and I wanted to check it out."

Even though Hannah claimed not to like baseball, seeing a World Series trophy seemed to pique her interest, if her raised eyebrows were an indication.

"Okay. Let's go."

Parker led them down underneath the center field bleachers and made a beeline for the trophy case with all the memorabilia the organization put on display. Luckily, it was small because after about five minutes, she noticed thin lips and yawns from her companions.

"Thank you for humoring me. We can head to our seats now." They didn't say anything, but Parker noticed their eyes brightened at the mention of moving on. They took the elevator to the concourse level and were re-enveloped into the Pride celebration. Hannah's and Morgan's excitement improved, and Parker sighed in relief that she didn't botch up this outing so soon after they'd arrived. By the time the first pitch was thrown, they'd found their seats on the elevated first base side. Morgan beamed as she saw other fans decked out in both Dodgers shirts and rainbow socks, shoes, or whatever rainbow swag they could get their hands on. She nearly bruised Parker's shoulder when she saw a Pride jersey on a young girl three rows down.

"I need that," she exclaimed.

"Do you?" Hannah asked in her mom tone. "Or do you *want* it?"

Morgan playfully pondered the answer. "Both."

Hannah shook her head like an exasperated mother. Parker felt the familiarity of the moment—different yet the same. She saw them going to more Dodger games with Hannah fully dressed in a jersey, hat, and socks, cheering on the Dodgers like they were her team the entire time.

"Where can I get that shirt?"

Morgan's question broke through Parker's haze.

"Um, they probably sell them in the fan store around the corner."

"I'll be right back."

Morgan jumped up, but Hannah grabbed her arm and pulled her back down.

"You're not going off by yourself and getting lost, young lady. Do you even know where this store is?"

Morgan looked at Parker expectantly. She'd hoped to talk to Hannah in Morgan's absence, but it looked like that wouldn't be the case.

"I'll go with her, and while we're at it, we can grab some food. Any requests?"

Hannah shielded her eyes as she looked up at Parker. "Water to drink, but I'll defer to your expertise on what kind of food to get. I can't go to a Dodger game without getting their signature food. Am I right?"

The raised eyebrow and flirty smile did something to Parker's insides. Match that with the trust Hannah had that she'd bring her back something good to eat—it might have seemed small, insignificant in the bigger scheme, but it meant a lot to Parker to have that trust. Now she was happy Morgan pulled her away. No sense in getting emotional right here in the middle of Dodger Stadium.

"Come on, kid. Let's get your shirt and hit the snack line."

Morgan clapped excitedly as they poured out into the aisle and walked up the stairs.

The fan store knew who their clientele was and made the Pride jersey easy to find. Parker even grabbed a few items to update her collection, and then they made their way toward the concessions. The line was longish, but it moved. Morgan's nose was in her phone, and Parker's curiosity got the better of her.

"What are you looking at?"

Morgan smiled. "Oh, nothing. Just the picture of us. My friends have some interesting comments."

"What kind of comments?"

"See for yourself."

Morgan held up her phone and showed the text thread. The first response made Parker laugh with the *I'm so jealous!* followed by three crying emojis. The second one gave Parker pause. It read *Awww, Parker is making heart eyes at your mom* with an actual heart eyes emoji next to it.

She cleared her throat and handed Morgan's phone back as the heat of embarrassment crawled up her neck.

"You're still not going to tell me?"

"Tell you what?"

"That you like my mom. Duh."

Parker sighed. It was no use avoiding the question, unless she wanted to explain to Hannah why they returned without snacks. *I was all googly-eyed in the photo, and your daughter asked me if I liked you. I freaked out and ran away, leaving your kid in the snack line with no money.* Probably wouldn't go over well. Looked like honesty was the only route to take.

"Yes, I like your mom."

Morgan nodded and stowed her phone. "About time."

"What does that mean?"

Morgan looked at her, incredulously. "You do realize I'm living in the same house? I see how at ease you are with each other. The joking, the flirting. How she looks at you when you're not watching and vice versa. It doesn't take a genius."

Parker closed her eyes and shook her head. "I'm sorry. I didn't realize we were so obvious."

"I'm not upset by it, if that's what you're worried about," Morgan said. "I know my mom likes women. I'm just glad she likes one as cool as you."

Parker smiled. "Thanks. I think you're pretty cool, too."

They paused the conversation as the line moved.

"*So.*" Morgan drew out the word. "Are you going to ask her out?"

Hope glowed in her smile, and Parker had no choice but to douse it. "I don't think it's a good idea."

Morgan pursed her lips. "Why not? Oh, is it because of what my dad did last year? I can assure you, she was upset about that, too."

"No. I would never be upset with Hannah over something Mike did. It's just…" Parker wasn't sure how to complete the sentence in a way Morgan would understand.

"Just what? You like her, she likes you. I'm not seeing the problem here. Other than distance, but that's not hard to navigate."

Parker nodded. Morgan really thought of everything. "It's not my ability to like your mom that's the problem. It's my capacity."

"What does that mean?"

Parker sighed. She opened this can of worms, and she was going to have to ride it out and hope for the best.

"When I like someone, I feel this overwhelming joy of being in their presence. I want to be with them all the time and do everything with them, too. I can be…intense…with my affection."

"Isn't intense affection supposed to be good?"

"Only if the other person feels the same. Otherwise, there's a chance to, unintentionally, disrespect boundaries."

"And that's what you did?"

Parker nodded. "I wasn't much older than you when I fell hard for a college senior—someone with a fiancé—and I sent her an anonymous letter declaring my love."

Morgan's eyes lit up. "My mom?"

"Mm-hmm. It's important to be respectful of the other person, especially when they don't share your feelings."

Morgan got quiet. She looked at all the people milling around them. Now Parker was worried. In trying to explain, she might have just ruined her relationship with Morgan. When she finally looked at Parker, Morgan's eyes didn't hold accusation, only curiosity.

"Do you still feel this intensity when you're with her?"

"Sometimes. I have a better handle on it. I don't let it consume me, but it's definitely still there."

"How do you control it?"

"I've learned to respect boundaries. Less chance of heartbreak, and the people I care about don't feel uncomfortable around me even when they know the truth."

Morgan's face morphed again. This time, she looked sad. "For what it's worth, I don't think feeling love and joy on any level is a bad thing. As for my mom, I think you're good for her. She smiles a lot when you're around, and I haven't seen a lot of that in a long time."

"I'm glad I make her happy. But I won't push her into something she doesn't want. You need to do the same."

Morgan sighed and nodded. "Okay. I'll leave it be."

They finally made their way through the concession line and picked up the drinks along with an armful of Dodger dogs.

"You know," Morgan said as they walked back to their seats, "I have no problem giving you and my mom time alone over the next few days."

Parker raised her eyebrow. "Don't get any ideas, kid."

"I wouldn't dream of it."

For some reason, Parker didn't believe her.

The stadium had grown considerably more crowded in their absence. Nearly all the seats were full, making it difficult to pinpoint where their seats were. Parker scanned the rows and saw the brim of Hannah's hat, but her smile wavered when she noticed Hannah wasn't alone. A woman about Parker's age sat in the seat next to her, smiling and laughing at something Hannah said. Parker didn't feel jealousy often, but she did in that moment. She knew she didn't have any right to Hannah, and she'd never tell her who she could see or not. But this woman was laying it on thick. Even from a distance, Parker saw the laughter was exaggerated. And the way she casually touched Hannah's arm had Parker seeing red.

"Who's that with my mom?"

"I don't know," Parker growled.

She walked down the stairs as quickly as she could with Morgan behind her and pushed past the other patrons to get to their seats. The physical relief she saw on Hannah's face told Parker everything she'd been thinking about the stranger was correct.

"Hey! You're back."

The woman turned, her smile faltering when her eyes landed on Parker and Morgan.

"Sorry it took so long. Lots of people wanted Dodger dogs." She glared at the woman, noticing for the first time her features weren't all that dissimilar from Parker's. Spiked hair, angular face. Only she looked more chagrined with them looming over her.

"I believe you're in my seat," Parker said politely, though she was thinking *Get the hint and leave*.

"My bad," the woman replied and stood up. The puffed-up chest said she wouldn't be intimidated. "You all enjoy the game."

She pushed past Parker with a shoulder brush and disappeared into the crowd. Parker closed her eyes and counted to ten. When she opened them, Hannah was smiling.

"Thank God, I was about to send out a search party. I'm starving."

Parker's eyes widened when Hannah snatched a hot dog out of her hand and began eating it like there was no tomorrow. She took her seat with Morgan on the other side, confusion settling in. "Are you okay?" she asked.

"I am now."

"No, I mean, with that woman…"

Hannah plucked a piece of bun off the end. "Nothing I couldn't handle. Overall, she was very nice, but I wasn't interested. Can't blame a girl for trying, right?"

"I guess not."

The nonchalant tone was baffling to Parker, but if Hannah could brush it off, she would do the same. She looked at her watch and sighed. "Well, we've officially been here for an hour. What's the final verdict? Stay or leave?"

Hannah opened her mouth but was cut off by the distinct sound of a baseball hitting a wooden bat. The crowd around them stood up. Parker looked up and saw a ball flying directly toward them. Reflexively, she lifted her hand to grab it, but in the end, it was Hannah who plucked the ball out of the sky. Cheers went up around their section. High fives were given to Hannah from every angle. Hannah sat back down, laugh lines present as she shook her head. Parker grinned. No, they were not leaving anytime soon.

❖

Hannah turned the baseball over in her hand. The flickering fire highlighted it with reds, yellows, and oranges. So many people wanted this souvenir, and she was the lucky one that had gotten it. She shook her head at the absurdity and only looked up when she heard the back door open and close. Parker strolled toward her with two drinks.

"You know, I've been going to Dodger games for years, and I've never caught a home run, much less a foul ball. You—who doesn't even like baseball—are there an hour, and you catch a foul ball."

Hannah laughed at the playful way Parker rolled her eyes and took the offered glass. She smelled it, recognizing the hints of mango and hops.

"You didn't poison my drink to get my ball, did you?"

Parker winked at her. "Only one way to find out."

Hannah sipped her beer—not poisoned—as Parker sat in the lounge next to hers and stared into the fire.

The temperature had dropped considerably by the time they got home, and Hannah had changed into the confiscated hoodie. She was wound up from the excitement of the game, though, so Parker suggested they light the firepit and hang out. Morgan begged off, claiming exhaustion, but Hannah didn't entirely believe her, given the way she'd carried on in the car. But she didn't call Morgan out. After all, it allowed her time to relax, alone, with Parker.

The mango hit Hannah's tongue, and she hummed her approval. "This really is good. What's it called again?"

She looked over at Parker sprawled out on the lounge chair. Her jersey was unbuttoned, revealing a white compression top. Hannah licked her lips and wondered what it would be like to crawl into Parker's lap. Would she freak out? Or would she wrap her arms around Hannah tightly and never let her go?

"It's called Mango Cart," Parker said. Hannah blinked back to the present. "A brewery named Golden Road makes it locally."

Hannah nodded, hoping the fire hid the blush in her cheeks. "Well, I like it. And I don't normally like beer."

Parker turned her head, her eyes laughing. "Too many keggers with crappy beer turn you off?"

Hannah cringed at the image. "That among other things. We didn't get a lot of variety in drinks back in school."

"Nope. Our choices were Bud Light, Coors, or wine coolers."

"I guess it's safe to say our tastes have grown more sophisticated."

"Or we have better incomes to pay for the better craft."

"That, too," Hannah agreed and raised her glass. She looked up at the sky, surprised to see so many stars, and an easy silence fell over them. Hannah closed her eyes and breathed deeply. It felt like the first time she'd been able to breathe in Parker's presence since she'd arrived, and it was wonderful.

"I have to admit, you were right. I had a lot of fun tonight."

Parker tsked. "Of course you did. You got the only ball hit into the stands all night. It made you very popular."

Hannah clutched her chest in mock horror. "Those are my new friends."

"They wanted your ball. Well, one woman wanted something else. I'm surprised we didn't see her again."

The tone in Parker's voice made Hannah curious. "Were you jealous?"

"Of course I was."

Wow. Hannah didn't expect Parker to admit it.

"My past experience with women hasn't been great—present company included—and a big reason is confidence. I don't have a lot of it."

Hannah was stunned. In her opinion, Parker exuded confidence. She opened her mouth to say as much, but her brain latched on to something else in Parker's statement.

"Wait. How many women have you dated?"

"Not that many," Parker replied. "I wasted my twenties chasing after straight women. The few that I actually revealed my feelings to were a mixed bag of *I'm flattered* and *You're very brave* and—my all-time favorite—*If I were gay I would date you*." She paused and stared hard into the fire.

"When I reached my thirties, I finally embraced who I was and could say it without cringing. However, all the twentysomething lesbians I'd missed in my search for romance were now all married and settled down with their partners." She turned to Hannah, a sad smile on her lips. "I got my heart broken so much in that time that it takes a lot for me to work up to talking to a woman now."

Hannah's heart ached. She swallowed the lump in her throat, fighting the feeling that somehow, she was at fault for Parker not being partnered up. It was an absurd feeling, she knew.

"You're a good person, Parker. Any woman would be lucky to have you."

A sarcastic laugh escaped from Parker. "That's another one of my favorites. Any woman would be lucky to have me, but not the woman I want to be with."

Hannah slammed the baseball and her glass on the wood table and crossed the small space between them. She was going to show Parker she was worth loving…somehow.

She shoved Parker's knee aside and sat on the edge of the lounge chair.

"I need you to listen to me." Parker turned sad eyes to her. "I was worried about coming out here. About being in this arrangement. I was afraid it would be cruel to both of us to be under one roof for two weeks, but it hasn't been. And you know why?"

"Because I'm so wonderful?" Parker said sarcastically.

"Yes, you are," Hannah replied, reverently and honestly. Parker's eyes changed. She no longer looked frustrated or upset. She looked intrigued, so Hannah continued.

"You're a wonderful person, Parker. I know there are some things we haven't discussed because I think we're both afraid to burst this wonderful bubble we've created. I see moments in you, where you want to push, but you don't. You respect my boundaries and my feelings and enjoy being in the moment. That means so much to me, and it has allowed me to be at ease with this entire scenario. You respect me. You respect us."

The fire allowed Hannah to see the shimmer of tears in Parker's eyes.

"Whatever happens, know that I am thankful for you being in my life."

Parker sniffed. "I'm grateful to have you in mine."

A shift happened. Hannah didn't know what caused it or why, but she felt bold.

"Can...can I hug you?"

A loud inhale punctuated Parker's wary nod. Slowly, she sat up until she was inches from Hannah's face. Those deep brown eyes held so much emotion and broke Hannah's heart. She reached up and wrapped her arms around Parker's neck and relaxed when the embrace was returned. The hug was simple, yet it said so much. *I care about you. I respect you. I...*

Hannah gasped as three words entered her head. She squeezed Parker and buried her nose in the crook of Parker's neck. The fragrance of spearmint combined with eucalyptus eased Hannah's heart, making her feel safe. After some time—minutes, hours, it wasn't clear—she pulled back and cupped Parker's cheek. Their breath mingled as their foreheads touched, and she allowed the emotion to wash over them.

The urge to close the space between them overwhelmed Hannah. They were there, alone, sharing an intimacy they hadn't allowed themselves to have until this moment. A kiss was only one step away.

As Hannah wrestled with the should-she-or-shouldn't-she war in her head, Parker pulled back and pushed a strand of hair behind Hannah's ear, a sad smile on her face. The smile morphed into confusion, then her gaze held realization. She must've seen something in Hannah's eyes because, suddenly, she slid back on the lounge and dislodged her legs from between Hannah's arms.

"I, um, I'm kind of tired now. I'm going to head to bed."

She stood and walked toward the house. Hannah cursed herself for not taking the chance when it was presented, and now it was too late.

Was it?

Parker was steps from the door, not even inside. Hannah had one chance to be bold or leave it be. She decided to be bold. She stood up and caught up to Parker in three quick strides.

"Parker," she said firmly. Parker turned yet said nothing. Hannah didn't wait for an answer or an invitation. She merely crashed their mouths together and took what she'd been desiring for months.

CHAPTER FIFTEEN

Devoured.

That was the best word Parker could come up with when Hannah crashed their mouths together. She was being devoured. This wasn't the tentative kiss of all those months ago. This was a full-on *I want you* kiss.

Parker opened her mouth to take a breath and assess the situation, take a step back. But Hannah wasn't having it. She slid her tongue inside, eliciting a sensual moan. Parker's knees nearly buckled as Hannah's tongue swirled and caressed hers. She could assess later. Right now, Parker wanted—this woman, this moment—with every fiber of her being.

She flattened her hands against Hannah's back and pulled her impossibly close. A low groan rumbled up from Hannah as Parker nipped her lower lip, then slid her tongue along the creases of Hannah's mouth. Hands slid up Parker's neck to her scalp. Hair was tugged with just the right amount of pain to trigger a flood of desire from Parker's core. In response, Parker slid her hand lower and grabbed Hannah's ass, pulling her flush against her crotch.

Hannah pulled back, panting, and rested her forehead against Parker's.

"What was that?" Parker panted.

Hannah glided fingertips lightly across her bottom lip. "Something I've wanted to do for a long time."

She clasped Parker's hand, then turned to open the door. Parker knew what was about to happen. At least, she hoped, but she needed to be sure. When Hannah opened the door, Parker used all her weight to slam it shut, trapping Hannah between her body and the solid wood frame.

"Morgan's in the house," she whispered roughly. Her breath fanned the hairs at the nape of Hannah's neck.

Hannah let out a frustrated groan and banged her head back against the door. All that stood between them was a sixteen-year-old whose room shared walls with both of theirs.

Hannah turned in Parker's arms and pulled their hips flush, her breath hot on Parker's cheek as she whispered, "I can be quiet."

Parker nipped at her ear and said, "I don't want you to be quiet."

A sharp gasp preceded a low whimper of frustration.

"I guess we could stay out here, but I don't want you to get into trouble with your neighbors."

Parker's eyes widened. Hannah wrapped a leg around her thigh and gave a wicked grin before bringing their lips together once more. It was hard to be coherent and come up with a solution to their predicament when Hannah reached for her belt, but Parker somehow found enough restraint to pull away, sucking on Hannah's lower lip before letting go.

"I have an idea," she whispered. She clasped Hannah's hand and led them to her studio.

The door was barely closed before they were kissing, nipping, tasting. Parker backed Hannah up until her legs hit the futon but stopped her from sitting. She gazed at Hannah, searching for any miniscule doubt.

"Are you sure?"

Hannah bit her lip and nodded.

Slowly—as if she wanted to savor every moment—Parker leaned down and caressed Hannah's lips. She didn't hurry or consume. She was languid but not teasing. Sensual as each meeting of their lips drew out more of her desire. Parker pulled back and smiled. Tentatively, she reached for the zipper on Hannah's hoodie and slowly pulled it down. She'd changed when they'd arrived home, but Parker didn't realize what Hannah changed into until now.

She gasped as Hannah's bare chest was revealed. Her breasts pebbled in the coolness of the room. Parker slowly slid the hoodie off her shoulders and to the floor, taking in every detail of the perfection in front of her. Parker cupped her breast and ran her thumb across a pert nipple. Hannah's breathing labored as she closed her eyes, and her body swayed.

"Hannah, look at me," Parker commanded gently.

Hannah opened her eyes, and Parker could see it was a struggle.

"Do you like this?"

"Yes," Hannah said.

Parker raised her other hand and gave the second breast the same attention. Hannah buried her head into Parker's chest, her grip tight on Parker's waist.

"Parker," she moaned. Parker's knees went weak. She closed her eyes and buried her nose in Hannah's hair.

"Yes?"

Hannah stabilized herself and looked up. "I need...oh God." She listed forward again, and Parker applied more pressure to her nipples.

"Tell me," Parker whispered reverently. "Tell me what you need."

She eased her ministrations, and Hannah raised her head and gazed into Parker's eyes.

"I want to touch you," Hannah whispered.

Hannah's eyes burned with lust when Parker stepped back and removed her jersey. However, she kept the compression top on and stepped close again. She wanted to have Hannah remove the top—for both of them. Sure, she knew Hannah would enjoy undressing her, but Parker wanted to experience Hannah's desire the first time she undressed a woman, and everything it entailed.

Slowly, Hannah pushed her fingers underneath the edges of the top. Because of its design, Parker knew her skin would be sensitive as the compression was released. When Hannah's fingernails scraped across her abs, Parker looked at the ceiling to stay in control. She almost lost the battle as Hannah inched the top higher and higher—scraping, caressing each expanse of newly exposed skin. Once Parker's breasts were exposed, Hannah stopped. A fingernail circled a nipple, then the other, a quiet, sensual exploration that had Parker teetering on the edge.

"Hannah," Parker growled.

"Yes?"

She chanced a look and saw Hannah's eyes fully dark and dilated.

"What do you need?" Hannah asked.

Parker swiftly ripped the top over her head and crashed her body into Hannah's. She meant to be gentle, but the feel of skin on skin propelled her to a place of carnal desire she'd never been before. Her lips consumed Hannah as she lowered them both to the futon. Parker stretched out on top of her and slid a knee between her legs and applied pressure. She was rewarded with a sultry moan and Hannah's firm hands grabbing her ass.

She trailed a line of kisses down Hannah's throat, clavicle, and chest. Parker took a nipple deep in her mouth and reveled when Hannah arched off the couch and dug her nails into her back. As her tongue worked diligently to stiffen the swollen flesh, her hand massaged the other breast.

Hannah's breathing shallowed when Parker switched breasts, and a low keening started as Parker brought her knee farther between Hannah's thighs, stroking lightly.

In all her daydreams, Parker never allowed herself to envision this aspect of their relationship. It would've been crossing a line in Parker's mind. With Hannah moving under her, matching her rhythm, Parker was glad she'd never tried to imagine this particular moment. The reality was so much better.

"Oh shit, Parker," Hannah said, panting. "What are you doing to me?"

Parker released Hannah's breast with a small pop and crawled back up her body.

"Do you like what I'm doing?"

"I do. But…"

Parker's brain flashed panic. "But?"

Her face must've expressed her worry because Hannah smiled. Then she grabbed Parker's face and kissed her hard.

"I want more," she said when they pulled apart.

Parker smiled and planted a kiss on her palm. "I can do more."

She covered Hannah's body and wrapped the hand she kissed around the armrest of the futon.

"Hold on," she said huskily, then drew Hannah into a slow, thorough kiss.

Parker was reluctant to pull away, but she had a promise to fulfill. She kissed a slow path down Hannah's body. Surprisingly, Hannah's gaze stayed on her as she licked and kissed her way to the valley between her breasts. Hannah's pupils dilated when Parker placed wet, open-mouthed kisses along her stomach. Parker only broke eye contact once to focus on removing Hannah's shorts. She flung the garment over her shoulder, and Parker sat back on her heels and stared in awe. The coiling desire from earlier traveled lower at the magnificence laid out in front of her. Her breathing stuttered past her lips. Was it possible to come just by looking at someone so exquisite? Parker was almost willing to find out.

Almost.

"My God, you're beautiful," she whispered.

Hannah looked toward the ceiling. Did she not believe it?

"Look at me."

Hanna obeyed the gentle command, and Parker noticed a light shimmer in her eyes. She knew then no words would appease Hannah. Parker needed to show her. She raised Hannah's leg and kissed the ankle. She worked her way up at a slow, methodical pace, all while maintaining eye contact. She wanted to read every nuance, every reaction from this woman. More importantly, Parker needed Hannah to know how much she wanted her.

A gasp was Parker's reward when she kissed a sensitive spot behind Hannah's knee. A moan when Parker licked her inner thigh. And a whimper of disappointment made Parker grin when she bypassed glistening folds to give equal attention to the other leg.

"Parker, please."

Parker set Hannah's leg back on the futon and guided her to bend both of her knees. She pushed them apart and adjusted her position until she lay on her stomach, her mouth in perfect alignment with Hannah's center.

"Do you believe me when I say you're beautiful?"

Hannah nodded. The metal frame of the futon creaked as her grip tightened. Parker thought about drawing out the expectation a little longer, but her own head was getting hazy from the tangy aroma coming from Hannah's core. Slowly—eyes locked with Hannah's—Parker slid her tongue into the folds and began a slow rhythm. Hannah immediately jerked her head back and screamed, breaking eye contact. Her hips bucked, and Parker wrapped her arms around strong thighs to anchor her.

"Oh God. That feels amazing."

Parker pulled Hannah closer and redoubled her efforts. The moans coming from above her spurred her into a quicker pace. Soon, hips moved in rhythm with her tongue, and Parker felt Hannah's interior walls begin to tighten.

She pulled her tongue out, Hannah whimpering at the loss. Parker didn't give her time to question her before wrapping her lips around Hannah's clit and plunging two fingers deep into her heat.

Suddenly, strong nails dug into her scalp, alternating between pulling her close and pushing her away. The interior walls tightened—Hannah's screams of pleasure plenty loud. Parker ran the pads of her fingers across hidden ridges at the top of Hannah's center, and it was

Hannah's undoing. She shrilled and lifted off the futon, despite Parker's anchor. Her chest heaved, and sweat coated every inch of skin.

Parker pulled back and ran soothing hands up and down Hannah's thighs, head resting softly on her stomach. She smiled when fingers gripped and, lovingly, tousled her sweat-soaked hair She looked up at Hannah—head tilted back, eyes closed. "You okay?"

Hannah ran a hand down her face, and her breathing slowed. "That was…I have no words."

Parker laughed and placed a kiss on the skin beneath her cheek.

"Come here," Hannah commanded.

Parker crawled up her body, but Hannah met her halfway and kissed her intensely. Could she taste herself on Parker's lips? On her tongue? The thorough, rough exploration said she did as Hannah's mouth turned insistent, her tongue probing. Parker was so lost in the carnality, she didn't realize Hannah reversed their positions until she heard the distinct sound of metal and leather being removed from around her waist.

"My turn," Hannah said, intent in her eyes.

Parker helped her take the shorts off with minimal issue, then Hannah straddled her lap, kissing her with fierceness. Parker relished the feel of full skin on full skin. She wrapped her arms around Hannah and pulled her fully against her, leaving no space between them. Somewhere in the haze of lust, Parker realized goose bumps were forming in some interesting places. She pulled away and saw Hannah's hand traveling south, searching for one thing. Parker gently stopped the progression and looked up at Hannah.

"You don't have to."

Hannah smiled and kissed her softly, then shoved Parker down onto the futon.

"Trust me, Parker. I *want* to."

The wickedness in Hannah's voice brought a smile to Parker's lips.

"Then, please. Don't let me stop you."

Hannah slowly opened her eyes and was greeted by the sound of the air conditioner pumping cold air into the room. She should've been chilled, but the warm body wrapped around her underneath the fleece blanket provided enough heat. She snuggled deeper into Parker's chest and smiled when—even in slumber—Parker sensed what she was doing and pulled her closer. Hannah sighed contentedly and recalled their marathon last night.

Whatever nerves she'd had about being with a woman for the first time were quickly abolished, thanks to Parker. She brought Hannah to a new level of desire, and intimacy she'd never experienced before. She also had no problem letting Hannah take control yet guided her in what pleasured her most. By the time they made it to round three—and had the sense to unfold the futon to a full bed—Parker's heaving chest and limp body illustrated the words that came out of her mouth.

"Okay. You know what you're doing."

Hannah merely laughed, then proceeded to crawl up her body and instigate round four.

The hot breath on Hannah's neck sent a shiver down her spine, but when she turned, Parker's eyes were closed, her face slack. Hannah caressed her cheek—so soft—then she turned back around with the intent to fall back asleep, only to be distracted by the arm cradling her so lovingly.

The tattoo was a music piece, obviously, but the melody was foreign. Carefully, she ran her fingers over the notes—eighth note, quarter note, a run of sixteenth notes. She twisted Parker's arm and saw the treble clef, four-four time signature, and the E-flat major key signature in tiny swirls on her wrist. Hannah was no tattoo expert, but the precision and the execution were incredible. To have notes so small yet legible was an artistic masterpiece. When she lifted the arm and followed the spiral higher to the elbow, she came face to face with a smiling Parker.

"It's a coda," she whispered.

"What?"

Parker shifted to lie on her stomach and draped her arm across the pillow.

"It starts up here. On my shoulder."

Hannah pushed up on her elbow and noticed the coda symbol in the center of the musical bar spiraling out and down. She tapped out the rhythm on Parker's skin and hummed the notes in time.

"I don't recognize it, but it sounds beautiful."

Parker rolled onto her back and gathered Hannah to her chest. She laced their fingers together and held their hands above them.

"It was one of my first jobs as a music editor. I was still learning the ropes, and the whole process was brutal. The composer redid the score twice."

"Ouch."

"Yeah. We were a week away from finishing the mix when the director decided to add a more uplifting scene at the end. By now, the composer was deep into his next project, so he gave me permission to sample his score and create a new cue."

Hannah sat straight up and peered down at Parker. She looked so sexy, but Hannah wouldn't be distracted.

"You composed this?"

Parker nodded with a cheeky grin.

"Why did you get the coda symbol?"

"Because I used part of the theme the composer originally wrote for the two leads. While it wasn't a traditional coda, it felt like one, especially since the new scene felt like a coda to their story."

"How so?"

"The entire movie was about how these two characters kept finding each other over the years. In the original ending, they decided to let each other go for good. The new scene had them meeting again after years apart. It gave hope that the characters would eventually be together, and the music needed to do the same. Despite the turmoil and overages to get this new scene, it really was a better ending, if you go by the test audiences."

Hannah traced her finger down Parker's arm, the bars running along the muscled line of her forearm. "Do you still have the piece?"

"I do. The file is on my computer. Maybe I'll play it for you sometime."

Hannah smiled and nuzzled closer. "Maybe. But not right now."

She kissed the spot just below Parker's ear, receiving a low rumble as her reply. Parker turned, and when their lips came together, Hannah easily slid under her body, relishing the feel of toned muscle flexing under sinewy skin. Parker sank into her, pushing her farther into the futon. Hannah arched her back and dragged her nails down Parker's side. They were unhurried in their movements, a far cry from the frenzy of a few hours ago.

Parker swooped in and started a languid massage of Hannah's mouth. The sensation stoked the remaining embers of the fire in Hannah's core, and she wasn't satisfied with following Parker's lead. She rolled until Parker was underneath her, compliant and willing.

She took her time running her hands down Parker's body until she encountered wetness between her thighs. She was poised to initiate another round when an alarm blared from Parker's phone. They both jumped, and Parker grabbed her phone off the table and silenced the alarm.

"What the hell was that?"

Parker groaned as she threw the offending object back on the table. "It's my reminder to feed the cats. It's easier for me to get up with an alarm than try to sleep in and have them screaming at me dramatically."

"Oh. I guess that makes sense," Hannah said. She slid her arms around Parker's shoulders and planted light kisses along her neck until she reached her ear. "Glad it wasn't an emergency or anything."

Parker groaned when Hannah nipped at her ear, but it sounded more frustrated than sensual. Parker's hand came up and gently moved her arm, then turned and gave her a small peck on the lips and sighed. Hannah hated the sound of that sigh.

"You have no idea how appealing it would be to say *fuck it* and spend all day in here with you like this."

"But...?"

"If I don't feed them, they'll start crying, and they might wake up Morgan."

Hannah sighed, realization settling in. "She'll come looking for us."

"Exactly. While she knows there's something between us, I'm sure you don't want her finding us together like this."

Hannah nodded. She knew Morgan would be supportive of them, but this was *their* moment. It was too important, too intimate, too private to have her daughter show up and undermine the culmination of what had been building for months. Still, Hannah hated the timing. She and Parker finally found their way to each other, and it was all thwarted by a couple of felines who wanted their food on time or there'd be consequences.

With a groan of disappointment, she rolled away from Parker and searched for her clothes.

"I'm sorry," Parker said. "I'll make it up to you."

Hannah turned and grabbed her chin, kissing her hard.

They dressed quickly, and by the time they exited the studio, the sun was peeking over the mountains. They walked back to the main house hand in hand, and Parker slowly opened the back door and entered the living room.

Hannah snorted at the slow, silent way they walked through the living room. "I feel like I'm sneaking back in my house so my parents won't know I've been out with my girlfriend all night," she whispered.

Parker hmphed and wrapped her left arm around her in a protective gesture. "Well, you have. Only we're not hiding from your parents."

Hannah shook her head and smacked Parker lightly on the arm. The house was eerily quiet. Even the floorboards sounded louder than normal under their footsteps. Suddenly, Parker stopped, and Hannah ran into her.

"What's wrong?" she whispered.

"We're busted."

Hannah turned toward the kitchen and saw two pairs of cats' eyes glaring at them. She pushed her face between Parker's shoulder blades to muffle the sound as she laughed so hard.

"Don't worry," Parker said, patting her hand, "they take bribes. Our secret is safe."

She turned in Hannah's arms and bent to give her a sensual, thorough kiss. When they pulled apart, Hannah hummed contentedly, and set her forehead against Parker's.

"Last night was wonderful," she said. She knew it sounded clichéd, but it absolutely was true, and needed Parker to know that.

"Do you think we'll have a chance to do it again?"

Hannah heard the tinge of worry in Parker's question and did her best to push it away. She slid her arm around Parker's neck and pulled her down until their lips were inches apart. Then she slid her other hand up and under the hem of Parker's shirt and raked her nails across her abs. A sharp gasp escaped when Hannah said, "You promised to make it up to me mere minutes ago. I plan to cash in at some point. Maybe more than once. Is that okay with you?"

She closed the distance between them and kissed Parker with everything she had until an angry *meow* pulled them apart.

"More than okay," Parker said. "And if there's any chance it will be as amazing as it was last night, best to rest up."

Hannah hummed her agreement, then gave her one last peck as she headed to the hallway. As she pulled back the covers and stripped down to her underwear, happiness washed over her. She wanted Parker. She *had* Parker, and she was going to enjoy being with her for all it was worth.

CHAPTER SIXTEEN

Parker's morning after with Hannah was comical. What better way to describe it, when she woke up with Hannah in her arms, then sneaked back into her own house so Morgan would be none the wiser to what they did all night. The thought had Parker laughing all through the morning cat feeding and the trek back to her own room.

She didn't go to bed right away. She showered first. Not because she didn't enjoy the scent of Hannah imprinted on her skin, her lips, or her hands, but Parker knew if she didn't wash it off, she'd be tempted to sneak into Hannah's room and finish what they couldn't as the sun rose. Around seven thirty, she finally fell into a heavy sleep and woke up just after ten when she heard a commotion. She stretched sore muscles—no need for boxing after her workout with Hannah—and pulled on some clothes to go and inspect the source. She saw Morgan standing at the stove wearing her new Dodgers Pride jersey and looking flustered.

"Morning."

Morgan looked up from the pan on the stove and smiled. "Morning. I made breakfast."

"I see that. What are we having?" Parker noticed sliced peppers and mushrooms in an egg mixture.

Morgan tapped the spatula against the pan and blew a strand of hair out of her face.

"I was going for omelets, but it looks like scrambles instead."

"As long as it tastes good, that's all that matters."

She gave Morgan a light pat on the shoulder, then went about grabbing plates and mugs from the cabinets.

"You and my mom were up pretty late, huh?"

Parker nearly dropped the mug on the counter but quickly caught it. "Uh, yeah. We were."

"Talking?"

"A little bit."

Warmth creeped up Parker's neck as she busied herself with putting fruit and silverware on the table.

"More than talking?"

This time, Parker didn't catch the two forks, and they clattered onto the table. She turned and saw Morgan, who smiled mischievously.

"Why do you ask?"

Morgan shook her head and scooped the eggs onto each plate. "I had to use the bathroom in the middle of the night, and I noticed both your doors were open and…your beds were empty."

Parker wished the ground would open up right then and there. Being caught was embarrassing enough. Have it be by your girlfriend's daughter was mortifying.

"I'm sorry."

Morgan snorted. "Don't be sorry. My mom's a grown woman and can do whatever she likes. But, please, don't give me any details, okay? I don't need that image in my head."

Morgan did a full-body shudder, and Parker laughed. "That will *not* be a problem."

"Do I smell scrambled eggs à la Morgan?" Hannah's voice drifted into the kitchen from the hallway.

Parker turned and nearly swallowed her tongue when she saw a freshly showered Hannah with damp hair in jean shorts and a tank top. She distracted herself with the coffee machine to get her libido under control while the conversation flowed behind her.

"Yes, it is," Morgan said. "Despite your best attempts to teach me, I still can't get an omelet to form."

"And I keep telling you, you're not letting the eggs sit long enough at the higher heat to solidify the base. You're too impatient."

"Yeah, yeah," Morgan grumbled and took the plates to the table.

A hand rested on Parker's lower back, causing her to gasp and straighten.

Hannah leaned in and whispered, "And how are you this morning?"

The sultry tone nearly buckled Parker's knees. She grabbed the edge of the counter until her legs felt steady, then leaned to Hannah's ear. "Are you trying to kill me?"

Hannah chuckled. "Just keeping you on your toes."

Her nails grazed the back of Parker's neck. A shiver racked her body, and a familiar stirring started in Parker's core. She glared at Hannah as best she could, and all she got was a devilish grin as Hannah sipped her coffee and joined Morgan at the table.

Lord, help me, Parker thought. She took a moment to compose herself, then joined them for breakfast.

Conversation flowed easily between them. The big focus was on David's housewarming that afternoon and what they needed to bring. They soon moved onto what Morgan had learned the past week and eventually ended up talking about the game the previous evening. Parker did a lot of nodding because talk of the game conjured images of Hannah kissing her, undressing her, writhing underneath her as she coaxed a third orgasm from Hannah's body. One look told her Hannah was remembering the same thing—if the dilation of her eyes was an indication.

"Will you two tone it down, please?"

Morgan's question broke the spell, and Hannah startled.

"What are you talking about, sweetheart?"

"I'm not an idiot, Mom. You two keep looking at each other like you're trying to say something but not let me know. It's so obvious you like each other. I'm totally cool with you two dating."

Parker stifled a laugh at being categorized as *dating* Hannah. *We're way past dating.*

Hannah, however, looked a little panicked.

"I'm sorry, honey. I wasn't trying to hide it from you. You're right, we do like each other"—she turned a sweet smile to Parker—"and we're still figuring some things out, including what you're comfortable with. I don't want you to feel weird around us because our relationship has changed. Does that make sense?"

"Uh-huh. Like I said, I'm totally cool with it. So stop hiding. But could you keep the flirting to a minimum? I don't need to see that."

"I'm sorry, too, Morgan," Parker said. "And I'm glad we have your approval. It'll make going forward so much easier."

"Just know if you hurt her, I'll kick your ass," Morgan retorted and winked.

Everyone laughed, and Hannah kissed Morgan's hair. She looked at Parker and sighed in relief. One hurdle conquered.

Suddenly, Parker's pocket vibrated. She pulled out her phone and noticed a text. "It's David. He needs some help setting up tables, games, and decorations for the party."

"I'll do it," Morgan said and stood and took her plate to the kitchen.

"Oh, okay," Parker said, surprised by her eagerness. "Are you sure?"

"Yeah. Besides, it'll give you two some alone time to do…" Morgan's face took on a reddish hue. She didn't complete the sentence. Instead, she walked toward the door.

"Do you want to know the address or do you plan to knock on all the doors?" Parker teased.

"Address, please."

"He's the third house up the street. Number 5247."

Morgan nodded and quickly left the house, leaving them with a lot to talk about. Hannah looked pensive, her lips pinched, and her gaze focused on the table. Cautiously, Parker stood and took the seat Morgan vacated. She placed her hands on Hannah's exposed thighs. The touch seemed to do the trick. Hannah's mouth relaxed and her gaze found Parker's.

"Talk to me. What are you thinking?"

Hannah sighed. "I'm happy Morgan is supportive, but I was hoping to have a little more time with you before she found out."

"Are you worried she's not telling the truth?"

"No, my reasons are more personal."

Parker clasped Hannah's hands and laid them on her lap. She looked at Hannah, really looked at her, and waited.

"Parker, I've felt something for you ever since you came back into my life. I wasn't sure how strong those feelings were until last night, and I'm not sure I want to give that up."

Parker smiled. "I don't want to give it up either."

"But there are so many variables. The big one is we're leaving in a week. What happens to Morgan if we break up? What kind of future do we have with—"

"Hey, calm down." Parker cupped Hannah's face in a tender caress. "We don't have to figure everything out right this minute."

"No?"

"Absolutely not. Let's enjoy this for what it is right now. Two women who are very attracted to each other and taking full advantage of the time they have together."

Hannah smiled and kissed the palm holding her cheek. "Thank you for understanding. I'll make it up to you."

"The same way I plan to make it up to you?"

Parker waggled her eyebrows and drew a laugh from Hannah. She was then tugged forward by her shirt, and Hannah teased with a light flick of her tongue across her lower lip.

"Maybe better."

Parker smiled as their lips met repeatedly. Then she wrapped Hannah in her arms and sighed.

"You know, if you want to make good on your promise from this morning, I'd be all for it," Hannah said.

"We don't know when Morgan will be back. Do you want to risk her walking in on us?"

"I guess not." Hannah groaned, and the eye roll nearly made Parker laugh. "So what do we do?"

Parker grabbed her hand and pulled her up, flush against her body. "You can be my sous-chef. I make a mean black-eyed pea dip."

"Lead the way."

As Parker pulled out ingredients and set up cutting boards, the impulse to ask where they were headed crept into her head. Quickly, she tapped it down. She didn't need to figure out what came next. Because right now, she had happiness next to her. And that was bigger than anything she'd ever expected.

Hannah was so happy David's house was within walking distance. While her dealings with LA traffic had been minor, she'd navigated it enough in April to know that if she had to travel far, she'd prefer to stay home. Maybe that was part of the reason she hadn't been upset they didn't do the touristy thing. That, and the people Hannah wanted to spend time with were only a few feet away in Parker's studio.

It was a beautiful day to be out, though. The sun was shining, and the temperature was in the low eighties. Hannah felt the temperature shift as they moved in and out of the shade trees. The fickleness of a desert climate made her happy she'd opted for capri pants and a short-sleeve blouse for the party.

Morgan walked a little ahead, Parker's food contribution firmly in her grasp. She'd returned from David's barely an hour after she'd headed over, claiming it had been easier than expected to get the rest of the decorations up. Parker had looked at Hannah knowingly, as if silently saying they were smart *not* to take advantage of their alone time. She'd only ducked her head and went about getting ready instead of dwelling on how embarrassed she would've been had Morgan come back and caught them…

No reason to finish that thought.

Hannah leaned into Parker's shoulder and entangled their fingers as she skimmed her nails along the exposed skin revealed by Parker's tank top. Parker placed a kiss on her head, and she smiled at the gesture. How was it possible to feel this happy after such a short time? Hannah wasn't sure, but she wanted to hang on to it for as long as possible. She knew what loomed ahead, but for now, she wanted to stay in ignorant bliss.

They turned into a driveway full of cars—another good reason to walk—and followed the music into the backyard of a Spanish-style bungalow. The atmosphere beyond the iron privacy gate belied the quietness of the neighborhood out front. People of all ages mingled around the fully concrete backyard. Kids ran around in swim trunks and bathing suits. A few adults dangled their feet in the pool while more kids splashed and played in the water. Parker guided them past the chaos over to a monster grill along the side of the house.

"Hey! You made it."

Hannah nearly laughed. David's arms were high above his head in a touchdown pose, tongs firmly gripped in his left hand. The last time she'd seen him, he was dressed in designer jeans and a button-down shirt. Now, he looked like the proverbial beach bum in a Hawaiian shirt, khaki cargo shorts, and flip-flops. The hair was still crazy, though.

Parker gently released her hand and gave him a big hug.

"Good to see you. You remember Hannah?"

Hannah stepped forward and shook David's hand. "It's good to see you again, Mr. Klotz."

"David, please. And it's a pleasure to see you as well. Thank you for lending Morgan to us this summer."

Hannah turned her eyes to Parker. "Well, I'm glad it worked out for everyone."

A light blush colored Parker's cheeks. She was thinking the same thing Hannah was. This worked out better than either of them expected.

"Oh, I'm sorry. Where are my manners? This is my wife, Lisa."

Hannah turned and saw a woman with long, bright red hair in a light, summery floor-length dress sporting the same pattern as David's shirt. The other thing Hannah noticed was her massive belly.

"Oh my, Lisa," Parker mused. "Haven't you had that kid yet?"

Lisa, obviously comfortable with Parker, punched her lightly on the arm. "Two more months, and then you're on babysitting duty."

Parker scrunched up her nose. "I don't remember agreeing to that."

"It was in the contract when you signed on to be my business partner," David said.

Everyone laughed, but Hannah only smiled politely. There was a familiarity between these people she didn't have, and it left her a little uncomfortable.

"Where can I put this?" Morgan asked, gesturing to the bowl in her hand.

"Ah, Morgan, sorry we didn't get a chance to catch up when you were here earlier. How's this one treating you? Not working you too hard, I hope," David said, putting his free hand on Morgan's shoulder.

"She made me do cue sheets."

Hannah chuckled at Morgan's scrunched-up face. David shrugged.

"It's a rite of passage, I'm afraid."

"That's right," Parker said. "I had to do it. I'm only passing the torch."

"Uh-huh," Morgan mumbled, but Hannah could tell her daughter wasn't really upset.

"Parker here has been keeping me abreast of your progress," David said. "In fact, I wanted to offer you a reprieve from paperwork. A promotion of sorts."

Morgan looked between him and Parker. "What kind of promotion?"

Parker put her hand on Morgan's other shoulder. "How would you like to spend the majority of your second week sitting in with David?"

Morgan's face morphed from grumbling to awe in less than a second. "Seriously?"

"Absolutely," David said. "I have to begin composing the score for a new series. Thought you might want to sit in on it."

Morgan bounced on the balls of her feet, speechless except for a few squeaks.

"That's my daughter's way of say she would love to join you," Hannah quipped. Morgan nodded.

"Wonderful," David exclaimed. "Have her be at my place nine o'clock on Monday morning. In the meantime, relax and enjoy the party. Food and snacks are around the corner, drinks in the coolers, and I'll have more burgers and hot dogs real soon."

He turned back to his grilling duties, effectively dismissing them. They dropped Parker's black-eyed pea dip at the food table, then mingled among the crowd scattered throughout the backyard. Morgan ran into a group of kids around her age and, after some mom encouragement, introduced herself and hung out with them. Hannah was sure David's son, Henry, was the first one to say hello and sat next to her on the concrete bench.

Parker introduced her to a few people. Most of them were in music or film, and Hannah felt a little inadequate, so she stayed quiet and absorbed rather than engaged. There was laughing, swimming, even a healthy, competitive game of cornhole between Parker and another music editor, which Parker won. Despite not being overly talkative, Hannah was having fun soaking up the atmosphere and watching Parker in her element.

"Do you mind if I sit here?"

Hannah looked up and saw Lisa standing over her. She immediately scooted over on the bench. "Please do. You must be exhausted."

Lisa widened her stance and eased backward onto the bench. She plopped down at the last second and sighed in relief.

"Thanks. It's hard to be hostess when you're carrying a bowling ball the whole time."

"I bet." Hannah laughed.

They sat in silence for a couple of minutes, watching on as the game got exciting when Parker landed a bag in the hole to give her team the lead.

"How long have you and Parker been together?"

Hannah turned to Lisa. She must've looked upset because Lisa backtracked. "I'm sorry. I didn't mean to be nosy. I've known Parker for a few years now, and while I know you're Morgan's mom...I don't know. You two just look so close."

"Is it that obvious?"

Lisa bumped her arm and smiled. "The holding hands when you walked in gave you away."

Hannah ducked her head to hide the blush. When she looked up, she ran into Lisa's compassionate gaze. Hannah relaxed. While she'd just met her, Lisa didn't look like the type to spread gossip or interfere in people's lives. She looked like someone who genuinely cared for Parker and wanted to be happy for her friend.

"We are close," Hannah admitted. "And the answer to your first question is...hard to say. Can you measure a relationship in hours?"

Lisa laughed. "Parker really is special. She puts her heart on the line a lot. But I guess that's how it is with artists."

Hannah smiled because it was the truth. She'd seen firsthand how Parker led with her heart with most things in her life. Whether it was her work, mentoring Morgan, or giving Hannah the best sex she'd had in years, Parker never did anything halfway.

"Unfortunately, it also opens her up to a lot of heartache," Lisa added.

"What do you mean?"

Lisa shrugged. "When I met David, he'd just ended another relationship in a string of relationships. He and Parker are a lot alike. They give everything to every aspect of their lives, including relationships. They need someone who wants to be the focus of their attention when they're not working. I'm a writer myself, so I understand what it's like to be so passionate in one aspect of your life it spills over into others. David and Parker do that as well. They give so much of themselves that when the rug gets pulled out from under them, it hurts."

Sympathetic eyes studied Hannah.

"You're going to be leaving soon, right?"

There wasn't accusation in the question. It was rhetorical. Of course, Lisa would know because David would know. And while she appreciated Lisa's concern, this was not a conversation she was going to have with anyone until she had it with Parker.

"Next Saturday actually, but I don't want you to worry. We'll figure it out. Like you said, Parker is special, and I'd be a fool to let her go."

Lisa smiled sweetly, then turned her attention back to the game. As Parker sank another bag into the hole, Hannah clapped and cheered, but a seed had been planted. She didn't want to lose Parker, but could she be someone's sole focus again?

They stayed until dusk, then made the short trek back to Parker's home. Hannah resumed her position at Parker's side, but something in the way she held Parker's arm this time felt different. Her grip was tighter, almost as if she was worried Parker would float away.

"Are you okay?" Parker whispered.

Hannah nodded and pulled Parker closer. "I was just thinking about something Lisa said. Nothing to worry about."

"What did Lisa say?"

She stopped at the walkway outside her house and turned Hannah to meet her gaze. The lack of light prevented Parker from reading Hannah's gaze, which made her nervous. Then Hannah planted a kiss on Parker's lips.

"She told me you were special," Hannah whispered. "And I agreed with her."

Parker smiled and leaned her forehead to Hannah's. She sighed and released her fear.

As they entered the house—Parker feeling all light and bubbly—Morgan immediately stretched and yawned.

"I'm heading to bed," she announced and turned toward the hallway.

"It's only eight thirty," Parker said.

Morgan waved her off. "I'm exhausted and full of food. I'll probably just read or something. Good night."

"Morgan, wait." Hannah let go of Parker's hand and went to her daughter. She spun Morgan around and guided her back to the living room. "What's going on? It's not like you to willingly go to bed early, especially two days in a row. Are you feeling okay?"

Morgan pushed Hannah's hand away from her forehead. "I feel fine, Mom. Promise. I think it's the adrenaline wearing off combined with being so busy this week."

While Parker agreed with Morgan's assessment, she, too, felt Morgan was holding something back. And she thought she knew what that something was.

Parker sat on the edge of the couch and asked, "Morgan, are you going to your room to give your mom and me some privacy?"

The sheepish look on Morgan's face said it all.

"Oh, honey." Hannah wrapped her arm around Morgan's shoulders and sat them opposite Parker. "While I appreciate your discretion, you don't have to disappear for us to spend time together."

"Yeah," Parker agreed. "We can wait until later to…"

The glare from Hannah stopped her from completing her sentence. She coughed and started again. "What I meant was, I want to spend time with you, too."

"We already spend time together," Morgan said.

"Work time doesn't count," Hannah replied.

"Exactly," Parker said. "So unless there's something specific you want to do in your room, stay out here and hang out with us."

Morgan bit her lip and nodded. "Okay. What do you want to do?"

"How about a movie? I have plenty on the shelf. Go pick one out."

"Can we make popcorn?"

"I thought you were full," Hannah said.

"Yes, but it's a movie. You need popcorn."

"Agreed," Parker said and headed to the kitchen. "You pick the film, and I'll make the popcorn."

Morgan went to the shelf and pulled out a Blu-ray. "You have *Tron: Legacy*?"

"Absolutely. It's one of my top five soundtracks."

"Mine, too," Morgan said. "The way the beats set off the colors in my head is so awesome. There's almost no difference between what I see in my mind and what I see onscreen. Cartoons are like that, too."

"Why is that?"

"That's when the motion of the picture is most in line with the shapes and colors of the sound," Hannah explained and pulled Morgan into a one-armed hug. "She goes gaga over old Looney Tunes cartoons."

Morgan rolled her eyes and playfully shoved Hannah away. "Jeez, Mom, can you embarrass me any further?"

"I sure can."

Hannah kissed her cheek, and Parker laughed when Morgan swiped her hand roughly across the spot.

"Well, we can watch *Tron* tonight, and tomorrow we can put in *How To Train Your Dragon*. How's that?" Parker asked.

"Sounds like a plan," Morgan replied.

Parker split the popcorn into three bowls, then took three bottles of water from the fridge. They all snuggled under blankets—Morgan stretched out on the sectional while Parker and Hannah sat opposite under their own blanket. A few minutes into the opening credits, Xena and Midnight joined them, curling into balls around Morgan's legs.

"Looks like they have a new favorite," Hannah whispered. "They're going to be heartbroken when she leaves."

So am I, Parker thought, but she didn't want to dwell on what was to come. As the opening scene came on the screen, two fingers tilted Parker's chin to the right. Soft lips met hers multiple times. When Hannah pulled back, adoration shone in her eyes.

"What was that for?"

"For being you."

Parker swallowed the emotion in her throat and touched her forehead to Hannah's. The words were there on the tip of her tongue, but not now. Too soon. Instead she settled on, "I'm glad you're here."

She turned back to the movie and settled farther into the couch. Hannah snuggled closer and wrapped her arms tightly around Parker's stomach underneath the blanket. She looked over at Morgan, stretched out with a bowl of popcorn on her chest and two balls of fur at her feet. If there was anything better than this, Parker didn't want to know what it was.

CHAPTER SEVENTEEN

Hannah rinsed the soap off the plate and set it in the drying rack. She looked out the window over the sink only to be met with the wood privacy fence surrounding Parker's property. Still, it made her smile.

The rest of the weekend had been busy with low-key activity. No more games or parties were on the agenda. They'd stayed up late long enough to finish the movie Saturday night, then made their way to their respective bedrooms. Hannah had almost followed Parker into her bed, but a quick nod to Morgan's door, and Hannah settled for a very passionate kiss good night before retiring to her room. They'd slept in Sunday, and then Parker walked them down to Magnolia Park for breakfast at Porto's and window shopping. They'd popped into a handful of shops that caught their eye with their window displays. Morgan was bummed Halloween Town had been closed but perked up when they found the Catnip Vintage store complete with kittens in the window. All the while Parker's hand stayed in Hannah's as they strolled without worry about time, place, or people. It had been the most relaxed, stress-free day Hannah had with someone she cared about in a long time. It made her happy, yet it also made her scared.

Hannah counted the days in her head. Only six left before they flew back to Arkansas, counting today. And then what? Her conversation with Lisa resurfaced, how Hannah said she'd do anything to keep Parker in her life. It was true, Hannah wanted to be with Parker, but it wasn't that easy. Relationships took a lot of work. She'd been in one for thirty years, and it was hard to keep one going even in the same room with the person. How would they navigate the extra component of distance? Did Parker trust her to stay loyal? Did she trust Parker? She grabbed the counter to steady herself.

That's where the real concern was for Hannah. Would the distance make Parker insert herself forcefully into Hannah's life? Mike had done that when he felt she was pulling away, to make sure he was the main character in their relationship. Would Parker panic and do something similar?

Hannah shook her head vigorously. Parker was not Mike, and it was ridiculous to start panicking when they hadn't even discussed a future together. They were too focused on the now. She was getting herself all worked up, probably for nothing. *Don't think about that now. Enjoy it for what it is.*

The heavy thump of Morgan's Doc Martens alerted Hannah. She quickly wiped her eyes and turned to find her daughter already dressed for the day.

"Morning, sweetheart. You're up early."

She knew David told her to come over around nine o'clock, so to see Morgan dressed and ready at eight confused her.

"I texted David. He said the family is up and ready for the day, so I can come over earlier and he can show me how to set up MIDI patches when he composes."

"Oh. Sounds technical."

"It is," Morgan said. "Where's Parker?"

Hannah shrugged. "My guess is she's sleeping in today. Taking advantage of David taking the reins on your internship this week."

She winked to make sure Morgan knew it was a joke. Her daughter's guffaw said the message was received.

"I'm surprised Xena and Midi let her sleep this long. Those two are like clockwork with wanting their breakfast."

"Maybe they chose sleep over food for once."

"Maybe," Morgan said.

She grabbed her satchel and flung it across her chest, then she pulled down the box of granola bars from the cupboard and grabbed two. "David says I should be done around three this afternoon."

"Okay. Will you be back for lunch?"

"No. David said he'll take care of it. I'll see you later."

As soon as the door closed, Hannah leaned against the counter, relishing the quiet that had been absent the past couple of days. Then she realized she and Parker would be alone. For hours. The anxiety from earlier gave way to a spark of lust at the thought of what they could do with that time. Enjoy it for what it is right now, her mind repeated. Hannah planned to do just that. Her thoughts turned to pleasure as she got a wonderful idea.

She reached up and pulled down a can of cat food. As soon as she popped the lid, the telltale *plop* of paws hitting the floor and the jingle of two collars traveled toward the kitchen. Sure enough, once the food was distributed into their bowls, Xena and Midnight waltzed in and circled her legs. She laughed as they impeded her progress and let out the most sorrowful cries.

"Enjoy. This is as much for my benefit as it is for you."

They nearly knocked her over when she set the bowls on the floor and started scarfing their way through the wet mush. Hannah shook her head and gave them one last pet.

"Eat slowly, please. I expect this to take a while."

All the kids taken care of, Hannah walked down the hall to Parker's bedroom with purpose. A light push on the door revealed Parker asleep on her back. The sheets were pooled around her waist. Her sleep tank rode up, revealing defined abs. Hannah bit her lip. Parker really was gorgeous. How she'd been able to stay away for two nights showed how much she loved and respected Morgan. But Morgan wasn't here, and it was time to make up for those lost nights.

Hannah slowly eased through the crack and pushed the door closed, just short of clicking it shut. Then she walked slowly over to the bed and gazed at Parker. Her hair was ruffled from sleep, and her chest rose and fell in slow, even breaths. Hannah's first instinct was to crawl under the sheets and splay her body along Parker's, kissing her awake. But her lust-filled mind came up with an even better idea, something a little more fun.

Carefully, Hannah climbed onto the bed and hovered above Parker on her hands and knees. Her face looked so relaxed in sleep. The sight made Hannah's breath catch for a second at the swell of emotion flooding her chest. She didn't let it deter her, though. Slowly—so she wouldn't shift the bed and wake Parker up—Hannah bent forward and placed light, open-mouthed kisses against Parker's neck. A low rumble came from Parker's throat by the time Hannah reached the top of her breasts. When she nipped at the small mound of flesh peeking out of her tank, Hannah was rewarded with a sharp gasp.

Strong fingers caressed her scalp as she moved lower and placed firmer kisses across Parker's abs. A slight tug, and Hannah looked up, only to be caught in Parker's desire-filled gaze. She looked fully awake—no residual sleep—and Hannah decided to change tactics. She crawled up Parker's body and sank into a carnal kiss, a meeting of lips and tongues. She clasped her arms around Parker's head. Parker groaned, and her hands pushed Hannah's top up to caress the skin on her back. Hannah pulled away, sucking on Parker's lower lip.

"Good morning to you, too," Parker said.

Hannah sat up and straddled her waist, gazing down at the exquisiteness laid out before her. She pushed the tank top up, past small breasts. Parker understood the mission and removed the shirt, tossing it off to the side of the bed and settling back into the mattress. She rested her hands on exposed thighs—her thumbs making light circles—and her eyes solely focused on Hannah.

"Morgan has left for David's, and the cats are having breakfast. I wanted to take advantage," Hannah said. She ripped her pajama top over her head and flung it somewhere in the vicinity of Parker's shirt.

Parker licked her lips. Her eyes darkened. "I'm glad you did."

Those eyes. So focused. So intense. Whatever Hannah thought she wanted to do went out the window after seeing so much desire focused on her. She wanted to reward Parker for her intensity. Parker's hands moved under the hem of Hannah's shorts, but she stopped them. When Parker's gaze asked a silent question, Hannah quirked a smile and kissed both of Parker's palms before placing them back on her thighs.

"Have you ever watched someone get off before?" Hannah whispered huskily.

Pupils fully dilated. Parker gulped loudly. Hannah leaned forward and kissed her, then whispered seductively in her ear.

"Has anyone ever been so turned on by you watching them, that they want to show you how you make them feel? How hot you make them?"

"No."

Hannah nipped an earlobe. "I want you to watch. I want you to see how you make me feel."

Parker whispered, "How do I make you feel?"

"Sexy. Beautiful." Hannah accentuated each word with a light kiss. She pulled back and gazed down at Parker. "Important."

Parker's breath shallowed, and she nodded her head. Hannah resumed sitting on her thighs, scraping her nails lightly down Parker's torso. A low groan reached Hannah's ears, and Parker bucked her hips lightly before settling back against the pillows. Parker nodded—telling Hannah it was okay to proceed—and Hannah realized that Parker would always listen to her. Respect her. Desire her.

She started slow and raised her hand to her own collarbone,

skimming her nails along the ridge. The light touch combined with Parker's intense focus caused Hannah's breathing to come in short gasps. She'd never done anything like this before. It felt foreign, yet erotic. Her hand drifted lower and circled the nipple on her left breast, but only around the areola—enough to tease. Goose bumps formed on her skin. Parker's hands flexed on Hannah's thighs, the only physical sign that what Hannah was doing had the desired effect. Slowly, she decreased the circle, and when she reached the nipple, Hannah clasped it between her thumb and index finger and gave it a small pinch. Parker's eyes went completely black, and she squeezed Hannah's thighs hard enough to cause Hannah to bite her lip. The two sensations combined made Hannah whimper. She threw her head back and pinched the nipple harder. Parker's grip on her thighs loosened, and soothing circles massaged the pain from the area. What started as a gift for Parker was now bringing Hannah to a level of intense sensation she'd never experienced. She needed to regain a modicum of control, or this would be over before she got to the good part.

Parker's hand worked its way into her hair and gently guided her gaze back to Parker. The reverence in the caress nearly brought Hannah to tears.

"Don't look away," Parker whispered. "Stay with me."

Hannah swallowed the emotion and resumed her journey. She kept light pressure on her nipple, and her other hand skimmed over her stomach, past the waistband of her shorts, until it reached the junction of her thighs. She let out a soft "Oh" when she encountered wetness, which wasn't surprising, but *how* wet she was shocked her. She pushed farther into the folds, the slickness coating her fingers. She groaned, but she kept her eyes on Parker. The simple act of looking at her lover while she touched herself nearly sent Hannah into a frenzy. Oh God, what had she done by starting this game?

Her hips took up a slow rocking motion as her fingers moved up and down her slit. She was too afraid to go farther inside. Afraid she'd explode if she did.

"Don't hold back," Parker said, her own breathing labored. Then she did something that nearly had Hannah tumbling into oblivion. She removed her hand from Hannah's thigh and shoved it into her boxers. "Ah. Oh shit," Parker gasped.

Hannah watched in awe as Parker's face contorted in sheer ecstasy. Her chest rose and fell in rapid breaths. When she finally gained enough control to look at Hannah again, she said one word.

"Together."

Hannah refocused and pushed two fingers into her core. Parker's movements mirrored hers, and soon they were totally in rhythm with each other. The moment was charged and should've felt strange to be so in sync without touching. But it didn't. Their connection went deeper than the physical. Hannah felt her internal walls start to contract around her fingers. She squeezed her eyes shut and braced herself against Parker.

No. No. No. Not yet. We need to do this together.

As if reading her mind, Parker said, "It's okay, Hannah. Let go. I'm right here with you."

Hannah increased her pace, her hips rocking up and down on Parker's legs. She groaned. "Parker."

"That's it, Hannah. Come for me."

Hannah screamed as the orgasm shot through her like a rocket. She slowed her movements and watched Parker lift her hips off the bed, then collapse in complete satisfaction.

Hannah rested her hand over Parker's heart, felt the rapidness of its beat, and closed her eyes when fingers threaded through her now damp hair.

"That was…unexpected…and amazing," Parker said.

Parker flopped her arms to the mattress as her breathing returned to normal. Hannah chuckled, then kissed up toned abs and pert breasts, and sighed when insistent lips met hers. They took their time, enjoying languid kisses after so much emotion. When Hannah pulled back, she smiled at the overwhelming affection in Parker's eyes.

"What time do you have to be at work?"

Parker smiled then flipped her onto the bed. "Anything I need to do can wait until after lunch." She bit the spot behind Hannah's ear, then soothed it with her tongue.

"Are you sure?" Hannah gasped.

"Oh yes," Parker replied, nipping Hannah's earlobe before moving down her body. "I'm pretty quick."

"Only when it pertains to work, right?"

Parker lifted her head and looked Hannah right in the eye. "I have no intention of rushing this."

Thank God for that, Hannah thought as Parker's lips wrapped around her clit.

❖

Parker leaned forward only to have the grape she sought pulled beyond her reach. "Stop."

She went for it again with the same result. Hannah laughed as she popped the grape into her mouth. Parker crossed her arms and gave her best stern look, which was hard since she wasn't really upset, but it was effective.

"Okay. I'm sorry. Here."

Hannah held out another grape. This time, Parker lightly clasped her wrist and slid her lips around Hannah's fingers. Her tongue swirled between the digits before sucking the grape into her mouth and chewing slowly. Hannah gaped at her, eyes dilated.

"You're mean."

"You started it," Parker said.

"Can you blame me? This morning has been…"

Hannah trailed off and gazed dreamily at Parker, a sexy smile on her lips. She ran her bare foot up Parker's calf to her thigh. Parker gasped.

"Now who's being mean."

Hannah laughed, her joy evident. Parker, somehow, mustered enough strength to not launch herself across the table and ravish Hannah again. She groaned when Hannah decided to remove her foot—out of relief or frustration, she wasn't sure. They continued eating breakfast like nothing had happened, and Parker took a minute to calm her libido.

"You're really making it hard for me to want to go to work. Sitting here, looking all sexy in your pajamas and post-orgasmic bliss. I don't hate my job often, but I do now."

Hannah let out a throaty chuckle. "I'm not going to apologize for stealing as much time with you as I can, especially since we have so little of it left." The sultry tone morphed into sadness.

Parker gulped down her emotions and summoned her courage at the same time. "What if there was a way to extend our time together?"

Hannah shook her head. "We can't stay longer. I have to prep for the new school year. Morgan needs to start prepping for college auditions—"

"I'm not talking about you staying longer," Parker interrupted. That was only a short-term solution. She gently clasped Hannah's hand and took a deep breath.

"Back in April, we agreed to work on our friendship and leave the door open for more. Well, I think we've reached the *more* part of our relationship."

"We have," Hannah agreed. "I think we blew the door off the hinges this morning."

Parker chuckled at the joke, but she wasn't deterred. "The only reason we no longer have a door is because we did this the right way. If we had given into attraction first, I don't think we'd be sitting here worried about what happens when you leave. Am I right?"

Hannah nodded. Parker took a deep breath. This was the moment that both excited and scared her. "Would you be interested in having a relationship after you leave?"

"You mean long distance?"

Parker nodded. The fingers in her grasp tensed, then slowly pulled away. Parker felt her pulse increase and a tightness form in her chest.

"I'll be honest and say the thought has crossed my mind. As recently as this morning, in fact."

The tightness eased. If Hannah thought about it, she had to be open to it. Right? The apprehension on her face, though, told Parker it wasn't all happiness and bliss. "What did you come up with? And be honest. Don't say what you think I want to hear."

Hannah sighed. "The thought is very appealing. I want you in my life going forward, there's no question about that."

"I don't think we can go back to being just friends after this. Do you?"

"I'm not saying we do that. I'm just..." Hannah paused and looked to the ceiling. Parker waited, knowing she needed to collect her thoughts. "I recently got out of a relationship where I lost myself to someone else's emotions and needs because he always believed he was more important than me. I'm worried about having that happen again."

Parker fidgeted in her seat. "Do you think I would do something similar?"

"Not intentionally. But a relationship like the one you're proposing takes a lot of trust."

"I trust you. Do you trust me?"

The hesitancy from Hannah did nothing to ease Parker's mind.

"I do trust you, Parker. Don't ever doubt that."

The problem was, the longer she stalled, the more Parker *did* doubt her. She opened her mouth to ask again, but Hannah quickly grabbed their dishes and went about washing them, leaving Parker befuddled and sad because she hadn't given an answer. Parker's heart cracked as she listened to dishes move in water and slide into the dish rack next to the sink. Once the last mug was clean, Hannah turned and leaned against the counter.

"This is a big decision, Parker. We can't be spontaneous about this."

"So is that a no?"

Hannah crossed her arms and sighed. "I'm not saying no. I will ask that you give me time to think this over. I want to be smart and think with my head, not just my heart."

Relief flooded through Parker as she stood and pulled Hannah into a hug. She tucked Hannah under her chin and kissed the top of her head.

"You take all the time you need. You're right. This is not a decision to be made lightly, so I'll wait."

She pulled back, happy to see a sweet smile on Hannah's lips. Parker kissed her softly, then headed to her studio.

It was okay. She didn't screw up again. However—despite Hannah's assurance she would consider the request—Parker couldn't shake the gnawing sensation that the outcome wasn't going to be what she wanted.

❖

Hannah lay staring at the ceiling in her bedroom with Xena curled up and snoring by her leg. She'd come back here to take a nap after the vigorous morning with Parker, but every time she closed her eyes, Parker's question and hopeful gaze penetrated her thoughts. She sighed as she scratched Xena's head, soft fur running through her fingers.

Hannah expected the question. Maybe not right then over breakfast and teasing, but she knew it was coming. Parker made it clear months ago she wasn't built for flings or no-strings sex. And while she had considered their future hours earlier, Hannah wasn't even close to a solution when Parker proposed the possibility. There were certain expectations that came with a long-distance relationship. Figuring out daily schedules, vacations, times best to talk…Was that a romantic relationship or a working relationship? Would Parker expect a phone call a day? A week? And what happened when one or more phone calls got canceled? Would Parker get upset, suspicious? All of the above?

And what happened after?

That question kept Hannah awake. Long-distance relationships fizzled out because the energy faded. Or—the alternative—someone uprooted their life to be with the other person. Hannah didn't expect Parker to give up her life and move back to Arkansas. Would Parker expect her to move to Los Angeles?

She rolled onto her side. Xena roused and glared at her, stretched, then jumped off the bed in search of a sturdier place to nap. She couldn't blame Xena for leaving. Too many questions in her head meant Hannah wasn't going to get that nap anytime soon. Questions that had her mind whirling, trying to see every possible scenario, every possible outcome to make the right decision.

A door slammed down the hall, rousing Hannah from her thoughts. She looked at her phone and saw it was three fifteen. It had to be Morgan returning from David's house. She rolled out of bed and padded down the hall to find her daughter staring out the window, Midnight cradled in her arms. She had a pensive expression as she stared at Parker's studio. Something was obviously on her mind, and—like any good mother—it was Hannah's job to find out what and help her solve it.

"Hey, sweetheart. Did you have a good day with David?"

A sweet smile formed on Morgan's face. "The best. He showed me how to make instrument patches, and then he gave me a small clip to play around with and compose some score."

"That's great."

"He listened to it before I left, and he gave me a few notes, but overall he really loved it."

Tears shimmered in Morgan's eyes. Hannah rubbed a soothing hand on her back and scratched the top of Midnight's head.

"That's wonderful to hear. Why are you crying, though?"

Morgan buried her nose into the soft fur of Midnight's neck.

"The scene David had me compose was a simple romantic scene from one of his shows. I could feel the emotion in their words, and I used that as my inspiration. Then, as I was composing it, the colors exploded in my head. When I placed the piece under the scene, I could see everything move like a painting along with the actors."

Hannah pushed back strands of Morgan's hair. "I'm happy to hear you were successful, but how is this different than the way you've experienced this movement of color in the past?"

Morgan set Midnight to the floor and straightened her spine.

"Do you remember when Parker said that the biggest thing music does in movies is guide the audience to have a particular emotion in a scene?"

Hannah nodded.

"I realized today that being a synesthete allows me to see emotions in music more clearly. The colors I see when I play music are the colors I expect to see related to certain emotions. So, if I want the audience to feel sad, I play the chords that have cooler colors. If I want them to feel happy…"

"You play the chords that have warmer colors," Hannah finished.

Morgan sighed, her shoulders sagging in relief.

"It sounds like you've discovered another level to your ability."

"I think you're right."

Hannah continued to caress Morgan's hair in a soothing gesture. "I'm not surprised. When we discovered your synesthesia, the doctor did say you could have more than one type to discover as you got older."

"I guess I have."

Hannah was puzzled.

"If you're so happy for this newfound awareness, why are you crying?"

"I'm afraid to tell Parker."

"Why?"

"She's been so wonderful showing me how to be a music editor. How am I supposed to tell her that's not what I want to do anymore?"

Hannah pulled Morgan into a strong, comforting embrace and soothed her.

"Oh, sweetie. Parker's not going to be angry with you over that. She'll understand, I promise."

"How can you be so sure?"

"Because she cares for you. She also understands you the same way I do."

"And what way is that?"

Hannah clasped Morgan's face in her hands and stared her daughter straight in the eye.

"You have a wonderful, unique view of music a lot of people don't understand. Yet it has allowed you to see the potential in music most people take for granted. Parker will want you to pursue the path that allows you to utilize your gift and bring you the most joy."

Morgan gave a small smile, then went in for another hug and whispered, "I love you, Mom."

Hannah sniffed back her own tears as she said, "I love you, too."

They pulled apart, laughing as they wiped away tears.

"I'm going to go out and talk with Parker."

"Okay, sweetheart."

"I'm surprised she's still working. Usually she's done by now."

Heat crawled up Hannah's neck, remembering the reason why.

"I don't think she got up until around ten, so she's running a little late."

"Wow. I guess she was worn out from the weekend."

Hannah bit back a snort as Morgan straightened her shirt and opened the back door. "Wish me luck?"

"You don't need it. Everything will be okay. I promise."

Hannah tracked Morgan until she entered the studio. She admired her daughter's courage to tell Parker exactly what was happening and the decisions she'd made about her future. Hannah wished she could find hers to do the same.

Parker saved the session on her screen and hit all the keys to export it for David. She leaned back in her office chair and stretched toward the ceiling. The exhaustion from the morning had vanished as soon as she'd stepped through the door that afternoon. The current exhaustion was due to some of the most convoluted edits she'd ever had to match from the picture editor's session. She looked at the clock on her screen and groaned when it said seven thirty. Her arms flopped to her side, and she slid farther down in the chair.

Today had been an emotional roller coaster of epic proportions. The lust-filled morning with Hannah. A concerning lunch after she asked Hannah a question that probably could've waited. Then Morgan coming back from David's and saying she wanted to be a composer. Parker smiled at how nervous the girl was to get the message out, only to be shocked when Parker showed nothing but support.

"You're not mad?"

"Why would I be mad? In fact, I envy you right now. You didn't take nearly twenty years to figure out what you wanted to do with your life."

"So you don't think I'm wasting your time?"

Parker had scoffed at the idea. "I *wish* more people would take the initiative and learn what you've learned. It would make my job so much easier. Plus, when you start negotiating your rates, knowing how the percentages and clearances work will be very beneficial."

Morgan had left lighter than when she'd come in, but the discussion put Parker farther behind. Well worth it, in her opinion.

She moved over to the futon and opened her laptop when a knock sounded on her door. She settled back and called for the person to enter. Hannah peeked around the corner, carrying a plate of food. Emotion erupted in Parker's chest at being so cared for.

"Hey you. I brought you some dinner."

"Thank you. Sorry I missed it. Since I lost my assistant, I have to do my own cue sheets."

Parker dug into the breaded chicken with rice and veggies, content to enjoy the presence and the comfort of being in Hannah's company without saying anything.

"I'm willing to do them if you show me how. I'm pretty sure I'm also responsible for your late hours."

Parker shook her head and swallowed before replying, "It's because of what happened this morning that I'm going to decline your offer because I believe *no* work would get done if we're in the same room—alone—for too long."

Hannah blushed and tucked a strand of hair behind her ear. "Duly noted. I just hate that this morning's activities prevented us from an encore."

Hannah slid a hand onto her thigh. Parker gasped and stopped her progress.

"I'm more than willing to have an encore. Let me refuel first. Please?"

"Fair enough. I also had an ulterior motive for bringing you dinner. I wanted to see how you were after talking to Morgan."

Parker shrugged. "I'm fine."

She mustn't have sounded convincing. Hannah's gaze turned serious, and she crossed her arms. Parker sighed and dropped the fork to the empty plate.

"A part of me is bummed, but the bigger part is not surprised. No one sets out to be a music editor. Well, I did, but I don't know anyone else who chose it as a career before exploring other options in film or music."

"I'm sorry."

"Don't be. Even though Morgan wants to explore composing doesn't mean she hasn't learned anything valuable here. In fact, I told her when she got her first gig, I'd send her my rates."

Hannah gaped. "You didn't."

"The rate for a music editor would be calculated into her overall budget. She'll be able to afford me."

Hannah shoved her playfully, easing the tension the conversation caused.

"Honestly," Parker continued, "I think it's the right move for her, and she'll excel at it."

"How can you be so sure? She also has a passion for playing. How do you know she won't change her mind again next week?"

Parker smiled and crooked her finger. "Come with me."

They walked the short distance to her computer, and Parker pulled up an old session. Hannah settled in the chair next to her, confused eyes staring at the screen. Parker hit the space bar and smiled.

"Do you recognize this?"

Hannah's brow furrowed, and she closed her eyes as the few beats of the song came through the speakers. Suddenly, her eyes popped open, and Parker grinned.

"That's your tattoo. The piece you wrote for the film."

"Precisely. When I wrote this, I felt it in my soul and was able to write it effortlessly. Morgan feels this all the time. Playing is in her heart, but composing in rooted in her soul. I don't know if it's because she can see the music as well as hear it, but she gives so much of herself when she composes. I'm sure she feels overwhelmed, and that's why she hasn't been decisive about what she wants to do. She's learning, though, that giving a part of herself to music isn't terrible. If anything, it'll make the piece more relatable and reach audiences in a way they don't realize is happening until the performance is over."

The piece came to a natural conclusion, and Parker chanced a look at Hannah. Tears were in her eyes, and Parker knelt in front of her. "I'm sorry. I didn't mean to make you sad."

"You didn't. Hearing you describe Morgan's abilities as a gift shows me the kind of person you truly are. Loving, caring, supportive, passionate. You're truly amazing. I'm so happy to have you in my life."

Parker smiled and whispered, "Thank you."

Hannah surged forward and took her mouth in a less-than-gentle kiss. Tongues explored, caressed, devoured. Parker stood and wrapped her arms around Hannah's waist and guided her back toward the futon. As she unbuttoned Hannah's blouse—slowly, methodically—she reminded her heart this was not the answer to the question she'd asked earlier. It was a connection, a validation, that what they had was real. The answer had to be verbal. A simple *yes* from Hannah's lips. Nothing else would do. She would wait. She would be patient. As Hannah pulled Parker down on top of her naked form—blindly touching, tasting, searing Parker's skin—she hoped that answer would come sooner rather than later.

CHAPTER EIGHTEEN

Hannah was playing with fire.

Parker had kept her word and not brought up the idea of a long-distance relationship again, but it was obviously on her mind. For two days, the physical intimacy they'd established stayed the status quo. As soon as Morgan was out the door, they'd seek each other out, as if there was an invisible string pulling them together. The heat and the passion would take over, and all of Hannah's worries and thoughts about tomorrow vanished.

By Wednesday, things changed.

Parker's touch became more reverent. Her gaze lingered on Hannah's face, her breasts, every inch of her body as if trying to commit it to memory. She no longer teased in her touches. They were firm, intentional. There was expectation evident in her gaze after every interlude that this was the moment Hannah would give her an answer to her question.

Unfortunately, Hannah was more of a coward than she anticipated. She dodged, distracted, and swept Parker into the bedroom. But by Thursday, the easy, flirty, after-sex banter they'd established was gone. Parker wasn't cold or cruel, but her replies were short, her smiles forced as she dressed for work. Her kisses? They didn't linger as long either. Those were Hannah's first clues to Parker's frustration. The second clue, surprisingly, came from Morgan.

Morgan's curiosity had shifted from music editing to getting to know Los Angeles, and Parker readily told them about all these great places only locals knew. She hinted at the beauty of the ocean on the Pacific Coast Highway one night when they sat in the backyard during a sunset. Little hints and suggestions placed in conversations about mundane, everyday subjects were starting to annoy Hannah because she wanted the old Parker back. The one that flirted and consoled and understood. That Parker was locked away now, and Hannah knew she had no one to blame but herself.

She needed advice. Now.

Her knee bounced as she sat at the kitchen table and waited for the call to connect. Muffled laughter drew her attention to the backyard. She smiled when she saw Parker and Morgan talking around the firepit. That was the other issue Hannah needed to address. What were Morgan's feelings about all this? Sure she'd shown her support, but was that only because it was a brief fling or would she accept having more of Parker in their lives?

The call clicked.

"*Hi, this is Stephanie…*"

Hannah ended the call before the voicemail message finished, and groaned. They left LA the day after tomorrow. Time was running out. She needed Stephanie to give her the proverbial kick in the ass to decide. However, it looked like Hannah was on her own.

Maybe she'd get lucky, and Parker wouldn't ask again before she left. Doubtful, but it was a possibility. Was it wrong to hope she wouldn't mention it until after Hannah was back in Arkansas? Not to Hannah. Her brain was sex-addled. Was it too much to ask for distance to achieve clarity? No, it wasn't. Not when so much weighed on Hannah's final answer.

Hearing laughter again, Hannah resigned herself to ask for more time, but right now she wanted to enjoy this last little bit of happiness with Parker and Morgan. She slowly made her way to the backyard and smiled at the sight in front of her. Morgan was conducting animatedly around the firepit while Parker lounged in the chair, cheering her on.

"What's going on here?"

Hannah laid a hand on Parker's shoulder. Emotion swelled in her chest when Parker clasped it.

"Morgan was showing me her best Gustavo Dudamel impression."

"Who?"

"The conductor for the LA Philharmonic," Morgan said, breathless from all her turning. "He's very wild with his conducting style."

"I don't think he loses control enough to fall into a firepit, but he is very animated," Parker teased.

"Uh-huh," Hannah replied.

"Parker said that the orchestra season starts next week. Wish we could stay and go see a performance."

"They are pretty impressive. Maybe next time you're in town," Parker said.

"I thought we were going to—what's that place…Solvang?"

"We can do that, too," Parker said. "But Solvang is much better to see at Christmastime."

The easiness of their interaction, normally endearing, annoyed Hannah because her daughter still got the happy, smiling Parker while Hannah got the brooding Parker.

"I hate to be a Debbie Downer, but I finished folding the laundry, and I put your clean clothes on the bed, Morgan. Would you go and put them away, please?"

Morgan rolled her eyes. "Fine. I should start packing anyway."

Once Morgan was in the house, Parker's hand slid away.

Hannah crossed her arms and stomped around the lounge until she stood directly in front of Parker.

"What's wrong?"

"I understand you want me to make a decision about our relationship, but it's pretty shitty of you to pull away from me while I'm still trying to decide, then use my daughter to manipulate me."

Parker stood, her eyes narrowed. "What are you talking about? I would never use Morgan to manipulate you."

"You just did," Hannah argued. "Saying it's too bad she won't be here for the LA Philharmonic season. Taking her to this town that is God knows where. Your hints and innuendos weren't working on me, so you dragged Morgan into it."

Confusion morphed into pain. Parker closed her eyes, her breathing loud in the quiet of the evening. When she opened them, there was disappointment and sorrow.

"First off, Morgan asked to visit me when she returned for her audition, and I was giving her ideas about what we could do when she came back."

The fight drained out of Hannah. "Oh."

"Second," Parker continued, "you're right, it is an important decision. I'll admit, I started getting nervous the last few days, when you didn't give me an answer. So I started rambling about the area and things we could do. I'm sorry for that, but I will not sit here and be accused of using your daughter to get what I want. That is not me, and you should know that by now."

Parker's words sank in, and Hannah's anger dissipated.

"You're right. I'm sorry for the accusation. I know it's not true, but I'm frustrated."

"With me?"

"Partially. Mostly with myself because I've noticed a change in you. In us, and I know it's my fault."

Parker shrugged. "I thought giving you space would help you make a decision."

"While I appreciate that, I don't think that's entirely why you did it."

Parker turned and sat on the edge of the lounge chair, her elbows on her knees, apprehension on her face. "You're right, and I'm sorry, but I also didn't feel right continuing as usual knowing that you weren't sure about our future."

"Unfortunately, I've been so frustrated that I haven't been able to think about what I want going forward," Hannah admitted.

"What are you saying?"

Hannah groaned and rubbed her temple. This was harder than she thought.

"I need more time."

"How much more? You leave in two days."

Hannah stared at her, hoping to convey what she was asking without saying it.

"You want to wait until you're back in Arkansas before you decide."

"You said I could take as much time as I needed."

There was agony in Parker's gaze. That was the only word that seemed appropriate for what Hannah saw before those eyes dipped and looked at the ground.

"I didn't realize you were planning to wait so long, especially when you continued to sleep with me. I told you I'm not good at flings."

"You did. I know that's how it looks, and what I did wasn't fair, but I didn't want to ruin our time together. Being intimate with you has come easier than I expected, especially when…"

Hannah trailed off, unsure how to complete that sentence.

Parker filled the silence. "It's easier to be intimate when you know how much time you have left."

Hannah rushed over and touched Parker's shoulder, but her hand was shaken off. Parker stood and turned toward the house, her quiet sniffs causing tears to form in Hannah's eyes.

"You know what? Forget I said anything," Parker said. "We were just living in the moment, right? And that moment is ending."

She wanted to run after Parker, tell her it wasn't true. What they had was special. But she didn't. She stood rooted to the spot. She jumped when Parker slammed the back door, leaving Hannah alone by the firepit, wondering what she had just thrown away.

❖

Parker moved her fingers over the mousepad on her laptop until the cursor entered the required field, and then she typed in the correct publishing information. Her head hurt, but it wasn't because she was doing cue sheets—she could do them in her sleep. The headache was spawned by the fight she'd had with Hannah the night before and the ensuing tension-filled twenty-four hours. She couldn't fathom how things had been so wonderful one minute, then scorched in the next.

She'd done her best to avoid Hannah, but—obviously—that was easier said than done. Morning had been the hardest with both Morgan and Hannah being early risers. Parker had done her best to be cordial in Morgan's presence, but it soon proved to be too much for her fragile heart, and she bolted for her studio under the guise of finishing up some loose ends before she went to the scoring stage on Monday. Morgan, smart kid that she was, knew something had happened and came to visit Parker for a while, expressing her gratitude for such an amazing opportunity. They talked about music, editing, and a few other things that had piqued Morgan's interest, but whenever the subject of Hannah came up, Parker diverted.

"You had a fight, didn't you?"

Parker only nodded. Pettiness had her thinking she didn't want Hannah to accuse her of manipulating Morgan again, so she kept her answers brief.

"Why don't you both just say you're sorry?"

Parker chuckled. "I love your optimism, Morgan. Don't ever lose that."

Morgan left the studio around dinnertime. Even though Parker was driving them to the airport the next day, Morgan gave her a big hug and said, "Thank you so much. For everything."

Parker nearly broke down after that.

With the last cue entered and accounted for, Parker put her laptop on the futon and sighed. How did this whole situation change so quickly? She rubbed her eyes because she knew. Parker always knew. The same reason she couldn't hold down a relationship. The same reason she'd buried herself in her career for years. She always wanted more than people were willing to give.

A light knock sounded, and Parker wiped the tears from her cheek. She knew who it was. Might as well face her now.

"Come in, Hannah."

The door creaked open, and Hannah slipped inside. She looked crestfallen, her eyes red and puffy. Her hands were stuffed deep into the pockets of her jean shorts. Parker sighed and gave a weak smile. Despite the fallout, she'd never regret being with this woman.

"Hey," Hannah whispered.

"Hey yourself."

Hannah's flip-flops slapped against the carpeted floor as she crossed the room and sat next to Parker.

"Morgan asked if we could be nice enough to each other to have one more movie night."

Parker snickered. "Sure. Have her pick the movie. I'll be in there shortly."

Hannah sighed. "You're still mad at me."

Parker looked at their hands on the futon. They were close but not touching. Felt like a metaphor for this situation they'd found themselves in. "I can't be mad at you for saying you need more time. The problem is I don't think having more time is going to help you come to a decision that you're not ready to make."

Hannah's brow furrowed. "You don't know that, Parker. I only asked because it's easy to get caught up in one another and block out the rest of the world. I know it sounds like a cliché, but I need space away from you, without the haze of sex and lust clouding my senses. You can understand that, right?"

Parker didn't answer. Honestly, she didn't understand. What Hannah was saying was she wanted to be away from Parker to decide *her* future. Not *their* future.

She pursed her lips and stared straight ahead.

"When my parents divorced, my dad started another family. As I got older, my time with him got less and less. Then one day—during summer vacation—I asked if we could have a private lunch. Just me and him without my sister or my stepmother there. You know what happened?"

Hannah shook her head.

"I was told I was being selfish for wanting all of his attention for myself. Can you believe that? Telling an eleven-year-old kid who got to see her father a few weeks out of the year that it was selfish to want to have one hour of his time without others around."

Parker's vision blurred with tears. She felt a comforting hand on her shoulder, and for the first time in twenty-four hours, she welcomed Hannah's touch.

"I realize now that it wasn't his attention that I wanted. It was validation. Assurance that even though I wasn't there with him all the time, my feelings mattered, my opinions mattered, my life mattered to him. Instead, I was called selfish."

Hannah covered her mouth and squeezed her eyes shut.

"I respect you need time to make this decision. But I don't think I'm wrong to want assurance that I am worth loving."

"No, you're not. And I'm sorry I can't give that to you right now."

Parker's heart broke in two. She took the hand on her shoulder and kissed the knuckles before letting go.

"Thank you for being honest."

She slowly walked toward the door and into the night, feeling heavy and deflated. Parker just lost the love of her life, and there was nothing she could do about it.

By the time Hannah had dried her tears and reentered the house, the movie was cued up and the popcorn divided into three bowls. Morgan came around and gave her a hug—probably Parker's doing because it felt sad yet loving—and Parker handed her a bowl filled with the fluffy popped kernels. She mouthed *It's okay* to Hannah on her way to the couch, choosing the spot at the end of Morgan's feet instead of their usual spot across the sectional. Fresh tears sprang to Hannah's eyes at the realization of what she'd let go.

No, it wasn't okay, but leave it to Parker to try to make it feel like it was.

The next morning, if Hannah had been pressed, she couldn't say what movie they watched. Two minutes in, she'd zoned out and gazed at Parker's face lit only by the flashing of the television screen. She'd racked her brain to find a solution, to fix this whole mess. But she couldn't. Bottom line, Hannah wasn't ready, and the need for her to be ready on Parker's timeline just reinforced her fears. Still, Hannah couldn't escape the thought that she was making the biggest mistake of her life.

The airport came into view quicker than Hannah expected. A feature she relished upon their arrival now left her full of dread as they entered the queue for the terminal. They somehow made it through the traffic in ten minutes—even Parker was surprised—and when they grabbed their luggage from the hatch, the inevitable had arrived and panic creeped into Hannah's chest.

She looked on as Parker embraced Morgan, both squeezing hard before letting go.

"You keep me posted on your UCLA application, you hear me? If you need any help, don't hesitate to reach out."

Morgan nodded and jumped into Parker's embrace, arms wrapped tightly around her neck before turning and grabbing the handles of their luggage. Then Parker's eyes found hers, and her whole demeaner changed. Parker looked shy all of a sudden and stuffed her hands into her pockets. Hannah's heart cracked at the uncertainty in the gaze she'd fallen into many times.

She didn't hesitate and walked right up to Parker, going up on her toes to embrace her fully. She buried her nose in the spot she loved just below Parker's ear. Spearmint and eucalyptus flooded her senses. Hannah breathed deep, knowing it was the last time she'd experience it.

"I'm sorry," she whispered.

Parker rubbed her back soothingly. "Don't apologize for looking after yourself."

Hannah closed her eyes. God, even when Parker was hurting, she still looked out for her.

When they pulled apart, Parker laced their fingers in a loose grip.

"Text me when you get back, so I know you're safe?"

Hannah nodded, not trusting her voice.

Parker gave a quick nod in return. Her hand slipped away, and she was in her car before Hannah had a chance to miss the contact. Two arms wrapped around her shoulders and squeezed.

"I'm going to miss her, too," Morgan said.

Together, they watched Parker's car take the turn and disappear.

CHAPTER NINETEEN

Parker cut the engine and leaned on the window frame. She closed her eyes and rubbed her forehead. It'd been another long, grueling day, and she was happy to be home. She'd be even happier if someone was there waiting for her.

They'd avoided a third strike in a year's time thanks to some eleventh-hour negotiations. Some were happy. Some said they should've had their own strike. All Parker cared about was that she kept working, and she'd gotten that in spades. As soon as the threat lifted, all the projects she and David had postponed suddenly wanted to get done in time for the fall schedule. It turned into a great distraction from the heartache she felt ever since Hannah and Morgan left.

She looked at the front of her little green house. It was so dark. No porch light was on welcoming her home. All that shone through the window was the kitchen light she'd left on before leaving that morning, to tell the cats she'd be back. She should be walking through her front door, grabbing a beer, and curling up on the couch with a mindless movie, Xena and Midi wrapped around her. But the bone weariness of being on a mix stage for twelve hours drove home how lonely Parker was. The feeling had been there a lot lately. It was as if her mind wouldn't let her run away from how she'd ended things with Hannah once she entered the door to her home, a place that should be her sanctuary from the rest of the world. All it did now was remind her of a time when it was full of laughter, warmth, and yes, even love.

Love had started embedding itself in every nook and cranny toward the end. Maybe that's why Hannah's rejection hurt so much. Parker hadn't been looking for love, but it found her in the most unexpected place with the most unexpected person. She reached into her pocket and pulled out her cell phone. She knew what she was looking for. She'd pulled up the text every night this week.

We're back safe and sound. Thank you for everything.

She ran her thumb over the words Hannah had sent six weeks ago. She'd tried to reply many times, but she couldn't think of anything that felt appropriate. *You're welcome* felt too simple for all they'd come to mean to each other. *I'm sorry* would've been condescending because Parker already apologized. Was she sorry for something else? Six weeks, and Parker sent no reply. In a way, that was a message in and of itself, wasn't it? Hannah probably thought so. Still, Parker believed it was better to say nothing than inadvertently say something to make the situation worse.

She moved to close the text app when a banner popped up from David.

Everything go okay today?

A thumbs up emoji was the most Parker mustered. She watched the dots bounce on the screen.

I imported your edits for American Gore Tales. Great job. Enjoy your weekend.

Parker smiled. One thing she liked about David was his ability to give praise when it was warranted.

Seeing no other texts coming in, Parker stowed her phone and climbed out of the car. She grabbed her computer bag from the back seat, then walked the path to her front door. She barely cracked it open before two little noses pushed through the space, crying loudly. Xena had the decency to back up, and her shrieking had Parker laughing for the first time in ages.

"You two are such drama queens," she scolded playfully. They circled her legs as she set her bag on the kitchen table and unpacked the laptop and hard drive. She paused and stared at the mail piled high on her dining table. She hadn't eaten at this table since Hannah and Morgan left. Meals that were fun and light. Then there was the brunch she'd had with Hannah after...

Parker squeezed her eyes shut and shook her head vigorously. Those memories were too painful and needed to stay under lock and key.

A high-pitched meow caught her attention, and she looked down to see Midi sitting next to the automatic feeder.

"I'm highly certain the food dropped an hour ago, and you're trying to guilt me into giving you more."

The crying grew in volume. Soon, Xena joined her sister's serenade. Parker rolled her eyes and went over to the cabinet.

"How about a compromise?"

She shook a few treats into her hand, then squatted down. They practically inhaled them from her hand, then trotted away satisfied. Parker brushed her hands on her jeans, then stood back up and went to the fridge. The cats skittered off in the direction of the couch, knowing the routine as well as Parker. She popped the top on her beer and walked toward the couch, only to stop and look at the back door. She hadn't been out there for a significant amount of time since Hannah left. It had been a week before she'd even entered her studio, doing most of her work from her laptop in the main house. Tonight, it was nice out, and the stars should be easy to see. Parker looked at the couch and the expectant eyes staring at her.

"I'll be back," she said, then went outside.

She lay back in the lounge chair and stared at the stars. Surprisingly, the ache in her chest wasn't so dense out here. Maybe it was because of the fresh air. Maybe it was because this was where she felt closest to Hannah. Or maybe Parker was finally beginning to heal.

❖

Hannah finished sorting her most recent sheet music into score order, then looked down at her phone.

"You're supposed to be getting ready for summer orchestra. Not checking your phone to see if your girlfriend finally answered your text after a month of radio silence," Stephanie said. She divvied up the stack of manila envelopes holding other compositions and continued the sorting process.

"I thought I saw the screen light up," Hannah replied, embarrassed she'd been caught for the umpteenth time. "And she's not my girlfriend."

"And whose fault is that?"

Hannah stopped, stunned.

Stephanie winced. "Sorry. That was harsh."

"You think? I thought you supported my decision."

"I do. It's just, the more I think about it—and getting Parker's side as well—I wonder what she did wrong."

Hannah's eyes widened. "She gave me an ultimatum, Steph. Tried to force me to decide before I was ready."

"Did she?" Stephanie dropped the folders on the desk and crossed her arms. "At any point did you tell her you would need longer than a week, besides the big blowup forty-eight hours before your departure?"

Hannah fidgeted and picked at her nails. "No."

"Why not?"

"Because I didn't think I'd need that long."

"Okay. When you realized you would need more time, did you go to Parker and tell her? Explain to her why?"

Hannah looked at her shoes. She'd worn sneakers today, with school not starting for two weeks and summer band another full week away.

"Look." Stephanie closed the distance between them and grabbed her arms. "I'm not taking Parker's side. You have every right to take as much time as you need, figuring out where and how to be with someone. After the shit Mike pulled on you, I expect it. But leaving Parker in the dark, thinking the worst possible outcome—while you're still sleeping with her—I can understand her fear that the answer you'll give is not the answer she wants."

Hannah rolled her lips and looked at the ceiling to keep the tears from falling. "It's been so hard to trust someone again."

"Did you trust Parker?"

The ache in Hannah's chest grew, and she nodded.

"Parker is everything I want in a partner. Kind, beautiful, caring. She listened when I told her about my bisexuality without judgment. She didn't push me away after I kissed her and ran. She opened her home and her heart to us. I…" Hannah gasped at the epiphany. "I think I fell in love with her."

"I *know* you did," Stephanie teased. She reached behind and grabbed the tissues off Hannah's desk and handed one to her to dab her eyes.

"And then I had to go and screw it up."

"I don't think you screwed anything up. You both got frustrated with each other. Instead of talking it out reasonably, you fell back on hold habits."

"Yeah. Parker pressed, and I ran away. We make a great couple," Hannah said sarcastically.

"I think you do. And not because your chemistry is smoking."

Hannah chuckled.

"The way I see it," Stephanie continued, "you and Parker are like two sides of a coin. You've each had people disappoint you in some way. Parker's fear is rejection. Yours is being stifled. I think, together, you can find a common middle ground where love isn't something to be feared. It's to be cherished."

Stephanie's eyes were so compassionate, a fresh batch of tears flooded Hannah's gaze.

"I didn't realize you were such a love guru."

"Eh, I have my moments."

Hannah wiped her eyes and blew her nose, then threw the tissue into the trash can.

"Oh, great romance guru, what do you think I should do now?"

Stephanie sighed. "I think both of you have to decide what you want. Parker needs to realize your needing time to make a decision was about you, not her. And you, well, you need to decide whether or not you're willing to take a chance on a relationship again and stop worrying every second that it might turn toxic."

She put an arm around Hannah's shoulders.

"I know it'll be hard. So I want you to think. Really think about what it is you want with Parker. Then, when she does reach out, you can have the conversation you should've had a month ago."

Hannah exhaled in relief. She could do that. She *had* been trying to do that, but her broken heart prevented her from looking past the hurt.

"Thank you."

"My pleasure."

The emotional moment was broken as Morgan ran in, huffing and gasping.

"Mom! Guess what?"

She was all energy and excitement until she took one look at Hannah, then her face contorted into concern.

"What's wrong? What happened?"

"Nothing you need to worry about," Hannah said. "What's going on?"

Morgan didn't look convinced, but she shrugged and continued on like nothing happened.

"I got the email notification from UCLA. They've announced when they're holding their admissions workshop."

"That's great, honey."

"I agree," Stephanie said. "And hopefully this workshop will help you figure which track to take. Unless you've chosen already?"

Morgan groaned and rubbed her neck. "I know you think I should play it safe and do performance, but I can't help but drift toward composition."

Hannah gasped, remembering Parker's words. *Performing is in her heart, but composing is in her soul.* Apparently, she'd been right. Hannah took a deep breath to stave off the ache that would surely come from the suggestion she was about to make.

"Why don't you reach out to Parker and David. See what they have to say."

"Are you okay with that?"

The hesitancy in Morgan's eyes hurt more than saying Parker's name. In fact, saying *Parker* didn't hurt at all. There was a different feeling. Not as foreign, but definitely unexpected. That meant something.

"Parker is still your mentor. She has helped you every step of the way. She'd be hurt if you didn't let her know, and I'd be upset if you stopped being friends with her because of me."

Morgan thinned her lips and nodded. "Okay, Mom. Thanks. I'll email her right now."

She ran out of the office, phone in hand.

"How do you feel?" Stephanie asked.

Hannah turned and smiled. "I think I'm ready."

And she was ready. Despite the fear and the anxiety over the unknown, Hannah was ready to consider her future and Parker's place in it.

Parker grinned as she read Morgan's email. Even Xena's full weight on her chest as she lay on the sofa couldn't dampen her joy—though Xena was constricting Parker's breathing. She inhaled deeply, and Xena reluctantly leapt off and trotted somewhere else. Parker sat up, pride building inside her. Morgan was going after her dreams.

The last few sentences of the email gave Parker small concern. Morgan wanted to explore composition, but she knew if she went with performance she could prepare a better application. David's reply was encouraging. He told Morgan to choose whichever one she was most passionate about. Parker agreed with David but added a little caveat. She didn't like the idea of Morgan putting unnecessary pressure on herself, so she made sure Morgan knew she had their full support, and they would help her with whichever one she chose, then she sent off the email along with her congratulations.

Parker continued scrolling through her other messages, expecting notes from a supervisor about the edits she'd done the previous day. She noticed a familiar name on a message that came in two days prior. How had she missed it?

The subject line read *An Educational Opportunity* below Keith's name. Parker was suspicious. What did he want with her now? Before she could tap to open the message, her phone started to ring. Stephanie's name popped up with a request to FaceTime. She'd been dodging Stephanie because she didn't want to talk about Hannah. *Can't do that forever.* Parker plastered on her best smile and accepted the request.

"Hey, stranger. How have you been?"

The stern glare combined with the raised eyebrow caused Parker's smile to fade.

"Are you done moping?"

"I'm not moping."

"Okay. Are you done pining? Sulking? Whatever word you use. Have you stopped your pity party?"

"I think I have enough in me for another month of pity," Parker said. The joke didn't land as Stephanie looked ready to give her hell, so she backpedaled. "I'm sorry I've been avoiding you. After our last conversation, I was upset, and I needed some time to clear my head."

Shortly after Hannah left, Stephanie had called, and Parker broke down. Told her everything that happened during the visit. Apparently, Hannah had told her side of the story first. Not to say Stephanie was cruel, but she hadn't been the supportive shoulder Parker needed at the time. They hadn't talked since, despite Stephanie's attempts to do so.

Stephanie's gaze softened, and she sighed heavily.

"I'm sorry, too. You needed a friend. I should've just listened and supported you."

"Thank you. Apology accepted."

Parker felt a weight lift. She hated being mad at her friends, and Stephanie was one of the best.

"I do want to explain why I came down so hard on you."

Stephanie's eyes bored into her. Whatever she had to say, it was serious.

"What do you need to tell me?"

"I'm sure you know some of the details surrounding Hannah and Mike's marriage."

Parker nodded. "She told me some of it. How he manipulated her into doing things he didn't want to do. I got a sense there was more, but she didn't want to give too much detail since Morgan was only a few feet away at the time."

"The manipulation was the tip of the iceberg. There's more you don't know."

Parker felt weird hearing this from Stephanie instead of Hannah, but if it could give her a better understanding of why Hannah jumped to the worst possible scenario so easily, she believed it was best to hear it now.

Stephanie looked at her hands. When she returned her gaze to Parker, there was a definite sadness.

"It got bad for her toward the end. Mike got jealous when she completed her National Board Certification and did his best to cut her down in front of her students."

"She told me that was an inflection point, but not about the students. What an asshole."

"That's not the most asshole thing he did," Stephanie continued. "In public, he always kept her close and needed to steal the spotlight. At home, he rarely acknowledged her unless he needed something. The few times she *was* able to get away, he traced her cell phone. Then he'd text her and ask her where she was. Hannah couldn't even go see a movie without him throwing a fit over not taking him with her."

Parker was speechless. How did Hannah survive that?

"I had no idea."

"I'm not surprised. She still feels ashamed she let his mental and emotional abuse get as bad as it did before finally walking away."

"Did she ever report him?"

"I think she wanted to avoid that for Morgan's sake and not make her choose sides. If he hadn't allowed the divorce, though, I think she would have."

A thought fluttered into Parker's mind. "Do you think...I could've become like that?"

Stephanie face showed shock. "Oh, Parker, no. Absolutely not."

"How can you be sure? *I'm* not even sure."

"Because you respect boundaries. Even when you were eighteen, once you knew she wasn't interested you stayed away. You respected Hannah's decision. Hell, you still do even though it's painful. Mike never did."

Tears formed, and Parker didn't try to stop them.

"I respect her because I love her."

Stephanie rolled her eyes playfully. "That's a no-brainer. You two have been through so much before you got together and after, and you both deserve happiness."

"It may be too late for that."

Stephanie's eyebrow rose. "Don't be so sure. Reach out to her. See what happens."

"We'll see."

They talked a little longer about mundane things, Parker feeling lighter than she had in weeks. When they hung up, they did so with the promise to stay in touch more.

Parker held her phone in her hand, contemplating the best way to reach Hannah after so much time. A smile formed as she figured it out. She typed up the simplest belated reply to get the ball rolling. Message sent, she turned her attention back to her inbox.

Now, what was this opportunity Keith wanted her to look at?

Hannah's heart nearly leapt from her chest, and she hugged her phone when she saw Parker's name pop up.

"Ms. Wells? Everything okay?"

Hannah looked at the confused faces of her students sitting around her podium. Did she gasp? Or worse, squeak? Or had she merely lost her train of thought altogether?

"Um, what was I saying?"

Brent raised his hand. "You were going over the change in tempo at bar forty-six."

"Thank you, Brent. Yes, the tempo picks up at bar forty-six, and don't miss the key change at bar sixty-four. Everyone with me?" Heads bobbed and her phone screen dimmed, but her heart rate stayed elevated. "If everyone is ready, we'll try our first run-through."

Hannah somehow made it through the two hours of play, including three pieces she'd chosen for the fall concert. However, when the moment presented itself, she peeked at her phone, and her heart did a little happy dance when Parker's name appeared two more times. She was patient until her last student left for the day, and then she grabbed her phone and locked herself in her office. When she saw the first text, she smiled hard.

Thank you for letting me know you made it home safely. I'm sorry for my delayed response.

Hannah pursed her lips and cradled the phone as if it was the most precious thing in the world. The second text caused a lump in her throat.

I'm sorry for what I did. Can we talk?

Hannah blew out a slow breath, her hand resting on her diaphragm. She closed her eyes and took two long inhales and exhales to calm her nerves. When she opened her eyes, she dialed the number she'd avoided for weeks.

It rang three times, and Hannah's heart plummeted to her stomach. On the fourth ring, the line clicked.

"Hey."

Hannah covered her eyes and fought back tears of joy. She missed Parker's voice. "Hey yourself. Are you busy?"

A heavy sigh filtered through.

"No. I, uh, didn't want to be too eager and answer on the first ring. Ridiculous, right?"

Hannah chuckled, feeling lighter. "No, it's not ridiculous. I probably would've done the same."

A snort filtered through the line, then silence. Hannah wasn't worried the call dropped. She believed Parker was having the same thought as her. *What do we say now?*

"I got Morgan's email. I'm so happy she's determined to get into UCLA and willing to put in the work to do it."

"Me, too. Thank you for your encouraging email. She really needed to hear that."

Hannah remembered when Morgan had received Parker's reply and how relieved she looked. Despite Morgan's announcement of wanting to be a composer in June, she was still working through some trepidation and indecisiveness due to coming to the decision late. Morgan was faced with switching focus at a point when others were solidifying theirs. Then Parker sent her words that not only encouraged her but also told Morgan to be smart.

Do what you love and learn the skills needed to pursue your other passions. There are always other avenues available for those who are determined and disciplined. No matter what, David and I will help you get into UCLA, whatever track you choose.

"I was inspired by her bravery. I also realized I should follow my own advice."

"What do you mean?"

Another deep sigh. Then, "I love you, Hannah."

Hannah covered her mouth to keep a sob from escaping as Parker continued.

"I knew it that first day in LA when you were all sleepy-eyed and adorable, petting Xena like it was an everyday occurrence. It scared me, but as we grew closer, it felt amazing. I wanted to hang on to that feeling. So I asked you to continue the relationship without giving any thought to what you wanted. When I didn't get a reply, I went about trying to coax you into giving me the answer I expected. That was wrong, and I'm truly sorry for that. I should've given you the time you so rightly deserved to make such an important, impactful decision about your life."

Tears flowed freely now. Hannah wiped her eyes and grabbed a tissue to blow her nose.

"I've made you cry, haven't I?"

Hannah chuckled. "These are good tears." She got herself under control then pressed the phone closer to her ear. "I accept your apology. Will you accept mine?"

"Why are you apologizing?" Parker asked.

"I knew I wasn't ready to give you an answer. I should've told you I would need more time. Past that week, probably longer. I wasn't honest with you up front, so you panicked and dropped hints. When that didn't work, you pulled away from me."

"Yes, I did. I shouldn't have done that."

"You were protecting yourself from heartache. Honestly, if I had told you I needed more time, maybe I could've given you an answer before we left."

"What do you mean?"

Hannah bit her lip. She felt her cheeks warm. Was she really about to confess this?

"Being with you physically awoke something inside me I'd never felt before. This deep, emotional euphoria. At first, I was frightened by it, and then you gave me an out by saying we should live in the moment. I embraced it, and soon I was afraid I'd have to let it go or allow it to change. I wasn't ready to do either." She took a deep breath. "I didn't say *yes* to your question right away because I needed to be sure that when I did, I was saying *yes* to all of you, not just the physical. That's why I needed time."

"And what is your response after having this time?"

"I miss you, Parker. I miss how you care for your cats like they're your children. I miss how passionate you are about your work. I miss watching your interactions with Morgan. Mostly, though, I miss how much you treated me with respect and care. I miss everything about you, and I don't want to lose you."

A loud gasp came through the speaker followed by telltale sniffs.

"Are you crying now?"

"Yes, and I have no problem owning it."

Hannah laughed. She wished Parker was there with her.

"I guess the question is what do we do now?"

"Believe it or not, I've been thinking about that," Parker said.

"Oh?"

Hannah's stomach rolled at the thought of picking up where they left off. While the physical aspect had been wonderful, they'd left all the important relationship components by the wayside. She didn't want to start a long-distance relationship based on sex. They wouldn't last long if they did, and then Hannah would lose Parker for good.

"Do you remember what I told you about my tattoo?"

"You said it was to remind you that even though the journey was rough, the ending could be beautiful and perfect," Hannah replied. Where was Parker going with this?

"I believe that's what our journey has been like. Tumultuous, difficult, but also passionate and full of love. I want a better ending for us, Hannah. We deserve a better ending for all we've endured and created together."

A sense of dread settled over Hannah. "Does it mean starting from the beginning?"

Hannah didn't think she could go back to the beginning and not be able to touch Parker the way she wanted.

"We already returned to the beginning at homecoming. We can pick up fresh from here and get the ending right. I want to get to know you, Hannah. Your likes, dislikes. What makes you happy and sad. In whatever way you feel comfortable doing that—phone, text, FaceTime—and as often as you're comfortable."

Fresh tears sprang with the gift Parker was offering. But something about it still felt off to Hannah. "I don't think I'll be happy with that arrangement."

"Oh. Okay."

Parker's disappointment was evident, and Hannah quickly moved into action.

"What I mean is, I don't want to be the only one making decisions in this relationship. I was in that kind of relationship for thirty years. I don't want to get to a point where you start resenting me having all the control. We need to be equal in this. I won't take anything less."

"I think I can deal with that."

Hannah heard the smile in Parker's voice.

"I'm going to ask you a question, Hannah, and I want you to be honest with me."

She gulped. "Okay."

"I got an email from Keith Booker the other day. He's somehow been able to finagle a little money from his department budget and asked me to come teach an introductory music editing seminar during the winter term at UCA. I would like to do it. Would you be okay if I accept his proposal?"

Hannah nearly jumped out of her chair.

"Parker, that's great! You don't need my permission, though."

"I don't want you to be uncomfortable with me showing up in your town."

"Oh, Parker." Hannah was going to need Gatorade after all the crying she'd done during this phone call. "You tell Keith to expect you in December on one condition."

"What's that?"

"You come talk to my students again, and we go out for dinner."

Parker laughed. "That's two conditions, but I'm willing to satisfy both."

Hannah joined in her mirth, and they fell into an ease and comfort that hadn't been there for some time. It wasn't long, though, before it was broken by a high-pitched meow coming through the phone.

"Sounds like dinnertime," Hannah said.

"Yes, and unfortunately, I haven't been able to get to the store, so I need to go."

"I'll let you go then, so you can keep them from starving and withering away."

"That's my little drama queens." There was a slight pause and then a hesitant, "Can I call you next week?"

Hannah smiled. "I look forward to it."

They disconnected the call, and Hannah leaned back in her chair, content and excited about this new future with Parker.

CHAPTER TWENTY

Parker felt a familiar tingle race up her spine. Someone was watching her. But it wasn't one of the students sitting with rapt attention behind her. It was a specific set of eyes. Blue. Intense. Probing.

The corner of her lips turned up. Unlike last time, she didn't feel nervous or uncomfortable, or squirmy. Now she felt warmth. She felt seen and wanted. Parker cued up the score demonstration on her laptop and turned back to the class. In the back row, she found those eyes crinkled at the corners, smiling at her. Parker wanted to fall into that gaze for the rest of her life, but she had a job to do. She quickly cleared her throat and focused on her lecture.

"I've done a lot of telling, and you've absorbed a semester's worth of technical language in three hours. I'm going to give your brains a break and show you how this all works."

She directed their attention to the split screen video and the side-by-side clips with matching music cues. As the students watched and listened, Parker's gaze drifted back to the redhead in the back row. Hannah looked good in her purple cardigan sweater. Her hair seemed shorter since their last Zoom conversation. That, or the beanie she wore hid the length. No matter, Parker would know soon enough. After all, this little visit had been planned.

Four months had felt like an eternity when they'd first decided to ease into a long-distance relationship. Now, it felt like no time had passed at all. And in a lot of ways it hadn't, since they talked as recently as the previous Saturday before Parker hopped on a plane to Little Rock, but the road hadn't been smooth getting to that point.

She'd started slow. A phone call a week with no specific day or time set. A quick text asking if Hannah was able to talk, and then her phone would ring. Parker struggled, mainly because she wanted to tell

Hannah every detail about something that happened, and there were a lot of somethings. She wanted to talk to Hannah every day and had to remind herself that just because she *wanted* to didn't mean she should. The line between healthy and smothering was a bold line in the sand that Parker did her best not to cross. So, she relegated herself to one phone call a week—on weekends—so Hannah knew she wasn't like Mike. That lasted about three weeks before Hannah sent a text.

You know we can communicate during the week, right? My phone works Monday through Friday, too. ;)

Parker had chuckled and explained that she was respecting Hannah's space by not being overbearing. That sparked an immediate phone call.

"Parker, I want to hear from you. I *expect* to hear from you throughout the week. What I don't want is to get sixty texts in an hour because I didn't respond right away. I don't expect constant communication because we both have jobs and responsibilities. Do you understand?"

Parker had been thoroughly admonished and changed her approach. Surprisingly, it was an easy accommodation. She didn't freak out when Hannah's replies came an hour after her initial text. Hannah would leave a voicemail stating she was heading to bed early after a grueling day, and Parker would leave a voicemail filled with nothing but support and compassion. Slowly, they were building a solid foundation. Parker wasn't sure what that foundation would be used for, but one thing she now had was assurance. She had certainty that her future would have Hannah Wells in it in some compacity.

Parker hit stop on the video clip. "As you can see, the director wants the note to hit as soon as the pirate's feet hit the ground, so the music editor put a punch—which looks like he took a hole puncher and punched out a circle in the middle of the film frame—to signal that beat to the composer, and the streamers—the three lines running left to right across the film—are the warning to the composer that the punch is coming up soon."

A young man with dark hair and glasses raised his hand. "How does the composer know how fast to conduct to hit the beat on time?"

Parker sat on the desk and dangled her feet, explaining the technique as the boy wrote furiously in his notebook. She scanned the crowd for any more questions and smiled when a hand popped up.

"The woman in the back row. What's your question?"

Confused stares turned to look at Hannah.

"Have you ever composed anything for a film before?"

Parker clicked her tongue against the roof of her mouth. "As a matter of fact, I have…once. I was asked to compose a piece for a new end scene for a movie I worked on. Two characters find their way back to each other after being apart for years and fall in love. This scene was added long after the composer had completed his work, so I wrote a piece for the scene, and the director loved it."

Oohs and aahs went up around the room.

"What movie was this?" the young man from earlier asked.

Parker broke her stare from Hannah and sighed dejectedly.

"Unfortunately, there is no physical copy of the film available because the budget was limited. But I do have a copy here with me that I'm willing to play for you…tomorrow." Everyone groaned. She looked up and caught Hannah's wink, and she returned it before looking back at the class. "Yes, I'm afraid that's all our time today. I'll see you all again tomorrow, and I can play that cue for you so you see how hard it can be."

The students' spirits lifted as they filed out of the room, leaving Parker and Hannah alone in the same space for the first time in months.

Parker stayed on the desk as Hannah glided down the steps, smiling devilishly. She hopped off the desk but kept her distance as Hannah stopped below the podium, her eyes raking up and down her body. A rush of heat spread to Parker's core. Intimacy was the one area they'd never touched in their conversations—past or possible future—but the heat in Hannah's gaze gave Parker a little hope that might change.

"Teaching looks good on you." She bent and looked at Parker from shoes to vest. "Or maybe it's the outfit."

Hannah stepped closer and rubbed the lapels of Parker's vest between her fingertips.

"Did I black out during some of our conversations the last few weeks? Don't get me wrong, I'm enjoying this flirty side of you, but I'm also confused. I thought we were taking things slow."

Hannah closed what distance was left between them. Parker looked into her eyes and saw something she'd never seen before. Desperation. Need. For her? She gulped when Hannah brushed a hand down her chest. Desire-filled eyes darted to her lips once, twice. Hannah's breath fanned the little hairs on Parker's cheek. What was going on?

"Hannah," she whispered, "if you don't step back, I can't be held responsible for what I do next."

"Good."

"Good?" Parker said, daring to hope.

Hannah grabbed her hand and rubbed light circles over her knuckles.

"These last few months have been a trial run for me. You wanted a long-distance relationship, and I was afraid I couldn't give that to you. Not without sacrificing parts of myself that I'd just gotten back after my marriage. But you proved me wrong. You've been the most understanding and respectful person throughout this entire thing, and I know it hasn't been easy for you."

Tears blurred Parker's vision. "There were days when it hurt so much to see you that I nearly hopped on a plane to do just that. Reason always won out, though." She paused and intertwined their hands. "Then—as if some higher power saw my struggle—you'd text or call, and I would feel whole again."

Parker worried she said too much, but she needed to be honest with Hannah. Especially since she was standing in front of Parker, looking at her as if she, too, had something important to say.

"These last few months have shown me one thing. This *can* work. You, me, us. We don't need to be in the same room. Your love for me is big, but I don't feel small next to it. I feel encouraged by it. I feel whole because of it."

Parker gasped. Hannah laughed through her own tears and cupped Parker's face.

"I love you, Parker. I'm sorry it took so long for me to say it back, but…"

Parker surged forward and kissed Hannah with all the passion she'd been holding since the last time they saw each other. Strong arms wrapped around her waist, and they sank farther into the kiss—exploring, remembering. Parker slowly pulled away after minutes and leaned her forehead against Hannah's.

"I would've waited forever to hear you say those words, Hannah. You're it for me. I know it's scary for you to hear it, and it's scary for me to say it—"

Hannah placed a gentle finger on her lips and shushed her.

"I'm not scared. Because you're it for me, too."

Parker slid her arms around Hannah and buried her nose in auburn locks. She cried silently and felt small tremors as Hannah did the same. Parker knew this wasn't a definitive happily ever after—they would have to put in the work to gain that prize—but it was a start.

The start of everything.

Epilogue

Two years later

Hannah looked around the tiny, one-bedroom suite and gawked at all the boxes piled high in every space. "I don't think I had this much when I moved into my dorm room."

Stephanie laughed as she opened one box and started pulling out linens and towels. She'd made a special trip—good friend that she was—to make sure she and Morgan settled into their new lives in Los Angeles.

"That's because when we lived in the dorm, we weren't allowed any style. Nowadays, kids have interior designers."

"I don't need an interior designer," Morgan said.

She walked through the door with two more boxes, Parker bringing up the rear with another two. Hannah rushed over and grabbed a box off Parker's stack before it toppled to the floor.

"Thanks," Parker said and rewarded her with a quick peck on the lips.

"Please, stop," Morgan whined.

"I thought you were supportive of our relationship," Hannah quipped.

Morgan shrugged and unpacked the box with speakers and wires. "I am, but I've had to watch you two make out the last two weeks. It's getting old."

Hannah felt heat creep up her neck. Parker, however, smiled like the Cheshire cat. "Well, now that you're out of the house, you don't have to worry about that anymore."

Morgan rolled her eyes while Stephanie laughed. Parker winked at Hannah, then helped unpack the rest of the audio gear they'd hauled up—a graduation gift from Parker and David. Hannah looked on as they set the speakers on the desk in the corner, then proceeded to run cables behind it, and reflected on how they'd got here.

After their first Christmas as an official couple, it was as if a pressure valve released for both. Communication was a daily occurrence. Text, email, phone call. It didn't matter. And they weren't just words of love—though there were many—it was also everyday life. Parker had shared news of jobs, friends welcoming new family members, and award nominations.

Hannah had flown out for the Golden Reels to celebrate Parker's nomination for best music editing. They stayed the entire weekend at the host hotel, enjoying the amenities and each other. Hannah had worn the purple gown from homecoming, which matched Parker's custom-tailored tuxedo with purple tie. And when Parker won, well, Hannah was surprised she'd been able to walk onto the plane the following day, happy she'd had the foresight to book an afternoon flight since the celebration went until the early morning hours.

While their bond strengthened, so did Parker's relationship with Morgan, which was a relief. Hannah would've been hard-pressed to say she'd never worried about her daughter, but she did, especially when Mike left Conway High for another teaching job in northeast Arkansas and reduced his contact with Morgan. It wasn't that he didn't care what was happening in her life—he had shown up to Morgan's graduation and, begrudgingly, congratulated her when she got into UCLA—but his absence was hard on her. Morgan, sensitive as she was, thought she was the cause for the rift, despite Hannah's attempts to convince her otherwise.

If for some reason she and Parker ended, would Morgan blame herself for their breakup as well? Hannah had voiced her fears to Parker. In the end, though, she had nothing to worry about, and Parker told her as much. She'd continued her mentorship of Morgan, and—ultimately—helped her daughter finally decide to apply for the composer track at UCLA. With Parker's and David's help, Morgan was able to write compositions not only for orchestra performance but also film use, giving her a range that the admissions board ate up.

Hannah smiled, remembering the day Morgan learned she'd been accepted.

It'd been their spring break, and Parker had made the trip to see them. The acceptance letter had arrived in Morgan's email on a

Wednesday, and Morgan was too nervous to open it. Parker took them out for the day. "They're not going to expect an answer right away. Let's go and have fun. It'll be a good distraction." It had failed miserably, but Hannah loved Parker for trying. In the end, Morgan worried for nothing. She not only made it into the UCLA School of Music, but she received a full scholarship, which made Hannah happier than anything in the world.

A light touch on Hannah's shoulder brought her back to the present. She turned and met Stephanie's concerned gaze.

"Are you okay?"

Hannah looked over at Parker and Morgan discussing how to run the audio cables efficiently, then looked back at Stephanie and smiled.

"Oh yes. I'm great."

And she was. So was her family. What else could Hannah ask for?

"Hello. Am I interrupting?"

Everyone turned and looked at the tall young woman standing in the doorway. She smiled easily, her green eyes searching the faces in the room.

"I'm looking for Morgan Wells."

"She's right over there," Hannah said, pointing across the room. Stephanie smiled automatically, but Morgan...well, Morgan looked like a deer in the headlights.

"Hi, I'm Kai," the young woman said, arm extended. "I'm your RA."

Morgan didn't move. Was she okay? Hannah moved to go and check on her, but a quick elbow from Parker shook Morgan out of her stupor.

"Sorry, hi. Yes, I'm Morgan."

She shook Kai's hand slowly. Something peculiar was happening, but Hannah couldn't put her finger on it. Stephanie shook her head and stifled a laugh. She looked to Parker and saw the same reaction.

"What am I missing?" she whispered.

"Oh, nothing," Stephanie replied. "I think Morgan just discovered her first crush is all."

Hannah sharply turned her head. Morgan's calm demeanor was gone, replaced with unsteadiness. She fidgeted her feet and folded her arms.

"Should I be worried?"

Stephanie shook her head. "Not right now. Let her figure it out for herself."

"I just wanted to come by and introduce myself," Kai said. "My room is right down the hall, so if you need anything just knock."

She left quickly, probably to go and introduce herself to other incoming students, and everyone resumed their unpacking duties.

"Gee, Morgan, could you *be* any more obvious?" Stephanie asked.

Morgan's face turned bright red as she opened her computer box. "I don't know what you're talking about."

"Uh-huh."

Parker snorted and continued with her cables. Hannah rolled her eyes and prayed whatever spark Kai ignited in Morgan wouldn't cause the chaos hers and Parker's did.

Later that night, after Morgan was settled in her dorm and Stephanie was back at her hotel—"I don't need to hear the soundtrack of you two having the house to yourself for the first time in weeks" had been her reasoning for that—Hannah snuggled back against Parker's chest in the lounge chair in their backyard. The weather was too warm to ignite the firepit, but the moon was bright and provided enough illumination along with the stars. A low hum of approval vibrated against Hannah's back. Two strong arms wrapped around her waist. Hannah sighed contentedly and nuzzled her cheek against Parker's shoulder.

"You sound happy."

"That's because I am," Hannah confessed. She nipped at Parker's chin and soothed the spot with the tip of her nose. "I just can't believe this is my life now. Morgan is going to her dream school. Though I worry about her budding interest in Kai."

"It's part of life, I'm afraid," Parker replied. "She's probably going to get her heart broken. All we can do is be there for her when it happens."

"Then I'm *really* happy I'm out here."

"Gee, thanks. And here I thought you moved out here because of me."

The sarcasm was playful. Hannah chuckled and kissed Parker softly, sweetly. "You're the main reason. But can't I also be happy that I'm nearby if Morgan has trouble adjusting?"

"Of course. I wouldn't expect anything less because I know how much you love your daughter."

Parker squeezed her for emphasis, and Hannah smiled.

"And I love how everything has worked out. Morgan got into her dream school. I start my new job as band director at Hollywood High next week—never thought I'd say those words."

"I have to say I'm very happy you're still able to work and do what you love. I know you were worried about that when we started discussing you moving out here."

Hannah hummed her agreement.

She always knew they'd discuss living together. They couldn't do long distance for the rest of their lives. Plus, the more Hannah visited Parker—and vice versa—the harder it got to say good-bye. So, when the subject went from a future idea to a very serious plan, Hannah had done her due diligence and reached out to people with music education ties in Los Angeles. Surprisingly, it was Stephanie who gave her a line on a possible position opening in Hollywood—a friend-of-a-friend type prospect.

"Having that certification from the National Board helped. All that work finally paid off."

"Yes, it did."

"Even if I hadn't gotten the position, though, there was no way I was *not* going to move out here. You're the love of my life, Parker. My place is with you."

Strong arms pulled her closer. Hannah melted against her chest and lightly ran her fingers up and down toned biceps.

"Can I tell you a secret?" she asked.

"Of course," Parker replied.

"I dreamed of this." Hannah turned her head and was met with the most beautiful smile. "You, holding me like this. Us, looking at the stars, loving each other the way we were meant to."

Parker leaned down and kissed her lightly on the lips, then touched their foreheads together.

"I have more dreams for us," Parker confessed.

"So do I."

"Do you think we can turn them into reality?"

Hannah turned her attention back to the stars and sighed contentedly.

"Every day for the rest of our lives."

About the Author

Anna Gram was born and raised in Arkansas by a mother who taught her to always chase her dreams. And she has done just that. She currently resides in Southern California, where her day job is sound editor for some of television's most popular shows. Writing has been a part of her life since she was nine years old, and she is overjoyed to finally have her stories come to life on the page for all to read. When she's not working on a new story, she enjoys relaxing with a round of boxing at her local gym, attempting to pare down her TBR pile of books, and snuggling with her cat, Xena, who refuses to be ignored at all costs.

Books Available From Bold Strokes Books

Brooke Takes Queen by Alaina Erdell. Brooke Staley faces personal and professional upheaval when Elizabeth Bettancourt, the emotionally scarred new owner of the resort she works for, considers selling. (978-1-63679-886-8)

Coda by Anna Gram. Parker is intriguing, magnetic, impossible to ignore—and completely wrong for Hannah. But sometimes love's melody refuses to end. (978-1-63679-926-1)

The Debutante Dilemma by Jane Walsh. Two debutantes are engaged to wealthy and titled brothers...but discover they only have eyes for each other. (978-1-63679-896-7)

The Love Book by Gun Brooke. When literary agent Rowan Cross receives an anonymous manuscript that deeply resonates with her, Verity realizes she has accidentally sent her own manuscript, complete with her very real feelings for her boss! (978-1-63679-850-9)

Secrets Under the Junipers by Suzie Clarke. Who killed Hallie Lynn Peeples? Cecilia McConnel needs to know. Bitsy Hanover holds the key. Can love uncover secrets? (978-1-63679-845-5)

Traveling Toward Forever by Erin Dutton. When almost-strangers take a road trip through America's national parks, love may be the final destination. (978-1-63679-894-3)

Beautiful Things by Emma L McGeown. A warmhearted romance of missed chances, undeniable chemistry, and a stubborn love that maybe, just maybe, can find its way back. (978-1-63679-934-6)

The Great Popcorn Romance by Georgia Beers. Opposites attract, and Riley Shaw stands no chance of resisting Hannah Kramer's magnetic pull. But opposites know just how to drive each other crazy... (978-1-63679-910-0)

Love Takes a Village by Karis Walsh. As Lena Preiss struggles to manage a busy restaurant in the Bavarian Christmas village of Leavenworth, Washington, chocolatier Devin Meyer brings an unexpected richness into her life, along with her delicious desserts. (978-1-63679-902-5)

Secrets of the Heart by Jenny Frame. When a beautiful stranger starts asking questions about Nikki Sharkey, head of an infamous crime syndicate, Nikki will stop at nothing to protect her daughter Isla. (978-1-63679-653-6)

Talon and the Songbird by Julia Underwood. In a world where survival depends on strategic alliances, Makayla and Talon must navigate not only complex politics but also the dangerous territory of their hearts. (978-1-63679-970-4)

Three Blissful Days by Dena Blake. Kendall Jackson attempts to make her ex regret dumping her by announcing she's dating beautiful park ranger Ivy Patterson. But there's nothing fake about how attracted Ivy is to Kendall. (978-1-63679-707-6)

Chasing Her Scent by MJ Williamz. When Sheridan Rousseau walks into Lisette Mouton's charming little bookstore in Quebec City, she unknowingly holds the key to a mysterious box hidden in a secret room. (978-1-63679-900-1)

Heart's Run by D. Jackson Leigh. Hoping to recover an escaped racing mare, stock transporter Tobie Mason locks horns with local wild horse advocate Maggie Wilkes. (978-1-63679-825-7)

Scandalous by Kris Bryant. When a Hollywood actress trades places with her twin sister, everyone's in an uproar about getting duped, but Lindsay's more concerned about finding out which twin she made out with. (978-1-63679-874-5)

The Art of Love by Ali Vali. When Mimi and Bianca both set their sights on Jolly, sparks fly, loyalties are tested, and hearts collide as they navigate the unpredictable nature of their hearts. (978-1-63679-719-9)

Iceberg by Gun Brooke. When Lady Arabella hires Zandra, she never expects to find love, especially not as a disaster looms on the horizon. (978-1-63679-908-7)

The Secrets of Rhydian Hill by Ronica Black. A doctor in need of a new start. A woman running from a killer. A love story that could end in tragedy. (978-1-63679-880-6)